SAY WHAT?

TALES WITH A TWIST

D.D. HUDDLE

Some tales herein include bits and bytes from the author's personal knowledge and/or experiences. However, any resemblance to actual persons–living or deceased–sites, groups, or events is entirely coincidental. A few stories are adaptations of out-of-print works.

ISBN 13: 978-1503078598
ISBN 10: 1503078590

Douglas Publishing LLC
P.O. 326
Plymouth, IN 46563

Other books authored as Don Huddle

The Stony Crossing Mystery Series:

> *Murder In Stony Crossing**
> *Cock-A-Hoop Justice**
> *Father Love Will Call The Roll*
> *Smut-Surfer Justice*

Also:

> *Route 3, Stony Crossing**
> *I Had To Walk Twelve Miles To School**

*Out of print

Acknowledgements

Thanks to Cathi Norton, Pody Gherardi, Lori Perkins, and John (Hawkeye) Wraight for editorial help. *Waaay* too many more to list each who contributed, but *you* know who you are. THANKS, y'all.

Dedication

First, of course, for Grace, the Bridge Queen.

Next,

for the last 10 (at least) generations of yarn-spinning ancestors,

and,

last but certainly not least, this book is for those who read it.

TABLE OF CONTENTS

TABLE OF CONTENTS (cont'd.)

CLARABELLE

HOWDY, HOWDY! Glad'n happy y'all come by. Firstly, I be Clarabelle Cadwallader comin' atcha. Then, I reckon I oughta say right now that pert-near all the other folks 'sides me in these tales don't talk 'zactly like I do, but y'all'll ketch onto their uppity way with words purty soon. 'Nuther thing. Y'all'll be learnin' bout me'n my boy'n Judge Hand soon's I git done with this here little bit. After that, I'll be back now'n agin, lettin' y'all know it's time to take a break.

Now 'fore y'all go readin' on ahead, iiffin ya kin kindly see a way to hold off jist a mite, I wanna give out some stuff that'll be fittin' in with that readin'.

Thank ya kindly. I 'spect a'body might wanna know somethin' 'bout these here thirty four tales. Well, they be happenin' all over creation from way back yonder to tomarra. An, they be happenin' from amiddle'a the hill country to way past the moon and like that.

'Member' what I said 'bout everbody in 'em talkin' considerable more hoity-toity'n me? I should'a said, too, that it hadn't oughta holdja back none from enjoyin'.

Lastly 'bout the tales. Most ever one has a endin' that'll keep y'all tryin' to guess what it's gonna be.

Now then, 'bout this guy D. D. Huddle that writ this here book. (Gotta funny name, ain't he?) He be whelped'n reared in Indiana and did all kinds'a jobs whilst he was learnin' school kids how to do stuff and gittin' his own extry learnin' so's to get to be a perfesser at Indiana University in Indiana. He did all kinds'a jobs, all right, like workin' buildin' roads. Bein' a cop. After that, a race-track ambulance guy. Workin' in guvment, too. All kinds'a others.

Doin' such like, he come onto lots'a stuff helpin' 'im in his writiin'a these here tales. That'n his past kin livin' years'n years in the Blue Ridges'n there about. He don't do no work no more. Jist writes stuff.

Well, I be done 'cept to say agin that one'a the real good enjoyin' things 'bout these here tales be tryin' to guess the endins'. Whilst ya'all be readin' 'em, a'course.

I be beholdin' fer so kindly payin' me some mind. OK then, y'all kin go ahead on with readin'n guessin.

JUDGE HAROLD ("HEAVY") HAND

Judge Harold Hand didn't get the middle moniker of "Heavy" for nothing. Named to the bench twenty years previously, soon his judicial philosophy was described as "Save six for pallbearers, then hang them, too."

Odds were great that any mischief-maker found guilty by him or a jury better refrain from thoughts of future plans. In the vast majority of cases, the State penal system would be assuming that role for the foreseeable future. Some suggested that, while the possibility of being caught in the act didn't deter criminals, the very thought of appearing before Hand lowered the county crime rate.

Defense attorneys made an almost automatic motion for a change of venue or judge, and being named as a public defender by Judge Hand came in a very close second to being chosen to lead the seventh cavalry's stand at Little Big Horn.

And, woe to any guilty-as-sin wrongdoers or their lawyers who entertained ideas of an end run around the law to get leniency or outright dismissal of charges. They learned the hard way that there was no room for such fancy antics in *his* court.

The razor-edged response left the legal lump-heads feeling as though they were sliced into nano-thin wafers preparatory to broiling. Therefore, what happened in the case of the town-drunk became local lore practically overnight.

****

Once again, Willie Cadwallader stood before Judge Hand. Over the years, the routine varied little. Arrested for the umpteenth time for public intoxication, this morning it was right after 3:00 a.m. Six hours later, Willie had barely slept off enough whatever alcoholic substance resulted in the current incarceration to appear before Judge Hand. As usual, he offered a blurry-tongued "Guilty" plea. Preliminaries hurriedly completed, Willie expected the usual, a stern lecture and ten days in the pokey.

Even in his bleary state, immediately after his "Guilty, Judge Shir, yer honor," Willie realized this time was going to be different. Through his developing hangover-headache, it penetrated that Judge Hand's hand was going to indeed be heavy. That was also obvious to Willie's nervous-newbie public defender, two attorneys waiting with clients, and the usual court hangers-on.

"Mister Cadwallader, be seated." Willie stumbled to his chair, and the judge continued. "Drunk again last night and still boozy! My patience is exhausted. Time after time, you have entered a guilty plea and vowed to cease your drunkenness. Often in only a matter of days after your release you are before me and pleading guilty again to yet another public intoxication charge. Obviously, your promise to mend your ways means absolutely nothing.

"As a habitual drunkard, this time my inclination at first was to sentence you to a longer term than the usual ten days. Perhaps thirty days would cause some change in your behavior. On further thought, I concluded only twenty days additional time would not be sufficient. Something like a year on the chain gang came to mind."

Willie's public defender, serving as such only because he was brand new in the firm, started to intervene. A glance from Judge Hand put a stop to such nonsense. Willie shuddered at the thought of a year-long alcoholic abstinence, never mind the hard labor.

Judge Hand cleared this throat to continue. "Therefore…," but a disturbance interrupted. Before the bailiff could attend to it,

2

someone stood and was asking in a small voice, "Judge Sir, your honor, could I jist maybe beg'a little favor to say a word?"

Such was the *outrage* in *his* court that The Honorable Harold Hand was temporarily speechless. Shocked silence could almost be *felt* throughout. Willie's lawyer was stunned silent.

Taking the judge's silence as consent, a slight figure stepped into the aisle, started toward the bench, and said as she approached, "Judge Sir, I be Willie's momma."

Judge Hand stared at the late-fiftyish lady, clearly from deep in the back-woods of the adjacent county. Briefly taken aback and caught between politeness and protocol, he remained silent.

"Judge Sir, I know Willie be forty and a couple or so and ain't done the right things all'a time. He be brought up knowin' if'in he does unruly things, he hasta take his punishment. But, he ain't lived at home fer months'a Sundays, and he's backslid.

"I ain't askin' y'all to let 'im off total, but Judge Sir, somethin' come up, and he's the onliest one that kin hep me. Now that Monty's gone, he was my husband and Willie's daddy, I got nobody else. Our big ol' house is gittin' too much fer me, and I got a lesser place to git to.

"That's why I need Willie to hep. I cain't be totin' all'a my belongin's by own sef. I come lookin' fer 'im this mornin; but heard tell he be in jail agin. If'in ya kin see y'all's way to puttin' off his punishment this time for jist a mite, he could hep. 'Sides, I might could tend to his overdrinkin' some. He be too big to take to the woodshed, but they's other ways." Willie shuddered again.

"Judge Sir, I'd be beholdin' to y'all and certain-sure he come back to git his punishment when he gits done totin' my belongin's and me seein' to his overdrinkin'. He'n I know he's got punishment comin', and I kin git on without 'im for a spell whilst he be doin' it.

"That's all I gotta say, Judge Sir. If'in y'all kin see yer way clear to hold up on his punishment jist a few days or so, I'd be beholdin' to y'all."

Judge Hand responded, "The court recognizes that there can be extenuating circumstances in some rare cases. The court also fully understands that at times justice must be tempered with mercy."

He hesitated and one of the waiting lawyers silently forecast and mentally mocked the judge's next expected statement. *("However, this is not one of those times.")*

The judge was well into what followed before his astonished audience suddenly realized they could be witnessing judicial history. Was Judge Heavy Hand flirting with *mercy!*

"The accused will stand alongside his mother." Head down, Willie complied, and Judge Hand continued, "In view of the extenuating circumstances recounted by Missus Cadwallader, it may appear that this is one of those rare cases in which some exceptions to hard and fast rules apply."

All ears were at full extension and vibrating. Was he *really* gonna do what it was beginning to sound like?

"However, it is the belief of this court that modifications of sentencing usually occur in cases involving first-time offenders."

Spectator's antennae returned to normal. It was gonna be the same Judge Hand. Ol' Willie was gonna get got good.

"Mister Cadwallader, your current guilty plea is a matter of court record. Therefore, you are subject to immediate sentencing and incarceration. You may recall that my earlier thought was to sentence you to a year at hard labor."

The Judge let his next word hang in the air to gain Willie's attention. "However...," All antennae snapped to full extension.

"However, for this one time only, I am modifying the usual sentencing procedure as follows. You are released in the custody of your mother for ten days to assist her in her moving activities. Ten days from today, you are to be returned to this court for sentencing relative to your guilty plea to current charges.

"Your mother in effect becomes an officer of this court and will report any drinking on your part...even *a single drop*. In addition, you are to participate fully in any attempts on her part to help you stop drinking.

"Should you violate these conditions, you will be immediately returned and sentenced. You will be well advised to remember that any sentence will include a stipulation for hard labor long enough to convince you to consider reforming your ways and not remaining the town drunk and an embarrassment to your mother.

"You appear still somewhat in the throes of your most recent drunken episode. Are you sure you fully understand and agree to the conditions set forth relative to being placed in custody of your mother for ten days?"

"Yeschur, I shertain' do. Yeschur, I shertin' do. Both of 'em... shertain do."

"One more thing. If after you finish helping your mother, should she give me a favorable report, it could well be a consideration in determining the length of the sentence for your current offence. Do you understand?"

"Yeschur. Do what Momma says."

"Very well. Now Missus Cadwallader, do you fully understand your responsibilities and agree to fulfill them?"

"Certain do, Judge, and y'all kin be certain I'll do 'em right."

"Very well. You may take your son. Probably a good idea to rest him the remainder of the day. Still looks a bit wobbly." Courtroom curiosity junkies could hardly wait to spread the word.

****

Next morning, Judge Hand was coldly *furious*, each word scalpel-edged. He began a verbal evisceration of Willie Cadwallader with, "Not *a day* has elapsed since you pled guilty to

5

being drunk, and here you are before this court accused for the same offence.

"Not only am I disappointed and disgusted with your continued drunkenness, I am likewise with my decision to allow you to remain free pending sentencing for your current offense. Furthermore, surely your mother standing right there beside you must feel as the court does regarding your broken promises."

Another five minutes of scalding, and Judge Hand threw up his hands. *What's the use!* Nothing I say will make any difference. The best I can do is keeping you out of circulation as long as possible to protect the public. We'll move ahead to sentencing right now. Where is your lawyer?"

"Ain't got 'im no longer."

"And, why not?"

"After me and Momma talked to 'im 'while ago, I didn't want 'im no more. He didn't talk akin to what we told 'im. He said what she wanted to do wasn't good. She told 'im she could do better."

"You must be represented by an attorney."

"Mama said she could do it."

"What!"

"Momma said anybody I wanted could, so I want 'er to." Judge Hand only stared. Spectators smiled—inwardly of course.

Mrs. Monty Cadwallader spoke. "Judge Sir, there be a law sayin' a'body kin stand fer anybody who wants 'em to.

"*Madam*! Are you *instructing* the court!"

"Reckon y'all'd be the one to answer that, Judge Sir."

Judge Hand straightened and prepared to assess this feisty female a healthy fine for contempt of court. The observers collectively inhaled. Wow, was this old lady gonna catch it!

But then the judge only sighed deeply and asked, "Just when did you attended law school?"

"Never, Judge. My departed husband Monty told me wunst."

Judge Hand sighed again. What difference would it make? Willie Cadwallader would plead guilty anyway. "Oh, very well. Mister William Cadwallader, you have been charged with public intoxication. How do you plead, guilty or not guilty?"

"*Not* guilty, Judge Sir."

Judge Hand snapped in disbelief. "*What did you say!*"

Willie's new "attorney" broke in. "I told 'im to say that."

"On what possible grounds?"

"It bein' what they call *'jepardizin' twice.'* Means ya cain't git 'im twice fer the same mischief."

Judge Hand glowered at another "instruction," but only responded, almost as an aside, "I assume the departed *Monty* told learned counsel that the term was *double jeopardy.*" Palms up, he raised his arms, and added, "Well, go ahead. Explain why this is a case of *double jeopardy.*"

"Well ya see, me'n Willie was jist on our way home from court yesterday when we hadta stop at the market for extry vittles, Willie be stayin' with me for a spell. Well, like y'all said, he looked some boozy when he was in here yesterday. Y'all even said so, and that I oughta rest 'im some so he could hep me better.

"Reckon he *was* shaky, 'cause when we come out, he tripped'n scattered the vittles. That there po-lice fella right yonder seen 'im and come over. Reckon the way Willie tried to 'splain things, made 'im look tipsy to the po-lice, so he give 'im this here tippy-toe walkin' test. Willie didn't do good and got arrested for bein' drunk.

"But, Willie weren't drunk *agin* like you said *today*. If'in he be a mite drunk like y'all said *yesterday* jist 'fore we'uns left, he'd be *still* drunk jist a mite later, not drunk *agin*. So, him bein' arrested twice fer the very same drunk'd be jepardizin' twice, Judge Sir."

The court-curious crowd swore later that Judge Harold ("Heavy") Hand showed the briefest trace of a smile just prior to announcing, "Charge dismissed."

7

PONGALIU ISLAND

Zack Gilbert, founder, owner, president, and CEO of **GILBERT INTERNATIONAL**, was *waaaay* beyond frustrated. The word for it hadn't been invented. His long-time personal assistant, Marty Clevenger, was bearing the brunt. "**Con**-found it Marty, I don't *care* what it's gonna cost! Stop whinin' about it. We're less'n two whoops and a holler from twenty billion this year, and you're standin' there like we're goin' belly-up if I do this thing I've been plannin' before you were a gleam in your daddy's eye.

"Dang it, son, we've talked about this a gazillion times! What is it you don't get? You gotta know the drill, but I'm sayin' it one more time. I've done everything on my bucket list—also visited every place that meant anything to me. I gotta do this last one. *Gotta*, I tell ya! Gotta see the place where that Banzai skum-sucker did this." He held up the stump of what was once his left arm.

"It isn't the cost, Zee Gee. Heaven knows, you can afford whatever you want. But, we're right in the middle of the China deal and the planning for those two European plant expansions on the Norwegian coast. Then ...."

Gilbert ham-fisted the desk. Three times. Harder each time. "*Criminitly* Marty! I'm eighty-eight years old! Think I'm gonna make two-hundred? Every single time I talk about doin' this thing, somethin' else comes up. This time, I'm *goin'*. Besides, what am I payin' five VP's for? Let 'em earn their high pay once in a while."

"But Zee Gee, the company jets...."

"Which word didn'tcha understand? *Dagnabbit* Marty, I know both jets are in for maintenance. Buy another one or lease one, I don't care which. I'm gonna be at the hanger tomorrow bright and early. Any problem understandin' that? Wanna hear it again?"

"No sir, but the nearest airfield to Pongaliu Island is light years away from it."

"Marty, you know very well that this thing has always been the top item on my bucket list. Why am I still hearin' all this *can't do* crap! Choppers still land on a dime, don't they? Go, Marty, go. Get a good night's sleep. We're gonna be on our way real early."

"You're the boss, boss."

****

Initially, Gilbert was aggravated that no helicopters or seaplanes were available, and the nearest safe landing site for land-based was still an overnight boat trip from Pongaliu Island. However, he relaxed when informed it would be taking the exact course his outfit took on the way to invade what he always called "that nothin' chunk'a coral crap."

Gilbert sat on the anchor's capstan forward of the decrepit seagoing trawler's wheelhouse, thinking back to a time more than 60 years previously. In size, speed, and about everything else, the rusty tub that Marty Clevenger more or less commandeered was a far cry from the LST (officially, "Landing Ship Tank" or "Large Slow Target" in their crew's lingo) of his last trip. The LST's design enabled them to move right up the beach, lower a ramp, and deploy tanks. This time, only troops would disembark, the site being unfit for tanks to maneuver with even minimum safety.

To no one in particular, Gilbert remarked aloud, "Well, at least those bucket's got one thing in common with this leaky scow. A flyin' fish could penetrate either one."

His thoughts drifted to Pongaliu Island, his "nothin' piece'a coral crap." Nothing distinguished it from any other of the endless string of atolls stretching roughly south to north for hundreds of miles in the South Pacific. Same size stretch of sandy beach fronting a seawall built eons ago by God knew who or why. Same line of palm trees up there beyond the seawall. Same everything.

Pongaliu Island's one brush with notoriety came as the result of a new U.S World War II strategy to bypass as many of these fortified atolls as possible, leapfrogging over one or more to take one further up the chain toward Japan. This eliminated the need to invade and capture every single of these tiny islands on the way to Tokyo. Thus, the end of the war would be speeded and fewer casualties suffered. The first two leaps having been successful, Pongaliu Island would be the next in line to secure.

****

No one was saying much in the pre-dawn as the LST moved slowly toward a speck on the map. As troops sat side by side in battle gear, 22-year-old Sergeant Beauregard "Bo" Calhoun, veteran of two earlier actions, shouted the usual *"listen up"* order.

"Y'all look to your right. Now, look to your left. You don't pay no attention to what I'm gonna tell ya, and one'a ya is gonna be dead by noon." They all heard a version of this before, but listened intently, anyway.

Calhoun continued, "'Sides, those yella sumbitches are dug in everwhere, even in little spider-holes with fake covers where they can pop out behind ya. And, there's snipers up in them palms. And the rest of 'em are in caves up in them cliffs. Y'all ever wanna see your kin agin, don't be fooled. They'll be waitin', all right.

"Y'all getcher sorry butts through that water'n down behind that seawall on the double or y'all'er gonna wind up floatin' out for the sharks. And when the beach master gives the word, y'all had better get over the wall'n move out. He's even meaner'n them heathens in front'a ya."

Zack Gilbert heard tales about beach masters, usually referred to by the troops as "beach bastards." Often top sergeants, they had absolute authority to do whatever necessary to keep the vast array of men, weaponry, and materials in order during the invading waves of each. Rumor had it that they also wouldn't hesitate a second to shoot any man not charging inland when the order came.

Standing six-six, a heavily tattooed gorilla-type was assigned to Gilbert's beach area. As if his stature, flinty eyes and unending scowl weren't enough, just the thought of what he might do with those twin pearl-handled holstered Colts stifled any thoughts of hesitation dead in their tracks.

Yards from the beach, Private Zackery Mason Gilbert was surprised how calm it all looked. He knew the Navy circled the island and bombarded it for 24 hours, but last night the sergeant said not to count on that helping all that much. "That Navy shellin' couldn't'a got ever big gun that's hid."

****

Hisashi Yamaguchi sat high above the cliff-side caves and watched as the little ship approached. During the decades since the white devils left Pongaliu Island, he never gave up hope that one day the followers of his beloved Emperor Hirohito would return for him. His people were patient. Yes, someday they'd come for him. And now they had! His thoughts returned to the time events began leading to this day.

Hisashi was honored to be chosen as a sniper for his unit. The extra hours on the rifle range paid off. As a sniper, he remained secluded high up in a palm tree from which he could pick off the enemy undetected. Whenever his location was threatened, he would just move to another palm.

12

The dug-in troops knew an invasion was coming. After the time-honored meal two days previously, there were Saki toasts and many choruses of the traditional shout given before the charge into battle. *"BANZAI! BANZAI!"*

****

The Navy's covering salvos shattered the calm, and Private Gilbert knew it was about time. Final cigarettes stubbed out on a boot sole, the troops lined up in assigned order.

Then the covering fire stopped to prevent it from falling among friendly troops, and Gilbert knew *now* was the time. The LST ground to a stop on the shallow bottom 30 yards from the beach, and still there was no return fire from the island.

The ship's bat-wing doors slowly opened and the landing ramp lowered into the surf. *Then*, there was return fire! Was there ever! Zack had never heard anything like it. Those hidden guns the sergeant talked about were laying down blanketing sheets of shrapnel all around and through the invading force. An LST farther down the beach suffered a direct hit. Then another tore through an advancing column.

Sergeant Calhoun stepped from the ramp into the thigh-high water and, rifle held high, began splashing and thrashing his way to the beach. Not far behind, Zack Gilbert followed, at first wondering what caused the strings of tiny splashes near his right. Almost instantly recognizing them as machine-gun fire, his splashing and thrashing reached record speed.

Ignoring waterlogged pants and boots, all of Sergeant Calhoun's unit made it but one. Billy Watson, Zack's poker-playing buddy, would never deal another hand. Last in line, the enemy machine-gunner corrected his aim a second too soon. Face down in the bloody surf, Billy rocked gently, studiously "unseen" by the next platoon pouring out of the LST on its way the beach.

13

Private Gilbert lay in the sand as close to the three-foot-high seawall as he could shove himself. The noise grew even more intense. Already, there were cries of, *"MEDIC! MEDIC!"* The din was so earsplitting that Zack almost failed to comprehend the repeated command to charge over the seawall. Seeing the seemingly-immune-to-enemy-fire beach master heading his way immediately sharpened his hearing.

****

Private Hisashi Yamaguchi and his comrades had very little trouble avoiding enemy shelling the previous day and night. The caves provided almost perfect protection. Today's bombardment from the warships stopped as the enemy's troop ships moved toward the beach. Suddenly, everything was strangely calm.

Hisashi watched silently as the ships of the white devils approached. Were there a lot of them! No matter, they and those in them would never prevail. Well concealed high in a palm among several farther back from the first rows, but within easy shooting range, he could see far up and down the beach.

He kept watching the white devils' ships dropping anchor just offshore. The hidden artillery behind him roared, and soon would come the order for him to fire. Nearly in awe, he saw the ships' doors open and soldiers stream down the ramps.

The firing order came. There were so many of the enemy that he was forced to fire so rapidly he couldn't tell for sure how many he hit. Soon, most of the cowardly infidel dogs were hiding behind the seawall, making individual targets much harder to pick out. Suddenly, they began pouring over it.

****

During the nine-day battle for Pongaliu Island, sniper Hisashi Yamaguchi was forced to retreat much farther inland and remain there during the nighttime hours. Thus, hidden and alone, he was not among the remaining troops who were secretly evacuated from a secluded bay on the north side of the island–those who hadn't committed a form of *hari-kari* by jumping from a cliff.

Next day, as he prepared to move forward into position for further action, Hisashi saw that the battle-line was much farther back toward the beach and there were no more sounds of it. To his surprise, he was able to creep far enough forward to take up a position much nearer to the enemy than he had for days. He was astonished to see them moving about on the beach as if nothing were happening. Well, maybe the others were fighting further away. But, wouldn't he have heard *something*?

It was no time for further questions. Many easy targets were available. He was so close to a big white devil that, through his telescope sight, he could actually see the bold tattoos on his sleeveless arms. Hisashi took steady aim and fired. The big white devil didn't fall but his left arm was dangling.

Hisashi grabbed the bolt on his rifle to eject the spent cartridge, but it jammed. Frantically, he jerked harder. Nothing moved–it was hopelessly stuck. He glanced up to see dozens of the enemy running toward him, weapons at the ready.

There was no choice but to retreat to fight another time. He raced toward the nearest cliff, scrambled up its face, dashed inside, and hid in a side-wall depression halfway back. Soon, he could hear the white devils all around outside firing into each cave. When they came to his, he pressed further against the cool walls. Many rounds ricocheted throughout before the shooting stopped. After what seemed an eternity, all was quiet.

****

On the hospital ship bound for home, Zack Gilbert, the last casualty suffered on Pongaliu Island, cursed that "sneaking rat-bastard-coward" in the tree who got off a lucky shot. After

15

surviving the battle described by a war correspondent as "Hell on Earth," fate just wasn't fair!

Would he ever like to get his hands on that sniper for about five seconds! He smiled sardonically. He'd like to get his *one* hand on him. *("Maybe....")*

The other wounded clowns around him sporting medals and displaying souvenirs didn't help either. The one always ribbing that Zack should get a special medal as the last casualty was particularly galling. The medals were only tin crap and the only souvenir he had wanted was the rifle that did the dirty work—the one the shooter ditched as he fled. The one that apparently jammed after that last lucky shot.

His other thoughts were all bleak. *(What good was a freak with only one arm? Those jerks keep talking about getting the million-dollar-wound ticket back home must be dumber'n dirt. What're they gonna do with half of 'em missing or shot all to Hell? What am I gonna do? College is out. Football after college is out. And who's gonna hire a one-armed cripple for any job?)*

****

With no rifle or food, Yamaguchi was reduced to stealing into the enemy area at night and snatching what food he could. After the white devils left, he was astonished at how much they left behind.

Six months later, the abandoned supplies were gone. Sitting above a cliff most of the day waiting for rescue, Hisashi was finally forced to realize help might be a little longer in coming. But daily, he still knelt at his makeshift Shinto shrine paying homage to the Sun Goddess and asking for deliverance.

Food remained a huge problem until he discovered he could survive on roots, crabs, coconuts, and the meat of the big black birds that were captured so easily. Even after he found an abandoned officer's sword and used it to spear crabs, the birds were a staple of his food supply.

However, he couldn't bring himself to kill and eat the one that roosted so close to his own sleeping spot. After a while, the bird became his "Shoichi," his soaring first son. When the creature died, Hisashi buried it alongside the shrine after repeating the ancient funeral chant of his ancestors.

With no noticeable change of season, one year melted into another, but Private Hisashi Yamaguchi remained certain rescuers would come. He was old, but not too old to return to Japan and revel in the rewards of having helped conquer the white infidels. How much better it would've been if he had fought alongside the emperor's troops. But, soon they would rescue him, and he could still celebrate the final victory with them.

****

Being rowed to the beach in a life raft wouldn't be quite the same as during the invasion. But, the builder of **GILBERT INTERNATIONAL** surrendered his fantasies of wading ashore several years earlier. Nevertheless, in a matter of minutes, he'd achieve the most important item on his bucket list.

Every inch of Pongaliu Island was burned into his memory, and he intended to visit every inch, especially the area where that sneaky-sniper-coward in the tree shot off his arm.

****

From his seat high above the cliff, Hisashi Yamaguchi sat watching as he had for decades. Suddenly, he thought he saw something! *He had!* He rubbed his age-dimmed eyes, then jumped to his feet and looked again. He *wasn't* seeing things! A small boat was out there! *At last! At last!* He *knew* they'd come.

Almost unbelieving, Hisashi continued to watch as the small vessel neared and dropped anchor well off the beach. Obviously,

17

the captain was wary of uncharted reefs. The ship was too far offshore for him to see its flag, but who could it be but those coming to rescue him?

Hisashi could make out a life raft being lowered and three figures taking places in it. They'd be here very soon! Better get his things together. Dashing about preparing to leave, he paused only to kneel at the Shinto shrine to thank the Sun Goddess. Then, he hurried to the adjacent thatched shelter he constructed so long ago.

What to take, what to take? He invented so many things to survive at first, then to make life easier later on, that choosing would be difficult. Which should he leave? As time passed, each one became a friend. The flat-stone table and log bench he couldn't take, of course. But, his favorite sun-hardened spear-grass chopsticks might come in handy.

One by one, he considered them, but it became harder to choose. There was the crab-stabbing sword, for instance. There would probably be little use for it, but he simply had to include it on the growing stack of items to take. He'd keep it as a treasured friend and reminder of what they shared.

Each time he placed one thing in a sailor's old sea bag that washed ashore, he thought of another he lived with all this time. Even the crude calendar he kept until it was totally covered with stone-made scratch marks for each change of the moon.

Hisashi kept walking out to the edge of the cliff to see how much longer it would be before his rescuers reached the beach. High waves were slowing their progress, but they kept coming.

Finally, everything was stuffed into the bag except the sword. Often, he used it as a cane. Hisashi sat. He'd rest for just a moment before starting down to the beach. For some time, he knew he was getting along in years. Even without a packed bag of belongings, it took longer each time. Rising, he looked around his home for all those years and smiled. The shelter, the shrine and especially Shoichi's grave flooded his memory. That bird was his family.

He took no time to check his rescuers position. They were sure to be on the beach by now, anyway. Hisashi hoisted the bag onto a shoulder. Soon, very soon, he'd he home.

****

Marty Clevenger helped his boss from the raft and handed him his hefty ivory-handled and Malaga-wood cane. "Here you are. Where to now?"

Turning in each direction, Zack Gilbert looked slowly up and down the deserted beach. "Gimme a minute, will ya Marty? Been more'n sixty years, y'know." He straightened, continuing to scrutinize the broad expanse of beach and jungle. Finally, he turned to his assistant. "Let's get started."

****

Using his sword as a cane, Hisashi Yamaguchi, bag of possessions on a shoulder, turned for one final look before starting down through the dense jungle. As he did, something shocked, almost staggering him, and he had to set down the bag.

One of the island's big black birds circled, then flew down and landed on the stone marking Shoichi's grave. Centuries of folk tales came crashing down. Was the spirit of his soaring first son coming to say goodbye?

Temporarily frozen into inaction, Hisashi soon shook it off and told himself it was nonsense. All those birds looked exactly alike. This was just a weird happenstance.

****

Zack and Marty walked and down a beach packed so surf-solidly that Zack had no trouble using his cane. Stopping occasionally to look around, he recalled a long-ago event to Marty,

19

then moved on. As the walk continued, the stops became fewer and the recollections shorter.

Back at their starting point, the old warrior stood looking into the jungle so long that Marty was debating whether to ask if he was going to try going in there. But, his boss only said, "Right from in there is where that sniper-sneak maimed me for life." He waved his heavy cane about. "Sure would'a liked to run across 'im."

"Ever think he could have done you a favor?"

"A favor!"

"Think about it. If he hadn't shot you, you'd just be another old ex-football star sunning himself on a park bench and boring everyone with tales you'd already told a hundred times."

Gilbert studied his assistant, then turned to stare into the jungle again. Turning back, he commented, "Y'know Marty, maybe you're not as slow-witted as everybody says." Marty grinned at the left-handed compliment by his long-time boss/friend.

****

Private Zackery Mason Gilbert, member of the U.S. Marines again stared into the jungle before announcing, "Old man's dumb idea…comin' here lookin' for somethin'. Just a nothin' chunk'a coral crap. Signal the raft to come back so we can start home."

****

High above, Private Hisashi Yamaguchi, member of the Emperor's Imperial Army hesitated once more before his trip down to the boat and his journey home. He walked over to the shelter to sit for a moment. The bird was still sitting alongside Shoichi's grave-marker. Looking around, memories of the shrine and many other ages-old objects and experiences filled his thoughts. *(So many things, so many years.)*

Memories were followed by a multitude of nagging questions. *(Will the victory over the white devils still be celebrated? Will I know anybody? I know my parents are gone, but what about my brothers and sisters? Maybe they are too. After all, I was the youngest. Will anybody know me? Suppose no one does, what then? What if my home isn't there anymore, where will I live? And, how will I live...get food?)*

He shook his head vigorously as if to clear away the questions. *(Stop this! Get moving! You've got your memories. Soon you'll be back in your home town and get your questions answered...get your problems solved.)*

Many minutes died and still Hisashi sat. More time elapsed. Memories–questions–problems.   Problems–questions–memories. Questions–memories–problems.

Slowly, Hisashi began taking items from the old worn sea bag. *(My memories are right here, and I don't know about finding answers in my home town. It's probably so much bigger now that I couldn't find my way around Hiroshima, anyway.)*

21

THE CAT FANCIER

David Allen sat looking over the sparse landscape in Six Sleep, Utah, thinking about how things had a way of working out. Just out of high school, he was on his self-awarded post-graduation-reward trip when his money ran very low and no one was picking up hitch-hikers.

The waitress at the café told him Six Sleep was so named by an Indian tribe because it was a six-day, six-night journey from the nearest camp. When he asked if she knew of any jobs around, she said that Jefferies Grocery might, but there was a catch. Because of Six Sleep's isolation, very few rooms for rent existed.

Therefore, non-local help sometimes boarded with the owner of the business. In David's situation, it was any port in a storm. He could endure anything long enough to earn bus fare back east.

Mr. John Jefferies of Jefferies Mercantile advised David of the live-in arrangement, adding that sometimes an employee became close to being considered a member of the family. After the evening meal, they often sat with the family in the living room. He even knew of an arrangement lasting for several years.

After stressing that he didn't want a fly-by-nighter who'd take off as soon as accumulating get-out-of-town money, he hired David. He felt a little guilty about his *back-east* plan, but as he told himself earlier, it was "any port in a storm."

David continued to gaze out over the scene that somehow became home and considered how time flies. After three years or so, he suddenly realized that the little pig-tailed kid he barely even noticed when he was hired somehow grew into a just-turned-eighteen, high-cheeked beauty. No one in his right mind would ever again dismiss Julia Jefferies as a pig-tailed kid.

****

As time winged on by, David got the distinct impression that the boss's daughter was also noticing how time flies. Nothing definite, but he was pretty sure she included him in her conversation oftener. He knew for a fact that she was spending more and more time in the living room when he was there. Seemed as though she listened harder to him than to her folks—laughed a little more at his occasional attempt at humor, too.

She even remarked that his new mustache looked good. He really got some food for thought when she told him he could call her by her first name, Julia, since he was now "a regular member of the family." Exchanging the favor, he allowed it would be fine if she called him "David."

Before long, both of them were smitten with the age-old intuition of sweethearts-to-be. Each sensed it would be jim-dandy with the other if they became more than first-name-friendly.

****

One problem—there wasn't a chance of them doing anything about it. Julia's mother would see to that. Maybe there was an outside chance her daughter would "keep company" with the hired help when Hell froze over, but not a snowball's chance before.

Her attitude didn't stop the electricity in the air each evening, but Julia's mother didn't appear to notice any change in the two. Oh sure, it wasn't long before "Julia" became "Jule," and "David" "Dave," but it caused Mom no concern. The young ones always sat across the room from each other; and apart from somewhat less formality in the conversation, everything went on about as usual.

The group read, watched TV and occasionally listened to mother or daughter play the piano. Sometimes, they petted the old white "Missy" cat that was always underfoot. That is, everyone but David. He didn't like *any* cat, even if it was a favorite of Julia's.

This hotbed of tranquility offered little else for excitement and no opportunity for fraternization. None. Nada. Mrs. Jefferies probably didn't even pause to consider the possibility of anything developing between Julia and Dave. She had her sights set on that well-to-do Williamson boy for Julia. He liked cats, too!

****

Julia and David simply must talk. Each just *knew* the other wanted to, but neither could think of a way to do anything about it. Even if one thought of a plan, how could that one possibly tell the other? No chance during the day and certainly not in the living room after dinner.

If only they could talk to each other without someone listening. They'd often heard, "Where there's a will, there's a way," but it didn't seem to apply in this case. Their wills were strong as could be, but a "way" didn't seem possible.

****

Sometimes the best answer is the simplest and most obvi-ous—so simple and obvious that folks look right on by. The solution may take some scheming and can be laced with a dram of danger, but that makes it all the more exciting.

One morning as Julia sat combing her hair, Missy-cat came over and did her usual figure eight against an ankle. Sometimes this caused a tiny spark of electricity. This morning it caused a *bolt of lightning* to smack Julia up 'side the head. Suddenly, she knew the answer to their problem, but patience would be necessary. Naturally, she couldn't tell David, but she was sure he'd catch on.

****

Great campaigns, like great plans, are also often simple. They start with little things such as, "Dave, I'll bet you'd really like cats if you gave them half a chance."

He couldn't imagine why she said that! Anyone with half an eye could tell how he felt about cats. Always had. Wanting to please her, he attempted a humorous but evasive reply. She wasn't particularly persistent right then, but in the days following, she became increasingly so, and it puzzled him considerably.

Finally, she started throwing haymakers. "Dave, you act like you just *hate* cats. I don't know how a nice Christian gentleman such as yourself can't seem to like one of God's creatures." *Wow!* Talk about hitting below the belt! It didn't sound one bit like Julia.

"I don't *hate* cats. Only, I've never been around them much." *(Been around 'em enough to know I don't wanna be around 'em.)*

"Well, that's just what I've been saying. If you gave them any chance at all, you'd like them."

Mrs. Jefferies began noticing Julia's badgering. She, too, often wondered why David disliked cats so intently, but it was no reason to let her daughter keep hounding him. "Julia honey, leave the man be. If he doesn't like cats, he doesn't like cats. Nothing says a'body's obliged to like them."

Julia stopped for a day or two before beginning again, this time with different tactics. "Dave, I just can't seem to get Missy's collar adjusted so I can fix her bell. Could you help me?" David, wanting no part of it, hesitated.

"Tell you what," Julia continued, "Why don't you just call her over there? I'll bet she'll come right to you."

Her mother broke in, an edge to her voice this time. "Julia, I thought I spoke to you about leaving David alone about the cat. Now you're at it again."

David, seeing he was about to get into the middle of things, but still wanting to keep in Julia's good graces, chimed in, "It's all right, Missus Jefferson. It won't hurt any to call the kitty. Once or twice, anyway."

Julia pointed Missy toward him, and was rewarded with a less than enthusiastic, "Here, kitty, kitty."

"Now Dave, you have to act like you really want Missy to come over. Animals can sense it if you don't like them."

David was about to remind her that he kept his end of the bargain when he saw that Mrs. Jefferies was about to get on her daughter's case again, and he didn't want to be responsible. "Here, kitty, kitty. Here, Missy, Missy." At Julia's urging and gentle pushing, the old cat took a grudging step or two, but no more.

"Oh, please try again, Dave, try again. You can see she's going to like you."

David relaxed in spite of grave doubts. "S'pose I could walk over and help with the bell," he offered, beginning to rise.

"*No, no*. Missy is starting to get a fondness for you! Just keep calling." David, noting the suspicious stare of the cat, tried again. But, neither then, nor any night for the next week did Missy venture all the way over. With very limited success, Julia continued her efforts to get the two very wary individuals closer together.

Eventually, still suspicious they might be, each was gaining a fraction more confidence that the other wasn't Satan-sent. Lately, Mrs. Jefferies observed the continuing playlet with good humor. Even if David hated cats, he didn't seem to mind Julia's nagging, so there was no harm being done.

Then one night it happened. Missy actually approached close enough for David to touch her on the head. She bolted to the safety of Julia, but the die was cast. A few nights later, the cat permitted David to stroke her a few times. Soon, the dams of dislike and distrust gave way. Believe it or not, Missy got so she went eagerly to him for her favorite, a neck and chin rub. And, believe it or not, David began to like it. Sort of, anyway.

****

The transformations of Missy and David didn't escape the eyes of the Jefferies, of course. Mrs. Jefferies chuckled, joking about whether David tamed the cat or vice versa. Husband John thought perhaps it was neither. It looked to him as though it was Julia who tamed both Dave *and* the cat, but he said nothing.

Later, Mrs. Jefferies decided maybe she should keep a *little* closer watch on the two cat lovers. But, after eyeing the cat-calling-and-caressing for a while, the feeling went away. Nothing was going on apart from the two calling Missy back and forth .

David's reputation for patience and playing his cards close to the vest would soon stand him in good stead. Had he been of a more impulsive nature, things most likely would've turned out quite differently.

****

The evening began normally enough. Julia sat toying with Missy's collar. "Dave, the bell on this fool collar keeps getting tangled. Why don't you call her over and fix it?"

The bell again? Oh well, it seemed a reasonable enough request, although he hadn't noticed anything wrong with the little bird-warning bell the last time he petted Missy. Looking around his newspaper, he called her over for her nightly rub-and-scratch.

The Jefferies didn't bother to look up from their reading. Those days, they only half heard any of the cat conversations between the young folks.

Missy hopped up onto David's lap and nosed under his newspaper. Absently, he began the routine they both knew well by now. He'd tend to the bell later. First came the stroking. Next, the head scratching causing a big increase in purring volume. The final bit, an under-the-chin-and-neck scratch, produced signs of sheer ecstasy from Missy.

Scratch-and-rubs one and two completed, David put aside his paper and ran his finger downward from the cat's upturned chin as he began, but something stopped him. Maybe the bell *was* getting tangled. He moved it sideways and tried again. Not much better. He started to turn the collar around to get at the bell. That's when he saw the first of many tiny attached notes to come.

Time, so fast fleeting in the past, now froze. Julia didn't dare breathe. Some very negative things could've occurred, but they didn't. Only David's look-before-you-leap nature and poker face saved the day. Julia began breathing again.

****

Time and more notes passed. Then it happened! On the way from Julia to David, Missy was detoured by Mrs. Jefferies offer to share a treat she was munching. Instead of holding the treat down to the cat, she picked her up.

"*John!* Come with me into the kitchen this very minute! There's something we need to talk about! *Now*, John!"

John Jefferies knew the tone. In the kitchen, she began, "Just look at this note! They've been passing these before our very eyes using Missy! *And, all the time he was pretending to like cats!*"

The lengthy discussion following ended with, "This must stop *immediately!* Our daughter's not dallying with any store clerk! *Why, who knows what could happen!* She might end up thinking about marrying him. Go tell him to leave tomorrow morning!"

****

At the wedding reception, Mrs. Jefferies saw David reach down to pet Missy and commented, "Julia likes cats so much, I always did think it'd be nice if she married a man who always fancied them, too."

A.K.A.?????????????

Central Springs was a small town. Not only did everyone know everyone else, the school enrollment was low enough so that the same group of kids passed together from first grade through high school. Patterns and behaviors formed in the early grades often followed students even beyond high school.

Therefore nicknames tacked on and interpersonal relationships that were developed as early as first grade could influence the recipient, positively or negatively, for life. Abel Kane Anson was a prime example. A biographical sketch of his school years bears witness to this.

****

Abel Kane's parents should've known better. Tagging a son with the first name of "Abel" was OK, but adding his mom's family name of "Kane" was not the smartest thing to do in such a religious community as Central Springs. It didn't take school kids long to make the jump to the Biblical story of Cain and Abel and begin teasing him about which he was.

Small, even for a first-grader, Abel Kane remained so all through school. As a result, he was the last one picked when two captains alternately chose those who would be on their team in pick-up basketball or baseball games.

As the smartest kid in is class, Abel was aware very soon of his place in the social pecking order. He compensated by retaliating against the teasing by showing off his superior intellect. First to

31

hold up his hand to answer a question, he also proudly announced his scores and report card grades. Of course, these actions only served to increase the distance from classmates.

Scrawny and undersized, high school athletics were out of the question. Ignoring participation on debate and speech teams, Abel audibly snickered when forced to attend their contests.

Abel Kane was pathologically organized. Everything must be in *absolute* order. The other kids, recognizing this in the first grade, rearranged his school books and material just to see him fume and frantically put things back in their assigned places. For a while, kids changed one of his nicknames from just "Awful Abel" to "Awful-Abel Organizer."

He was interested in girls, of course, finally working up his courage to ask his female counterpart for a prom date. Rejected, he retreated further into a social shell.

As the highest-achieving student in his senior class, he would be the obvious choice to deliver the valedictory address. However, the school administrators were fully aware of his classmate's opinion of him (therefore, community opinion) and changed the eligibility rules. Classmate William Frost would deliver the address, and Abel refused to attend the graduation ceremony. The superintendent then withheld his diploma, reluctantly relenting only after Abel's parents threatened to sue.

****

Unable to afford college, and still seething at his school treatment, he kept his resentment hidden enough to obtain employment as a clerk in the post office. Impressing supervisors by his organizational ability, he moved steadily up to become Central Springs' postmaster, youngest in the State's history.

****

Abel skipped his high-school classes' five-year reunion but finally decided to attend the tenth. He quickly found that after 10 years, nothing changed. He was left standing over there to one side during the meeting-and-greeting stage. A few classmates passed by with a cursory "Oh hello, Abel" on their way to mingle with others of their "in" gang.

That was it for his "meet-and-greet" with one exception. His chief tormenter from first grade forward, Gerry Anderson, stopped by long enough to jab, "Hey Abel, your brother Cain with ya? Get everything organized today?" Inwardly infuriated, Abel left before the *Hail, Hail, Hail, The Gang's All Here* intro to the "What've you been doing the past ten years" opening segment.

That's about all there is to relate about Abel Kane Anson. That is, if you don't count the fact that he became a serial killer.

****

That Central Springs' postmaster was boiling inside was in no way apparent. He continued to be an extremely competent, highly-organized individual, but a transparent one folks saw but looked right through. Jim Fennel once said Abel was like Antarctica. "Everyone knows it's down there, but don't pay much attention to it." Had they been aware of how Abel Anson would organize his actions, no doubt *that* perception would've dramatically changed.

Lately during any free moment, Abel's thoughts of how his classmates treated him all his life were only exceeded by those of revenge for their outrageous treatment. (*"Which are you—Cain or Abel?" was it! "Wee Willie Abel can't reach the table," was it! Didn't want me on the team, was it! "Smarty, smarty had a party," was it! Mary Sue Crandell turned me down for the prom did she! Changed the rules so I can't give the valedictory speech, did they! All of them ignored me at the reunion, did they! Still ignore me, do they! Always "Abel Organizer," is it! Well, I'll show them a thing*

33

or two about organizing!) Abel's long-festering rancor bred action. Oh yes, he'd show them! He fumed aloud, "Those high-minded hypocrites! Revenge is mine, sayeth Abel Anson." He chuckled.

Naturally, he took a great amount of time to plan. Abel Kane Anson would never do differently. Besides, there was plenty of time. After all, everyone in his school class was only in their late twenties. No need to rush.

First, he'd list and plan for every possible contingency which could arise in dealing with *any* chosen wrongdoer, no matter that one. After identifying a particular classmate, he would develop a very detailed plan specifically for that one.

General contingency planning underway, one item high on the list was concealing his motive. After some thought, he decided it wouldn't be of much concern. There was no discernible motive for Abel Anson to commit a crime, was there? After all, he was invisible, wasn't he?

Also demanding additional attention was how to explain his presence in the area of the action should that become necessary. Well, he had a yearly vacation didn't he? Anyhow, such a confrontation was extremely unlikely considering his planning.

Abel reviewed his list of general plans countless times before considering it ready. But, there remained one item he could not resist–leaving a clue that he did the deed proving it wasn't just an accident. Before he departed the area, he'd mail a short letter to the local police signed "A.K.A.?????????????," having added the same number of question marks as letters in his name.

Abel knew that law enforcement personnel believed those initials to mean "Also Known As." He chuckled. In addition to the satisfaction of having dealt with a miserable jerk, he fantasized about the cops trying to deduce just who "Also Known As" actually was. Or if the number of question marks–13–meant anything.

A. K. A ?????????????

****

General planning completed, it was time to prioritize the list of classmates upon whom justice would be administered. This was not as easy as Abel first imagined. After weeks of deliberation, he decided which ones and the order of retribution. As his chief tormentor from the first day of elementary school, it was only fitting that Gerry Anderson would be number one.

****

Abel's organizational ability stood him in good stead when formulating a specific plan for Anderson. As postmaster, he had no trouble tracking the movements and/or interest of his intended. He relieved or temporarily reassigned the employee who regularly sorted the mail and took over now and then. Doing so enabled him to discover that Gerry Anderson was now an avid hunter and made a yearly trek to northern Michigan during deer-hunting season.

The idea of a rifle shot doing in Anderson occurred to Abel, of course, but there were certain drawbacks. A major one was that he knew absolutely nothing about guns or hunting. However, the more he considered it, the more he became convinced he could do it–maybe not this year, but surely the next.

****

Jack Ellison, owner of Central Springs Hunt Club, was astounded when Postmaster Anson joined. Having known him for years, Ellison was further taken aback when Anson enrolled in the beginners LEARN TO SHOOT program. At the end of the course, the club-owner was even further bowled over when Abel Kane Anson won the accuracy competition by a wide margin.

Arranging for vacation time required much less energy. After all, he was the postmaster, wasn't he? Obtaining fake hunting and driver's licenses was also comparatively easy as were the remaining items on his tightly organized to-do lists.

Abel obtained the name of Gerry Anderson's hunting lodge from the return address on his mail and googled its website. In no time, he secured every scrap of information necessary for completing his mission.

Abel hadn't forgotten the "A.K.A." letter. He prepared a few simple sentences to be mailed to the police chief in the town closest to the lodge. Aware of DNA clues, Abel used latex gloves, the first of a box of self-sealing envelopes, and peel-off stamps which didn't need to be moistened.

When finished, he read the brief document with its initials-only and question-mark signature several times, each time experiencing more pleasurable anticipation.

> To whom it may concern:
>
> Today, Mr. Gerry Anderson was shot and killed.
> This was not the result of a hunter's stray bullet.
> I killed him.
>
> Very truly yours,
>
> A.K.A. ?????????????

Smiling, he carefully concealed it in his luggage as he reflected again upon the furor it would cause. Packed and ready to depart, Abel went over each item on both lists once again. Satisfied all was in readiness for the next step, it was time to deal with Mr. Gerry Anderson–*permanently*.

****

Using the alias of Wilson McGinnis, the day prior to the opening of deer-hunting season, Abel Kane Anson registered at HUNTER'S PARADISE LODGE. A mile away, Gerry Anderson was doing the same at *DEER TRACE INN.* The similarities ended there. Anderson went into the bar. Abel mushed a mile through the snow to inspect the staging area where **DEER TRACE** guests assembled to be transported to their assigned blinds tomorrow morning. There they would await the passing below of an unwary, unlucky or just plain stupid deer. Should the "big-game" hunter hiding in the flimsy structure a story or so up a tree be dumb-lucky with a shot, he could hang the unfortunate animal's head on a wall to collect dust.

Locating the staging area wasn't difficult with the help of maps and information provided in **DEER TRACE** advertising. Finding a spot with an unobstructed view and proper concealment was more time-consuming. After nearly an hour, Abel found one within easy shooting distance. Along with white coveralls and camouflaged rifle, the concealing underbrush would make detection virtually impossible, even if foul play were suspected.

Having packed everything and checked his rifle again this morning, Abel donned his camouflage gear and slipped out a side door well before dawn. A hundred yards beyond **DEER TRACE LODGE**, he pulled off the road and parked. During his earlier research, he found it not uncommon for cars to do so.

Barely dawn, he located his hiding place, arranged concealment, and checked his rifle twice. Even at this hour, shots by distant hunters could be heard. Minutes later, sounds of vehicles arriving at the staging area signaled hunters would soon be dropped off for transportation to their respective blinds.

Enough light now, through binoculars Abel almost instantly spotted the 300-plus pound bulk of his target. Putting them aside, he took up his telescope-sighted rifle and again spotted Anderson.

During the uproar following a very accurate 80-yard shot, A.K.A. ????????????? vanished quickly and quietly back into the deep cover of the woods. On the way out of the nearby town he stopped only long enough to drop a letter into a street-side mailbox.

****

Fellow workers at the post office remarked that their boss was so unusually upbeat, he must've had a good vacation. When asked, Abel said it sure was and he hoped to have another like it.

For weeks, his euphoria lasted, helped along at first by the local commotion resulting from news of one of Central Springs' citizens being "accidentally" shot while on a deer-hunting trip. When news of the letter to the police leaked out, local reaction was even more tumultuous, continuing to feed Abel's elation. He smiled at each rumor and revelation.

With the "alleged" homicide no closer to a solution after nearly a year and no hint of the actual identity of "A.K.A." the event was put into the cold-case file. As yet, the signature had not become a 24/7 cable-news channel's sensational-story-of-the-day. This would change soon enough.

****

A brief encounter with Mary Sue Crandell, the same Mary Sue who rejected Abel as a prom date, resulted in him moving her from fifth on his list to number two. He chanced upon her at the mall and greeted her warmly. Barely acknowledging him, she swept right on by. A.K.A. ????????????? dropped his research on Charles Collins that night and began hers.

Following his painstakingly organized methods, he soon put together another plan to deal with Mary Sue. Always a loner, she still avoided socializing with anyone, even to vacationing alone. Next year, it would be a solo hike down the Adirondack Trail.

****

A. K. A ?????????????

The Virginia police chief had no idea who Mary Sue Crandell was, much less A.K.A. ?????????????? Nor did he have the slightest inkling about any killing until another hiker rushed in to inform him there was a body beside one of the overlooks down there on the Trail. *"Looks like she's been shot!"*

Again, post office employees were surprised at the positive demeanor of the postmaster upon returning from his vacation. Again and again, he smiled upon overhearing their comments.

****

Abel Anson attended his second reunion, the class' twenty-year. Inwardly grimacing, he listened as William Frost began the remembrance ceremony for six of his classmates. Oh yes, he was the very same fellow who replaced Abel as valedictorian.

Frost began by summarizing the facts of six tragic deaths as if no one was aware that the first two still-unsolved homicides were followed by the cryptic A.K.A. ????????????? letters.

He followed with the "news" that after the second homicide, the letters became national news. Next, he again reported what everyone knew—the only similarities between them were that after being investigated and reinvestigated, there was not one shred of evidence of the sender's identity.

There was more "news." The third class member's demise was ruled a suicide, the fourth and fifth, accidental. The sixth an as yet unsolved homicide.

Frost finished with his own commentary about law enforcement failures, a lengthy prayer for the departed, and finding the perpetrator. Head bowed, Abel glanced sideways both ways and smiled inwardly. *(Eight more to go, but there's still plenty of time.)*

He left immediately after the ceremony, congratulating himself on his strategy for not sending letters after the third through sixth actions. Had he done so, the cops might've connected the dots, deduced everything was just too coincidental, and started snooping more intensely around Central Springs. Not sending letters took away much of Abel's satisfaction and he determined to start sending them again.

Enough time passed since number six that he figured the police would think the killer died or was in prison, leaving the old investigations in cold-case files. So, sending a letter after number seven was dealt with would have them thinking it was done by a copycat killer. Ah yes, things had been brilliantly organized and carried out. Soon it would be time to proceed.

Abel smiled at the paradox of William Frost leading the remembrance ceremony would be number seven.

****

During Christmas holidays, local regular daily news programs were interrupted by breaking news that another death involving a Central Springs resident had occurred. The body of a Mr. William Frost was found in the parking lot of a suburban St. Louis motel, apparently run over by a hit-and-run motorist.

At first thought to be the result of an accident, within the hour, it was reported that yet another A.K.A. question-mark follow-up letter had been received by the local police. That night, the latest accident-turned-homicide became the featured story on all 24/7 news-blabs and major networks. Next day, with few exceptions newspaper headlines shouted, **A.K.A. STRIKES AGAIN.** Or,**?????????? IS BACK.**

Virtually all media commentary was police-negative, whether directed at local or federal agencies. Pleas for help in solving the now notorious multiple murders came from two syndicated TV shows. One agency underling suggested A.K.A. ????????????? be added to a most-wanted list. His supervisor said it was a dandy idea if only they knew who it was.

All sources interviewed suggested that the perpetrator, or perpetrators, showed a genius for planning, organizing, and never making that tiny misstep leading to the downfall of most criminals. Also for incredible patience.

Except for possible psychological satisfaction, there seemed to be no apparent motive. One profiler said it could be revenge, but that was dismissed since revenge killing most often showed evidence of passion and was certainly less well organized, planned, and executed. All involved agencies agreed that this was indeed a new breed of serial killer.

Abel Kane Anson did a lot of smiling. *(Revenge is sweet, sayeth Abel! Maybe I should thank them for treating me so badly in school. Never would've had this much pleasure.)*

****

At his desk doing the morning business, Postmaster Abel Kane Anson looked through his open door to see Police Chief George Martin, the one person who always treated him civilly from their elementary school days onward. The chief strode to the doorway and looked in. Abel beckoned, rose and shook hands. "Glad to see you, George. What can I do for you today?"

"Just dropped by to check the mailbox. But, as long as you're asking, that fifteen-fingered clerk of mine fouled up our postage meter again. Last time you sent Joe Engle down, but I'd consider it a favor if you, yourself, could take a look at it. Got time? We're due to get out the monthly State reports this afternoon."

"No problem, George. I'll get my hat."

On the way, they passed the usual chatter about doings in Cedar Springs. At the station, the chief surprised Abel, guiding him right on by the clerk' office. "Come into the office a minute, will you? Something I want to ask."

41

Inside, Abel was again surprised to see two other men whom the chief identified. "This is John Armbruster. He's a police chief from down Saint Louis way. This other gentlemen is Harry Henderson. He's a fed.

"I've told them you're such a keen organizer and don't make mistakes. Since that's the case and you're the postmaster, they thought maybe you could help them come up with an answer to a question they have. Go ahead Henderson."

"Well, Mister Anson, obviously you aware that a great many law-enforcement agencies are working on the Central Springs murder cases. Also, that we have made no headway on solving them. Now, perhaps you can help us with a question we have."

"Mister Henderson, what question could I possibly answer regarding a crime occurring down there?"

"Well, Mister Anson, we need every bit of help we can get."

"I still don't…."

"Let me explain. After this most recent murder of a Central Springs citizen that happened in Chief Armbruster's jurisdiction, he received one of those now-notorious A.K.A. letters.

"Chief Martin's been telling us of your meticulous attention to every small detail in order to never make a mistake. So, perhaps you can help us with a question concerning this document."

Henderson held it before him and continued, "This is photo-copy of the envelope which contained the A.K.A. letter sent to Chief Armbruster. Here's our question. How is it that your name and address are on the stick-on return address label?"

FLORENCE BY ANY OTHER NAME

Agent Wendell Wilkerson at the Reeves Crossing train station had about enough. His record as Assistant Agent at Newport News was a good one. He was almost sorry he asked for a promotion, having no idea he'd get a station of his own deep in the mountains. Here, everything went haywire every *single day*.

Today was only going to be another example. Cattle got loose from the morning local. Then, the 9:37 hit a wagon down in the hollow and the engineer stopped to see whether anyone was injured. That bollixed up the schedule so all eastbounds ran late. Then, on this *totally* fouled-up day, the regional superintendent "dropped in" to inspect the books.

If all this weren't already bad enough, now a white whale of a woman was insisting upon buying a ticket for a nonexistent place. Wilkerson peered through the grill at her. "I tell you madam, I *can't* sell you a ticket for *Florence!* I've looked in all the books and there *is* no *Florence* on this rail line!"

The whale was adamant. "Don't know nawthin 'boutcher fancy books. Alst I want is git a ticket fah Flawnce."

Teetering on the rim of a shouted response, the agent hesitated. Recalling the regional super's departing lecture about the customer always being right, he kept a tight rein. Tersely polite, he responded, "Madam, I'm telling you again that I can't sell a ticket for Florence or any other place not in the schedule book."

"Don't see why'n the world y'all cain't see your way clear to sellin' me such a ticket. Other man 'fore y'all did."

"Madam, I cannot be responsible for what the last agent did. For the last time, *Florence* is not on this rail line!"

"Still cain't see why y'all won't sell me a ticket fah Flawnce."

This was the last straw. No job was worth all the other craziness, and now this! Wilkerson began breathing like a steam locomotive pulling away from the station—slowly at first, then puffing ever faster until it reaches full speed. Then, having inhaled every last bit of air his lungs allowed, he exhaled in a great bursts.

Nearly purple from extreme oxygen depletion, he grabbed the edge of the counter and, as he straightened to his full height, noisily inhaled another full charge. *By Jupiter,* he was gonna let this woman know where to head in! But, seeing her still waiting so doggedly unyielding, somehow caused the pent-up outburst to stick in his throat.

With clenched-teeth calm, he slowly exhaled and shoved the schedule books toward her. "All right, Madam, since you're so all-fired stubborn, just *show* me exactly where *Florence* is."

Displaying great patience, she pointed out Florence. "Why right there she be. Sittin' ovah yondah on that bench."

LETTERS TO EUNICE

Having finished mowing the front yard, Rex Keller was trimming the hedge bordering the front sidewalk. A couple years back, he began talking aloud to himself, but was careful to avoid this when someone else might hear. His wife, Anne, chided him as an old fud when she heard.

He stepped back and inspected the results. "Not bad for an old fud. Not bad at all. Eighty-seven on my next birthday and still doing my own yard. Thank goodness I'm still able. Gotta be honest, though. This could be the last year. My back is killing me.

"House is too big now for just the two of us. Been a good run. Sixty-five years. More for Anne. She grew up here, and we moved in with her parents right after we married, then stayed after they split. Been here ever since.

"Not gonna pen us up in one'a those warehouses they call 'assisted living.' We'll find a regular house and do the *assisting* ourselves. Get a little help in for Anne when she needs it."

Rex rested a moment longer, then stood and rubbed his aching back before beginning again. "Gotta get on with it. Everybody's gonna be here this weekend. House'll be packed. What a time! Kids, grandkids, great grandkids here all at once for our sixty-fifth wedding anniversary. Who' would'a thunk it?"

A half-hour and another rest stop later, Charlie Prost came swinging along. Rex couldn't remember how long Charlie had been the mailman, but it was years. How he managed to maintain such a cheery manner was a mystery. No one could recall seeing him unsmiling or failing to offer a happy hello. Big kidder, too.

This morning was no different. "Hey there, Rex. See you're talkin' to yourself. Anybody answerin' this time? See ya got most'a the work done. Should'a called me. I would'a done it for ya…for a small fee, a'course."

"Charlie, you're right on time. As usual, you've showed up just when the work's about finished. Whataya do, hide up the street and watch until you see the heavy lifting's all done?"

"Now, now, Rex. You know in spite of rain or sleet or heavy liftin', the mail must go through. Speakin'a the mail, I've got somethin' of a mystery maybe you can help me with."

"Need help finding your backside with both hands?"

"Not thatcha don't have experience in tryin' that on yourself, this is official. I s'pose you've heard of those really rare times when a letter may be delayed a little bit in delivery. Well, I got one here that's been delayed a little."

"Delayed? How little?"

"Well, several years."

"C'mon, Charlie. How many years?"

"Well, about sixty-six."

"Ye Gods! Sixty-six! Call that a *'little bit'?"*

"But, it *did* get here, Rex."

"Gotta be a record. What makes you think I can help?"

"Here it is, Rex. Kind'a beat up so you can't make out the return name and address. Can't tell much about where it was sent from, but it looks to me like it an APO mailing. You know, from a military post. You *can* see for sure that it's addressed to your house to somebody named Eunice Carmondy. Ever hear of anybody by that name livin' here?"

The instant Rex saw the name and address on the letter, he felt dizzy. *It couldn't be!* But, there it was with the telltale double underlining beneath her name. His head cleared, but he remained silent, staring at it.

Mailman Prost asked, "Everything OK, Rex? You looked pretty pale there for a minute."

"I'm OK Charlie."

"Well?"

"Well, what?"

"What's the matter with you, Rex? I asked if you knew anybody by that name."

"Matter of fact, I do. Just seeing her name like this set me back a bit. Charlie, 'Eunice' is my wife Anne's first name. She never liked it. After we married and her parents moved away, she wanted to be called by her middle name. She was a Carmondy."

"Wow! Won't she be surprised! She home? I'd sure like to see her face when she sees that letter! Can you call 'er?"

"'Fraid not. She's off shopping somewhere."

"Well, tell 'er I was glad it finally got here."

"Will do. Thanks a million, See you later."

As Charlie went on down the block, Rex Keller held the letter before him, still in a state of semi-shock. He knew what the blurred-out return name and address was, all right. His thoughts raced back sixty-six years when it was mailed.

****

Rex's first thoughts were of events in the field hospital just to the rear of an action later known as "The Battle of the Bulge." Sergeant Rex Allen Keller drifted in and out of consciousness for almost a week. Medics were successful in removing the three pieces of German shrapnel that penetrated his back.

The big tree limb that slammed onto his helmet when the shell exploded overhead was another matter. The doctor told him later that there was nothing they could do but wait to see if his brain would recover. Meantime, they watched him carefully to determine whether any changes might appear.

Rex recalled that in one of his more lucid periods, he seemed to have had a blurry memory of the same beautiful nurse tending to him. On the fifth day after the shell burst, his sight suddenly cleared, and he spoke for the first time. "Hello there."

The nurse rushed out to summon a doctor. He hurried in and began checking several signs. "Well now, it looks as though things are looking better."

The medic left after giving orders to the nurse. Among others, "Watch him carefully. If he wants to talk, encourage him. If he shows signs of lapsing into unconsciousness, come get a doctor immediately. I'll arrange for other shifts to do the same."

Rex smiled as he remembered remarking that they were paying far too much attention to a little something that "just happened yesterday." When the nurse stopped chuckling, she brought him up to date, not only about his "little something" that happened *five days ago*, but also how the battles were going. Good news, the allies were advancing.

After two more days, the medic decided full-time care was not needed, so nurses only stopped in routinely. By now, Rex and his day nurse became fast friends, learning much about each other.

At the memory, a smiling Rex said aloud. "In such a situation, it's only natural some personal information gets exchanged," then looked around. *(There I go again. Gotta break that habit.)*

As Rex learned more about the nurse, he was increasingly fascinated. Her name was Bridgette DuVal. Although French, she spoke perfect English due to having lived in England during the years France was occupied, returning soon after the allies fought their way ashore on D-day. She was his same age, their birthdays only three weeks apart. Her boyfriend had been a resistance fighter, but was captured and executed by the Gestapo.

Her parents were forced into a slave-labor camp near what was now the front. She had heard no word about them in years, but planned to go there as soon as it was declared safe.

Rex's memories continued as if only yesterday. Soon, he noticed Bridgette's "routine" visits were becoming ever more "routine." He joked with her about this and said he was going to miss them when he was returned to duty with his outfit.

Joking further, he suggested perhaps he'd need some "routine" visits there. To his surprise, she smiled, raised an eyebrow and responded, "When one is a nurse, one does what is necessary to see to her patient's recovery."

****

Rex jumped, startled when Anne called to him from the porch. "Rex, I saw Charlie Prost from the window. Anything for me? Sue Green is sending me her recipe for cinnamon rolls."

He turned quickly to retrieve his hedge trimmers, stuffing the ancient letter into a pocket as he did. "Don't know, Babe. Haven't looked through it. I'll bring it up. Need a break, anyway."

Rex went to the den and again began thinking back sixty-six years. He left the unopened letter in his pocket, but its heavy presence was no less felt.

****

Soon after he returned to his regiment, Rex was informed that he would remain there for at least six weeks while his condition was monitored, then be given a medical discharge.

Ecstatic, that night he wrote letters home with the good news, first to Eunice Carmondy, his high-school sweetheart. They pledged to marry after graduation, but the war intervened. He recalled almost every single word of that letter written so many long years ago.

49

My *dearest Eunice,*

I have time for only a quick note to you and my parents.

There is GREAT NEWS! I will be coming home in just over six weeks! It will be the longest six weeks of my life, but I'll be thinking every minute of how wonderful it will be to hold you in my arms again. And to think of our lives <u>together</u>. I know it will be a long time for you, too, but it's finally going to happen.

Must stop, my darling.

Forever yours,

Rex

****

The unopened "mystery' letter before him, Rex sat for a long time, staring at it as other thoughts returned. After his hospital stay, Sergeant Rex Keller was on a flight to Dulles airport for a final check-up at Walter Reid hospital.

He still mentally shuddered at the memory of the shock a millisecond after entering the airport. *There she was! Eunice!* He couldn't understand it–Eunice right there with his parents!

Why was she here! For five weeks, letters to her became ever more tenuous as he struggled to deal with what was becoming inevitable. Surely, Eunice *must've* gotten that *last* letter. The one sent the day he sent one to his parents advising them of his arrival.

In hers, he explained things, but there she stood! Was she gonna act as if she didn't get that letter still so clear in his mind.

Dear Eunice,

This is the hardest thing I've ever done and will always be, but it's the fairest for everyone. My heart breaks for you to hear this, but I cannot go through with a wedding. To be perfectly honest, I have met someone here in France and we intend to get married just as soon as she locates her folks who have been in a slave labor camp in Germany. She was my nurse when I was in the army hospital and is my true love.

I'm coming home to visit my parents for a couple weeks, then pulling strings to get back to France to marry. Or to get her to the U. S.

I'm not going to be stupid and say it just happened, but that's just what it did.

Eunice I will always remember you as the finest friend anyone could ever have and wish you the best of everything. It won't be long before you find someone lots more deserving than me.

Rex

****

Putting thoughts of the letter aside briefly, Rex recalled how happy his folks were, but nothing compared to the joyous feelings Eunice expressed over and over. In a brief hiatus, she explained that she was visiting his parents in Richmond when they got his arrival-time letter. They persuaded her to stay and come with them to Washington to meet him.

So, that was why she hadn't gotten his final letter. She was away when it arrived. She'd get it upon returning home. But, in all these years, nothing was said about any "Dear Eunice" letter. At the airport, Rex first thought it possible that it could've been on the plane that went down in the English Channel. His second thought was, *(But wouldn't the letter I mailed my parents the same day have gone down, too? Maybe not. Maybe on a different plane.)*

Later that day, when Eunice brought up the subject of not receiving an arrival letter, Rex's mother explained, "Don't you see, dear? He wanted to surprise you." Rex only smiled weakly as Eunice embraced him once again.

****

Tapping the letter on his desk Rex sighed, "Never can tell what's in store. How different things might've been if Anne had gotten this letter. And if, during a counterattack, some greenhorn Luftwaffe pilot hadn't mistaken the slave-labor camp for an allied target. The one where Bridgette was visiting her parents only two days before I left for home."

Turning the letter over and over, Rex debated whether to take one last look or just shred it. Maybe one last look would provide some closure. He reached for a letter opener. *(I just gotta know if this is my "Dear Eunice" letter arriving after all this time. If it is, that would explain why she never said anything about it. And, she wasn't just pretending not to have received it.)* At first, he had trouble processing what he was seeing.

My *dearest Eunice,*

I have time for only a quick note to you and my parents.

There is GREAT NEWS! I will be...

"*Drat!*" It was only the copy of his letter to Eunice telling her he'd be home in six weeks. Due to uncertainties of mail delivery, many GI's sent a copy of each letter a day or so later. Eighty-six-soon-to-be-eighty-seven Rex Keller sprang to his feet, knocking over a desk lamp. About to shout, "***Anne! Come in! You're not gonna believe this,***" he stopped in the nick of time. How would he explain opening her mail? Besides, showing her this letter might lead to a "chat" about a certain "Dear Eunice" letter. He fed it into the shredder.

****

Two days later, Rex was finishing the front-yard tree trimming when Charlie Prost came by with the mail. "Hey Rex! Who says lightning can't strike twice in the same place, you *lucky dog!*"

"Does the postal service have any restrictions about boozing while on the job? What're you talking about?"

"Why, that letter yesterday, Rex."

"You mean *two days* ago. You're confused, as usual."

"Rex, my good man. I mean the one I gave to Anne when she was out here with her flowers *yesterday*. The one just like the first one. Sixty-six years late and beat up a little. But, who says the mail don't go through? I betcha the TV would carry on about it if you tell 'em. Once might not be a record, but two's just gotta be, don'tcha think?"

HEY Y'ALL! KINDLY HOLD UP PLEASE!

THIS HERE BE MISSUS CLARABELLE CADWALLADER TALKLIN' ATCHA. 'MEMBER? I BE THE ONE THATCHA READ ABOUT BACK IN THE VERY FIRST TALE WHERE JUDGE HAND WAS GITTIN' READY TO DO JEPARDIZIN TWICE TO MY BOY.

SAY NOW, WEREN'T THEM TALES FOLLOWIN' THAT FIRST ONE SOMETHIN' ELSE! DIDJA KEEP ON TRYIN' TO GUESS WHAT THE ENDIN' WAS GONNA BE WHILST YA WAS READIN' ALONG? OUGHTA, MORE FUN THATA WAY.

ANYWAY, I BE ALSO THE ONE THAT'S S'POSED TO KEEP LETTIN' Y'ALL KNOW EVER NOW'N AGIN IT BE TIME TO TAKE A BREAK FOR COFFEEIN' UP OR WHATEVER. (NOW, Y'ALL KNOW WHAT I MEAN.)

GO AHEAD ON NOW'N I'LL BE COMIN' BACK ATCHA AGIN PURTY QUICK.

BACK FROM "WHATEVER" SO SOON? WELL, KEEP ON READIN'N GUESSIN' 'CAUSE THESE NEXT'UNS WILL KEEP Y'ALL SCRATCHIN' TRYIN' TO FIGGER HOW THEY TURN OUT. GARANTEE IT, 'LESS, Y'ALL BE'A OUTSTANDIN' GUESSER, BLESS YER HEART.

SEE Y'ALL LATER WHEN IT BE TIME FOR A BREAK.

COACH HEYNED

All high school basketball teams have one or more student "managers." Most would mortgage their future to play on the team, but most couldn't drop the ball through the hoop while standing atop a stepladder. Their only chance to associate with the "guys" is to become the team's designated "manager."

Team managers have a myriad of assigned duties, including distributing uniforms, collecting wet towels, soggy uniforms, and making sure everthing is ready for trips to name only a few. "Manager" it may be, but, "gofer" would be more accurate.

Aside from being "one of the guys," rewards for the manager are few. He gets to sit on the bench during games and ride on the team bus. And after his senior year, he's awarded a sweater emblazoned with the first letter of the high school's name. However, "**Mgr**" is embedded prominently in it to make it clear that he wasn't an actual team member. Those tokens are it for rewards. Anything else, he has to imagine or invent.

The new team manager for the Benston Battling Buccaneers, Roy Edward "Ned" Harkness, fit the mold as had so many others. So typical was he that "team manager" in the dictionary would've included his photograph.

Five-foot seven, scrawny and hereditarily non-athletic, chances for him doing anything agile afoot beyond walking to Friday night

Bingo were zero minus zero. Horn-rimmed glasses were the exclamation point.

****

Apart from adding a different name to the long list of all-the-same team managers, their careers varied little. To coaches and players alike, most often the manager's chief interaction begins with *"Hey...Theo!"* (Or the name of whoever is the currently designated vassal.) A "Gimme" or "Get with it" order often follows, and he jumps to obey. In Ned's case, as usual the only difference was that his demand-call to duty was *"Hey...Ned!"* preceding "Gimme" or "Get with it."

Not long after Ned became manager, somehow "Hey...Ned" became fused into only one word and "Hey...Ned" became *"HeyNed"* to the players, coaches and other classmates. Now and then even a teacher addressed him as such.

Ned didn't mind being asked, "Hey...HeyNed, 'What's happening," or "Gonna win this week, HeyNed?" It was a form of recognition as one of the "guys." His very own nickname was lots better than a semi-ignored, "Ned." Worse yet, "Edward."

A junior and into his second year as team manager, Ned became increasingly aware that there was more to basketball than only watching the player handling the ball or shooting. Sitting near long-time coach Bernie ("Alabamy") Beck during games, Ned heard all sorts of Beck's shouted instructions to the team and began observing more intently during practices.

When Ned sometimes asked questions about strategy, Coach Beck expressed surprise at a manager's intense interest in the game's finer points and his budding knowledge. Initially, the coach teased him about becoming a new assistant, then became genuinely impressed. Occasionally, he even allowed Ned to sit in on the coaching staff's meetings.

Before the season ended, Ned Harkness developed such a love for the game that it became not just an athletic event to him. It was an art form equaling ballet. By his senior year, Ned knew exactly what he wanted more than anything was to become a basketball coach. Finally working up his courage, he shyly expressed this to Coach Beck.

"Harkness, I've had lots of 'em say that. Can't think'a more'n one that made the grade. Rest of 'em didn't stay long at it."

Knowing Beck's manner, Ned squirmed in his chair and prepared for the worst. For a long moment what the coach added didn't register. When it did, the boy was so thrilled that he had trouble controlling his grin.

"Yeah, I've heard 'em talk that way before, Harkness. But of all of 'em, I think you got the best chanch'a cuttin' it. Never knew anybody to pick up the game faster. Kid, you bein' born with brains instead'a muscle don't mean you can't be a good coach. Tell ya what I'm gonna do. I'm gonna letcha sit in on all the coachin'-staff's meetin's. Whataya think'a that?"

Ned still hadn't recovered enough to speak and only nodded vigorously as Beck continued, "Knowin' the fix your family's been in since your dad busted his leg, you goin' on to college is gonna take some doin'. You bein' pretty nerd-lookin' and not a player either, I can't do much about tryin' to getcha a scholarship, but the university bein' only a couple miles down the road from your house, there's no reason you can't live at home and go there.

"'Sides that, you bein' brainy, you can probly get some other kind'a scholarship. You givin' that any thought? Talk to the Guidance guy 'bout that, have ya?"

"Well, yes. But, he said most of them don't furnish much beyond tuition and books. Said some offer more, but the competition is tough, and math and science majors get almost all of them. Computer geeks, too. Said he knew getting a summer job

61

could be hard, but maybe if I could get one and lived at home, it's possible I might make enough to go to the university."

"Sounds like he could be speakin' the straight skinny. What about a student loan?"

"My dad's dead set against it. Says it could make you broke all your life."

"Tell ya what, HeyNed, I can maybe help out a little with the job thing. I'm sure you heard'a old man Jake Jenkins. You know–Jenkins Hardware. He's a shirt-tail relative'a my Missus. You probly know he's a skinflint and the hired-help thinks he's meaner'n a stepped-on rattler. Awful borin', too.

"Well, Martha–you know, my Missus–she can handle 'im pretty good. I talked a'ready to 'er 'bout puttin' in a word for ya, and she's ready to. Just say the word. It'll mean you could work this summer and next summer after you graduate. Jenkins'll try to hire ya as cheap as he can, but you'll be able to save quite a bit. Whataya say?"

Still semi-flabbergasted at what was happening, Ned hesitated. Coach Beck took this as reluctance and figured he guessed wrong about the kid, then saw tears begin to well. "Aw c'mon HeyNed. You're not gettin' the world on a silver plate. You're gonna work your butt off for that old miser-tightwad, and it'll be pretty tough for a while."

Ned tried as best he could, but had trouble finding enough words for proper thanks. Beck stood. "Cut the crapola, kid. You're the one that's gonna be bustin' his butt. Speak'a butt-bustin', better get yours down to the locker room and make sure everthing's set for practice. Go on–git before I change my mind."

****

The summer job at Jenkins Hardware was indeed difficult, mostly due to Jake Jenkins himself. His instructions, repeated *ad nausea,* could soon be partially tuned out. However, his incessant nasal whining (a new subject daily), coupled with his expectation that Ned would verbally agree to each whine, was more trying.

A crazy opening hour twice weekly only added to the nuisances. Jake thought opening twice weekly at 7:00 a.m. would attract more customers than if he opened every day at the regular 8:30 hour. There was no good evidence for this. He always did it this way as had his father, beginning 65 years ago. In fact, it made no difference in sales whatsoever, but Ned and the other clerks had to take turns opening early.

Yes, these and other Jenkins idiosyncrasies made working for him a trial, but Ned's dream of a coaching career was the buffer making it bearable. Except for what he gave his parents, every dime of his minimum-wage pay deposited in savings was another step toward his goal.

Toward the end of summer, even penny-pincher Jenkins recognized that Ned was an asset. He brought in new customers, and some regulars began asking that he wait on them.

Two weeks earlier, Jenkins raised Ned's pay $2.00 weekly. OK, so what if it only amounted to about a nickel an hour, it was that much more in his college fund.

When Jake asked team-manager Harkness to work Saturdays during his senior year, he agreed, providing there wasn't a Saturday game. Things were looking up. The extra earnings accumulated while still in high school, and during his first college semester, would help put his growing fund over the top.

****

As team manager during his senior year, Ned became more committed than ever to becoming a coach. Most of his limited free time was spent reading or talking about basketball. The assistant coaches, as well at head-coach Beck, offered tips adding to his knowledge of the game. Occasionally, Ned would discuss the previous night's game with them. Once, even Coach Beck asked him what he might've done in a certain game-deciding situation.

Knowing Ned's coaching ambition, the assistants kiddingly began calling him "Coach HeyNed." Players picked up on this and soon did likewise. This didn't stop their usual "Hey...Heyned, Gimme this...," or "Get that..." demands, but it was now a less demanding, "Hey, HeyNed! Gimme, etc."

Prior to the opening game during Ned's senior year, it was apparent that the Battling Buccaneers were not going to set the basketball world aflame. This was understandable, with the starting five having no senior-year players and only two juniors. However, as the season progressed, the team's potential was obvious, and everyone looked forward to its further development and next year's winning record.

Ned expressed his disappointment to Coach Beck at not being involved next year to experience the expected success. "Way it goes, kid. Ya gotta remember that nothin' lasts forever. And when things go bad, ya gotta suck it up and keep plowin' ahead. Seein' you workin' the way ya have this past while, I think ya can keep plowin' when ya hafta."

****

Working Saturdays at Jenkins Hardware during his senior year and serving as team manager for the basketball squad had been hectic, but Ned minded not at all. College was one step closer. Then two days before graduation, a lightning bolt of good fortune struck! In the mail from the university came notification he had been awarded a privately funded scholarship which would cover his first college year's tuition.

Ned couldn't have flown higher. *Wow!* Everything was going his way. Enough savings and now a scholarship!

For Jenkins Hardware's star clerk, the summer seemed to crawl along. What a year it was going to be! Just entering college would be great, but knowing it was the first step toward fulfilling his coaching dream made it ever so much better.

****

Only two weeks before the Fall semester at the university was scheduled to begin, lightning struck Ned once more. This time, it was not flashing good news. That evening after a strangely silent dinner, Ned's mother said there was something about which they all needed to talk. Ned was all ears. This never happened before.

"Edward, I know how much you want to go to college, and I know how much you want to be a coach. But something has happened that might mean you'll have to think about putting off your plans for a little while."

Stunned? Shocked? Bewildered? Astonished? Dazed? All of those and more. Ned's heart seemed to stop, then race. He couldn't believe what he was hearing. Put it off! *Put it off!* He couldn't possibly have heard correctly. What on earth could be the matter!

As his mother dabbed away tears, she explained, "Edward, you know that since your dad broke his leg so badly, he's only been able to work part time. Today, the plant superintendent called him in and said the job descriptions for your dad's department had been changed and now required none but full-time employees. Your dad will be out of a job in two weeks.

"Oh Eddie, I just don't know what we're going to do. We were barely making it as it was." The tears became a torrent. "Oh, Eddie, Eddie, it breaks my heart to ask this, but can you help out a little more until your dad can find some other part-time job?"

Ned's father sat staring at his still barely-touched food, saying nothing as Mrs. Harkness continued. "I know John'll get work soon, I just know it." Between sobs, she added, "Eddie, we could lose *everything!* Can you help out with more, Eddie? *Please?"*

The debris of Ned's dreams came crashing down around him. The collision of them and his family was almost overwhelming, but, there was no choice. College and dreams would have to wait.

****

By mid-November, Ned's father still had no luck in finding a new job and his prospects looked as dim as ever. Ned's daily grind at Jensen Hardware remained just that. And Jake Jensen's monotonous mannerisms didn't help. The flame of the coaching vision hadn't died, but dimmed after a long day of selling nuts and bolts along with doing other menial chores.

Every day, there was nothing to look forward to but more of the same, plus twice weekly getting up at an ungodly hour to fulfill his now regular assignment of opening the store to keep the 7:00 a.m. senseless schedule. Coach Beck's advice to keep "plowin" helped, but gut-wrenching reality remained ever present.

Naturally, Ned attended all the Battling Buccaneer's games and was pleased to see their improvement. It looked as though they might even have limited success in the coming state-wide tournaments. After each game, his thought was the same. *(Maybe some day....")* But, it seemed a bit less emphatic each time.

The next to last regular-season game before the tournaments were to begin was on a Tuesday in February at a big-city school more than 50 miles distant. Winter driving conditions and the game ending late would make it too difficult for Ned to return safely, get a night's sleep, then open Jensen Hardware next morning at 7:00.

There was little conversation in the Harkness household at dinner. This was usually the pattern after another no-new-job day for Ned's dad. At 8:00, he tuned the radio to the local station broadcasting Buccaneer's games only to learn tonight's would be delayed because their bus was held up by bad road conditions.

During the ensuing know-nothing, time-filling babbling with a second-stringer at the mike, Mrs. Harkness remarked that it was a good thing Ned hadn't tried to attend the game. He didn't respond. After more prattle and seemingly endless commercials, the game began. Ned closed his eyes and saw every play.

At halftime, against a much higher-ranked team, the score was tied. Ned smiled. He knew the team had improved. Tired, he said he was going to bed and catch the last half on his radio.

****

Ned dropped off to sleep during the post-game wrap-up show, delighted that the team won. He had no idea what time it was when he heard voices, then his father calling him to come downstairs. Grabbing a robe, Ned hurried down.

To his astonishment Mr. Wilson Burns, the high-school superintendent and John Winston, the athletic director were there. Ned's thoughts raced. What was going on?

His dad spoke first. "Eddie, Mister Burns and Mister Winston want to talk to you about something very important. Are you sure you're wide awake? It's very important."

If Ned hadn't been wide awake, he surely was now. "Yes sir, I certainly am."

Superintendant Burns began, "Edward, let me say first that you are not in any trouble. We're here to ask your help in a difficult situation." Ned relaxed a bit, but his curiosity burned even more brightly if that were possible.

Burns continued, "Edward, on the way back from the basketball game last night, the team bus was involved in an accident. Fortunately, no one was fatally injured and the players suffered no significant injuries. However, the driver and all three coaches, sitting in front seats, were injured and hospitalized. Assistant coaches Maxwell and Foster sustained internal injuries and Coach Beck a badly fractured leg and other injuries."

Ned was alive with questions, but remained silent as Burns added, "Mister Winston and I spoke with all three coaches. All three expressed a strong desire to return to work at the very earliest minute, especially since the tournaments are scheduled to begin next week. However, the doctor attending them said this would be out of the question for at least a month.

"Edward, this circumstance leaves us in a predicament. When I informed Coach Beck of the doctor's estimate, he was quite naturally disappointed, but agreed we must find a coach as soon as possible. However, no one on our faculty is qualified. As you are no doubt aware, Mister Akers in the biology department played college basketball, but he has no coaching experience at all or any knowledge of Coach Beck's system. Finding a qualified coach would be virtually impossible at this stage of the season."

Former team-manager HeyNed was having trouble figuring how he fit into all this when Superintendant Burns didn't just explode one bombshell, he dropped a bomb barrage.

"Edward, after a lengthy discussion with Coach Beck, Mister Winston, and Mister Akers, we arrived at a possible solution. You would assume a significant role, and we cannot go forward without your participation." Staggered, Ned remained silent.

"Edward, Coach Beck says you are the only one who knows his system and has the ability to analyze changing situations during games and suggest the necessary changes.

"Now here's what we're proposing. Since you are not a regular faculty member, we can arrange for you to participate in coaching the team as a volunteer assistant coach. Mister Akers has agreed to be named interim coach and understands and agrees that you will do most of the actual coaching. The joint assignment would be announced publicly, but the actual details of how to carry out your duties will be left to you and Mister Akers.

"We apologize for coming at this hour, but the situation is extremely critical. Incidentally, since so much of your time will be taken, Coach Beck says he can see to persuading Mister Jensen to accommodate your absence.

"Edward, this is a great opportunity for you. We hope you will respond positively and help us through this trying time."

****

After a few remarks about the regular coaching staff, the following afternoon, Superintendent Burns introduced Mr. Charles Akers and Mr. Edward Harkness to the team, students and assembled media as the two interim coaches. They would jointly coach the Battling Buccaneers until the regular coaches recovered and returned, adding, "...perhaps by the time the team plays in the finals of the State tournament." The cheerleaders sprang into action, leading the student body through, "Three cheers for Coach Akers!" Then, "Three cheers for Coach Harkness!"

After the gym cleared and the team gathered on the floor for practice, Coach Akers explained how the new coaching situation would work. He emphasized that HeyNed, "Pardon me—Coach Harkness—was Coach Beck's personal choice, and when Coach Harkness spoke it was the same as Coach Beck speaking.

There was an understandably quiet acceptance. But soon after practice began, attitudes seemed to change quickly as Ned shouted instructions and encouragement. Players who knew Ned as student-manager "HeyNed" had some trouble at first with "Coach Harkness." But that also faded when a variation of Coach Beck's system suggested by Ned worked better than before.

During the three days prior to the final regular-season game, news of the unique coaching situation soon spread from local media outlets to national coverage. Both coaches and the team prepared for this and refused to let it interfere with practices.

Local fans, at first loudly expressing consternation concerning the coaching arrangements, soon changed course and began boasting about it to reporters. Jake Jenson even had a large sign made for his window informing all that it was his employee who was now the Buccaneer's coach.

Friday, a newspaper editorial warned it was time for a reality check. Everyone should remember that it was beyond reason to expect miracles to be performed by any team thrust into last-minute, get-by, coaching. "This will be acutely evident when the Buccaneers play the ninth-ranked team in the State tonight. However, fans should continue to support the team during the circumstances that have befallen it at this critical time."

To the astonishment of the local radio announcer and stringers from two national sports networks, the score was tied at the final buzzer. Back and forth it went during the first overtime, ending in another tie. Then in the closing seconds of the second overtime, the Buccaneer's center somehow got loose for a winning dunk.

The announcer nearly swallowed his microphone. "I must admit that in my pre-game remarks I said there was no way this small-town team with no regular coaching staff could win. But win they did, and...." For the one and only time in his career, he seemed at a loss for words.

The visiting "opinioneers" took the usual way out, blaming the highly rated team for an incredibly poor performance. Tonight's miracle would be celebrated by the winners, of course. But such an upset should not be expected when the statewide tournaments began the following week.

They were wrong. Not only did the Battling Buccaneers win the first tournament round, they won again the following two weekends and would now play for the State championship.

As this fairytale sports saga moved along, it continued as the headline sports story of area media. The national networks again began bombarding eager followers with every detail. Each member of the team was featured as were both coaches. A regular Sunday-night news-magazine chronicled Ned's bio, entitled, "Coach HeyNed–a coach by any other name."

Obviously, neither coach had any experience in dealing with the flood of attention raining down. How they kept themselves and their team focused on the games ahead was a story in itself. This was helped along when a still-convalescing Coach Beck made a surprise visit and warned players, "Your job is playin' the game. Wanna be part'a the cheerin' section, get a skirt and pom-poms."

A full week of hoopla over, it was time for the State finals. To the delight of everyone but the losers and their fans, the amazing Buccaneers continued winning and advanced to the final contest.

What a game it was going to be! Tonight, the Cinderella squad from out of nowhere faced the State's newly top-ranked and undefeated team to decide who would be State champions. By now, many doubters became convinced. The team was tagged "Destiny's Darlings" by a talking-head, and it stuck.

Nearing the close of the first half, it appeared Cinderella's glass slipper was not going to fit the Buccaneers this time. Destiny's Darlings were on the ropes. Their all-time leading scorer was having a miserable game. Shot after shot fell short or caromed off the rim, and he stopped shooting altogether. Ned's team went into the locker room trailing by 16 points, and it looked as if the second half would be even worse.

Some coaches rain down fire and brimstone at half-time after a team's bad showing. This wasn't Ned's style. After telling everyone to just relax, he discussed a few defensive changes, closing by reminding them they were the same team as the one that won its way to this, the final game. "There's no magic wand I can wave. Just become that same team."

As the team took the floor for the second half, Ned took his star scorer aside. "Bill, just relax out there and think about this. To be a star you have to put a *T* on the end of it."

"Whataya mean? I don't get it."

"What does *star* spell when you add a *T* on the end?"

Bill thought, then smiled. It'd spell *start*."

"Riiiight. It also means you can't score if you don't shoot."

Ned may not've felt he had a magic wand. But he did. From the start of the second half, Bill rained in shot after three-point shot, and the team morphed from so-so defense into defensive demons. At the end of the third quarter, they trailed by only five points. Still energized during the fourth quarter, they closed to within a point with six seconds to play.

Ned called a timeout and diagrammed a play slightly revised from one that opposing teams anticipated in this situation. His hot-shot shooter wouldn't take the last shot this time, but pass the ball to a teammate instead.

As the Buccaneers put the ball in play for the final six seconds, trailing by a point, a person just entering the arena may've mistakenly thought a wake was in progress. To say no one breathed was hardly an exaggeration.

The seconds ticked down–six, five, four. Guarded by two players, shooter-Bill barely managed a pass to a teammate. Three seconds, then two. Halfway through the basket-bound ball's flight, the game-ending buzzer sounded, and the red light flashed on.

****

The exploding crowd noise could've shaken a seismograph. Only the contingent of extra security personnel prevented the playing floor from a full-fan-invasion a nanosecond after the score.

Oh, it was grand, it surely was! *State champions!* Small-town heroes slay top-dog dragons. David/Goliath stuff from which dreams are made. Fan adulation immersed coaches and players.

Just as the coaches were about to join the Battling Buccaneers for the customary net-cutting and trophy-presentation ceremonies, Ned felt someone shaking his shoulder. He shrugged it off, but the shoulder-shaker was persistent. Coach Harkness finally turned.

****

"Eddie, Eddie! *Wake up!* You've overslept. Hurry and get dressed while I fix your breakfast. You know Mister Jensen won't like it if you don't get the hardware opened at seven."

Ned sat up and shook his head vigorously. Then again. This was real, all right. He was in his room, all right. Jensen Hardware awaited, all right. He shook his head again, the dream stubbornly refusing to surrender to reality.

Hardware-clerk Harkness sat staring at his breakfast, life's cruel truth slaying any appetite. Mister Harkness looked up from his newspaper. "Eddie, great game last night. Hear about the team bus having an accident on the way home?"

Lost in thought, Ned didn't respond, and his dad began again, getting as far as, "Eddie, I said...," when a knock interrupted.

Mrs. Harkness rose to answer. On the way to the front door, she exclaimed, "Why, it looks like Superintendent Burns from the high school! Mister Winston's with him, too! What in the wide world could they want at this hour?"

73

TWIN MYSTERY

Chief of Police Carl Morten knew what to expect when he met with Prosecutor William Henson to give him the latest report on the recent string of bank holdups. There'd be snorting, stomping, and hollering. Then more hollering. The chief was right. Henson slammed down the report. "Con-*FOUND* it, Carl! It's not like we're dealing with the greatest stickup-artist since John Dillinger! We know this perp's M.O. every bit as well as he does. We surely ought'a! This is the ninth time he's hit a bank around here!

"Not only that! You got an eyeball witness at every last heist. *And*, you got DNA from a cigarette butt. Why in Billy-Blue-Thunderation can't you get me something to get at least one of 'em? I don't care which. There's no way they're not the one's pulling these jobs. It's one of 'em alone or they're taking turns. Dag-*NABBIT* Chief, we're being made look like fools on this. You sure you haven't overlooked something?"

"Will, the best investigators in both hold-up jurisdictions where the holdups are going down, plus the feds, have picked over every scrap of the few clues we have so often that they can recite them from memory. The profiler says the bank heists fit either twin like a glove.

"We've interviewed the eyeballers so many times some of them won't come in anymore. The doer wears a hood and mask, so a facial ID is out. Nothing unusual about his clothes they can recall.

"Both twins' alibis are absolutely airtight. At first, I thought maybe they could be switching places where they work so it'd look like the same one was at work all the time while the other did the deed. No way. The time-line puts them both at their regular job all day when the banks were robbed."

"Anything new on the DNA?"

"Had it checked by two labs. Samo-samo. Identical twins are almost always identical in every way. The one tiny thing we found different between them was that they smoke different brands. Well, the DNA on the butt we found outside the Second National was from the brand one of them uses. Thought we had something on one of them right then."

The chief sighed and continued. "But, it turned out it was his payday, and both twins bank there. Bank stays open late on the plant's payday so depositors can come in after work. Jumped all over that, but both worked overtime that day past the stick-up time.

"I tell you Will, we're all about daffy trying to figure any other way to go. Either these two are the smartest crooks on the face of the earth or they're not the doers. I'm not ready to let either one off the hook. We'll come up with something sooner or later or they'll make a slip. Just gotta hope we get the goods before some citizen gets hurt."

"Well...looks like you've done everything possible with what little bit there was at the crime scenes. Nothing new on their backgrounds?"

"Not a smidgeon. Both clean as a whistle since they moved here twelve years ago. Not so much as a single traffic ticket. Church-goers. Active in charity work. Got the same story when I sent their names over to Barthville. That's their home town."

"Carl, I don't have to tell you the news-noses think they smell blood in the water, and the sharks are circling. I understand you have a press conference tomorrow. Any thoughts on that?"

"Nope. None. Nada. Lard on the usual BS, I suppose. Working hard on the cases. No new info for release at this time. Yata,Yata, yatida. I'll take a few questions. More yata, yata, yata. Thanks for coming, et cetera, et cetera."

"Well Carl, I have only one thing to say."

"And that is?"

"I'm glad it's you instead of me."

"I really appreciate that Will. I really do. It's a great help."

****

The news-noses thought they smelled blood in the water for sure. The questioning moved rapidly from aggressive to almost hostile. Back in the office after it was over, Assistant Chief Clifford Burns took a chair and remarked, "Man alive! Am I ever glad that was you and not me out there!"

Chief Morton didn't reply, just steely-stared across at his assistant. In seconds, he sprang to his feet, snapped to attention, saluted, and responded to the stare, *"Yes sir! Right away, sir!"* As Burns goose-stepped out, Morton chuckled in spite of his post-conference mood.

After reviewing the cases for the umpteenth time, Morton tossed down the last file and remarked aloud, "Maybe the sharks are right. Nah, they've just seen too many TV CSI's where the star finds a hidden clue and solves everything in an hour minus thirty minutes of commercials. Every last one of us can't be missing the magic CSI clue."

The chief paused before adding, "Or can we?" He picked up another folder, then tossed it back on the pile. "Heck with this. I gotta get out'a here for a while…talk to somebody else."

He thought a moment, then phoned his old friend, Chief Chip Olsen at Clemsen City. They began chatting about the case, but soon Olsen remarked, "You need a get-away break. Drive on over.

D. D. HUDDLE

****

Over coffee at Dippy Doodles, Chief Olsen listened closely as his counterpart brought him up to date on the bank robbery investigations, adding, "I hate to admit it, but those twins have outsmarted us so far. How am I gonna get the goods on either or both? We've checked them up, down and diagonally. They come out saint-clean. Same story over in Barthville, where they grew up. Nothing on either one. Nothing."

Chief Morton sighed and picked up his cup. "Chip, you've been around a long time. You were even chief in Barthville about the time those two would've been teenagers. Remember anything about them? Anything at all?"

"You said you checked them out thoroughly with Chief Wannell at Barthville?"

"Yep."

"Check out the whole family?"

"Got nothing there except that they moved away years back."

"Well, there *is* one thing I can tell you. When they were born, it caused quite a story. It was also quite a story when one of the kids went bad later, and the family disowned him. According to their religion, they could never acknowledge his presence on earth again—*never*—even if he *was* one of the identical *triplets*."

78

FINAL FLING

During the second year after her husband died, the constant badgering by 74-year-old Alice Abernathy's children to "get out more" were only bothersome. Lately, their hints and suggestions became a major nuisance. Her reticence wasn't a matter of stubbornness. Always very practical, it just seemed to her that with one great exception, most of the items she had on her mental "to-do" had been realized.

The one great exception was the longest-standing one she kept to herself all these years. Now, it fell into what she mentally called at this stage of her life an "old-fool fantasy." She quickly suppressed thoughts of it whenever they resurfaced. Usually, each time daughters Ellen and Carol Ann or son Meredith brought up the getting-out-more subject, all they got was, "I'm doing just fine, thank you," and that was that until the next time the nagging began.

Finally, she decided on a different tactic. She'd do whatever they put forward next time just to get them to stop with the "get out more" foolishness.

Within the week, they were back at it. The local parks and recreation department was starting an "Alive and Kicking" program for oldsters to be held in various districts of the city. Carol Ann enthused, "Go, Mom. You'll meet lots of new friends and have a good time." Her mother winced inwardly. *(Just what I've been looking for—mixing it up with a bunch of old fuds.)*

OK, just to shut them up, she'd go one time. Her "enthusiasm" remained at minus zero when a twenty-something, pony-tailed, blond-bombshell appeared, "sprightly" at the ready. At her bubbly best, she greeted the small group. "Welcome, welcome, welcome! How nice to see all of you on this fine morning. I see you found the breakfast bar OK. Now, since this section of our new program is for this district, you probably know lots of the others here. But, let's start by introducing ourselves for those who don't."

Alice Abernathy grimaced and sighed. *(Oh boy.)*

Blondie continued, "We'll start with the two of us up here in front. I'm sure this gentleman to my right needs no introduction. Everyone knows the owner of Reynolds International, Mister Jeffrey Reynolds! Mister Reynolds is the primary underwriting sponsor of this new city-wide program. He's taken some of his valuable time to be with us today."

Yes, everyone knew ninety-five-year old Jeffery Reynolds, the richest man in creation and a philanthropist. He waved and the obligatory round of applause that followed.

Blondie "bubbled" some more. "I'm Vicki Velson, Most everybody just calls me 'Vicki V,'" adding (again), "It's *so* nice to see you on this fine morning," adding (again), "I see you've found the breakfast table. There's plenty left, so don't be afraid to go for more." Chuckles rippled as Lem Lawson immediately stood. His sweet-consuming reputation was well known.

Vicki V continued bubbling. "This being the first meeting, learning more about the group could be lots of fun. I'll bet almost everyone has something that maybe their own spouse or best friend may not know about." Some restless stirring.

Vicki quickly counseled, "Now relax, folks. What I'm talking about is something you've always wanted to do, or maybe something you still plan. Like an item on what some call their 'to-do' or 'bucket' list. Others a 'final fling.' Maybe you've always wanted to see a Broadway play or write a book. Maybe do a parachute jump. Don't laugh, it's not too late. Incidentally, your item doesn't necessarily have to be a secret.

"So how about it? Want to have a little fun? How about you Mister Lawson. Will you go first?"

Lem put down his muffin. "Well, I tell ya. What I'm plannin' to do is make a break for it as soon as the grub runs out."

When the laughter subsided, he began again, relating his lifelong desire to be a chef in a big-time restaurant. "Since I'm not gonna get to, I'll just do my part by thinkin' about it when I'm eatin' in one." More laughter.

A humorous tone having been set by Lawson, the others relaxed and got into the game. Jolene Marie McAllister always wanted to be a ballet dancer. She weighed 190, and joined the good natured laughter.

Harry Valentine elaborated upon what most already knew–his wish to become a city councilman, eliciting still another round of laughter. A Republican in an overwhelmingly Democrat district, Harry ran unsuccessfully for the office so many times that voters lost count. "I don't care if they keep calling me 'Hopeless Harry,' I'm gonna keep running." He clapped along with the rest.

The others related their wish in the same humorous fashion. Last up was a somewhat reluctant Alice Abernathy, but she became animated as she told of her dream of touring Europe that began in the fourth grade. She continued speaking until, embarrassed at her colorful descriptions of the places she'd studied, she suddenly stopped in mid-description of yet another site and apologized for "babbling on so long."

Vicki V quickly reassured, "Not at all, Missus Abernathy. Not at all! Your descriptions make it ever so real. It's plain to see your wish has been with you a long time." She looked around. "Now, let's see. Is that everyone? Oh no. It looks as if there's one more. Mister Reynolds, how about it?"

Jeffrey Reynolds straightened in his chair, but didn't respond immediately. In the silence Cleve McGregor, his very best friend and the only one who'd dare, spoke up, "Jeff, you old buzzard, you've done about everything. What could be left to talk about?"

"Cleve, you're almost right...for once. Thank the Lord, I've been able to do or see about anything I wanted. Listening to Missus Abernathy describe her wish, it occurs to me I may've missed something by not having one.

"I've been to Europe on business several times and thought I'd seen a good many places she talked about. But, the way she depicted them makes me see I didn't really get to know much about any of them. Maybe I should put it on a bucket list to go back and do it right."

Again, Cleve McGregor jibed, "Is this what it sounds like to me? You hitting on Alice right here? The very idea! You sneaky old dog, you!"

Both Alice Abernathy and Vicki V participated in the hilarity. After the meeting, Jeff Reynolds hurried over to assure Mrs. Abernathy he wasn't proposing any such thing as that rascal McGregor implied.

Teasing, she responded, "Well, now I really *am* disappointed, Mister Reynolds. Here I was all set to make plans."

Searching for a reply, Reynolds stumbled a bit before catching on. Recovering, he again complemented her for her descriptive prowess and added, "One of the places I visited but failed to learn much about which you didn't mention was Amsterdam. Is that on your list?"

"Oh yes. One of the top ones." She started to describe some specific areas of the city, but abruptly stopped. "There I go again. I'm sorry."

"Oh please don't be, Missus Abernathy. Your descriptions are delightful." A pause, then, "Perhaps," but just then his chauffeur appeared. "Uh oh, there's Jack, the human time-clock come to drag me off to a far less interesting meeting. I'm afraid I really must go."

As he rose, another, "Perhaps," was again interrupted by the chauffeur's urging. Mrs. Abernathy also departed, giving no thought to either of Jeffrey Reynolds' "Perhaps." Before long, that would change.

****

The day after Alice Abernathy attended the Alive and Kicking social, daughter Carol Ann dropped by. "OK Mom, tell all. What happened at the Alive and Kicking meeting? Any good lookin' guys hit on you?"

"Shame on you! We had some breakfast stuff, then a blond honey-bun had us introduce ourselves and we chatted. Doubt there's much sense in going to another."

"C'mon Mom. Must've been more than that. Who'd you talk to? What'd you talk about?"

"Nobody in particular. We just chatted about this and that. Nothing important."

"Well, it's at least a start on getting out of the house more. I'm sure there'll be some interesting conversation later on."

"I doubt it. Most of them are as interesting as a banana slug."

Other small talk and coffee over, in the midst of Carol Ann preparing to depart, her mother's telephone rang. Mrs. Abernethy listened briefly before responding, "Oh, I don't know about that. I doubt there's much more I could say about them. After all, you've been there in person."

Another silence. Then, "Well, I suppose that would be all right, but I still don't see...." She was obviously interrupted again, then agreed to whatever the caller wanted and hung up.

Overhearing her mother's end of the conversation, Carol Ann immediately began pumping her for details. After putting it off as a "nothing call," Alice finally acquiesced. "If you must know, it was that old fool, Jeffrey Reynolds. At the meeting, I mentioned some things about places he'd been but hadn't learned much about. He was pestering me to have lunch and so we could talk about them some more."

"You mean *the* Jeffrey Reynolds! The one with the big bucks! He must be a hundred years old. What places?'

"Oh, just some places. I don't remember every last thing that was talked about. Just a couple places. Now that I think about it, I'm going to phone and beg off lunch."

"Oh, don't do that Mom! He's harmless at his age. Besides, it'll be fun to doll up and get out to fancy restaurant…and, with Mister Got Rocks himself."

"Oh shush, I don't…."

"Mom, you promised him. He can't be around much longer. Do it to give him a break while he still has a little time."

"Carol Ann Abernathy! How you talk!"

"Just do it, Mom."

****

Carol Ann was right about the restaurant being a fancy one. At **EMILE'S**, the moment the *maitre d'* spotted Mr. Jeffrey Reynolds, he rushed over to personally escort them to their table.

The usual amenities met, Reynolds began, "Missus Abernathy, I have three reasons for asking you to lunch. I wanted to apologize for leaving the meeting so abruptly. My chauffeur thinks the world will stop turning if I'm two seconds late for the next appointment.

"Second, your descriptions of places in Europe were fascinating, particularly since you've never visited them. I'm quite certain no tour guide could do as well.

"Now for the third and most important reason. An old man wanted to see and hear more about Europe from so informed, charming, and gracious a lady. Sharing lunch seemed to be my best excuse to do all three. By the way, may I address you as 'Alice'?"

"Mister Reynolds, you certainly may call me 'Alice,' and your apology is quite unnecessary. I wasn't in the least bit offended. Quite the opposite. I'm the one who should apologize for babbling on and on.

"As to your second and third reasons, I fear you are misinformed concerning your tour-guide comparison. Perhaps about the informed, gracious and charming description, also, but, I thank you very much. I'm flattered and hope I do nothing to change your opinion."

"Missus Abernathy–Alice–I have no doubts about that, and please call me 'Jeff.'"

Over salads, the conversation turned from discussing various European sites to the people who inhabited them. Reynolds said he never had time to learn much about the people who lived at each one. Could she tell him something of them?

Mrs. Abernathy began by talking about her keen interest in Winston Churchill's career after he'd been blamed for a military disaster years previous to the Second World War.

She spoke enthusiastically of one place she always wanted to see–the actual war room used by Churchill during England's desperate war years. "I understand the remains of one of his famous cigars are still in an ashtray.

"Then there's the...." She stopped. "There I go again. Just can't shut up an old lady's nonsense."

"Alice, my dear. Do you have any idea how interesting this is? Do you realize how *real* you make things sound? You could teach a course at the university. Now that I think of it, I have a certain amount of influence out there. I could make that happen."

"Oh Mister Reynolds–Jeff–there's no way I could do that. When the students discovered I'd gotten the information from books and TV, I'd be a laughing stock."

With the noon hour about over and diners departing, Reynolds' chauffeur appeared across the room and came over when beckoned. He stood stiffly as his boss instructed, "Whatever meeting I'm supposed to attend, go there and tell them I've contracted some deadly, very contagious, twenty-four hour virus or something, then come back and wait here."

"But sir."

"Jack, when is your next payday?"

With "I'm on the way, sir," the chauffer was gone.

"Now then Alice, you were talking about places and events in England. Go on please."

"Well, I'd like to visit all the usual places. Knowing more about the baths in Bath would be interesting. Also, the Spanish galleon that accidentally brought the potato-killing virus to Ireland which caused the Irish Potato Famine. Or, the fellow who invented the fortress walls that deflected Cromwell's cannon-fire. Or, what happened to the Dorchester pilots who finally torpedoed Hitler's so-called 'pocket-battleship,' the Bismarck. Oh, lots of other things, but there I go again."

Further encouraged by Reynolds, she continued for nearly an hour, including sites and events in continental Europe, ending with, "Please forgive me again for my wagging tongue. That stuff is just an aging lady's hobby and foolish dream."

"What was that line from a movie, Alice? The one delivered by a dying husband? The one where he said they hadn't realized all their dreams, but he was glad they had them? Well, dreams aren't foolish, Alice.

"I'll tell you something else. Remember at the meeting I said I'd seen and done about everything I wanted to? Well, with your descriptions, you've made me realize I missed a great deal by not having another dream or two. I can't tell you how very much I enjoyed this lunch, especially your word pictures. That's what they are–word pictures."

****

Not that she was expecting anything, but it was two weeks before Jeff Reynolds phoned. "Alice, I've been doing a lot of thinking during the past two weeks, and there's something very, very important I want to discuss. I don't want gossipy ears trying to listen at Emile's. Can you meet me at Friendship Park? I can have Jack pick you up."

"Whatever can be so important, Mister Reynolds?"

"Too much for over the phone. And, it's 'Jeff.' Can you come? It's important to me, and I hope it'll be to you, also."

"Well...I guess so. When?"

"As soon as possible. As I said, I've been thinking a lot about this. Is this afternoon possible?"

****

Sitting at an isolated picnic table, Reynolds wasted no time. "Alice, I am too old to delay a minute about something I'm going to suggest. It will no doubt come as a shock at first, so please give it serious thought before responding.

"That bucket-list talk at the meeting, then your wonderful descriptions, caused me to give serious thought to the remaining time I have. I want to do something besides making money. There's no sense in beating around the bush. I want a last fling, and I know what it is." He paused, "Alice, I want to visit Europe to do and see what I missed all those times I was there."

He paused again–longer this time–as he looked across at Alice Abernathy. Then, "Alice, I want you to go along."

87

Shocked? Yes. Stunned? *OH YEAH!* In the silence, she was aware of distant playground sounds, birds singing nearby, and traffic noise. She heard the words, all right, but was she hearing what she *heard* just now*!*

Reynolds hurried on. "Alice, let me finish. I'm not talking about a romantic entanglement, even if a guy my age was dumb enough to propose it, which I am absolutely not doing. I don't give a rap about what people think, but I'll make the arrangement perfectly clear to one and all. Just good friends we are, and just good friends we'll remain during the trip.

"Naturally, there will be no expense to you. Please don't even *think* any 'kept woman' thoughts. If you need a reason for going along, you can be a tour guide. I can think of no one better equipped to plan such a trip. If you are uncomfortable about receiving funds, I'll donate a sizeable sum to any charity you wish.

"We'll always have separate accommodations and you may return home any time you like. And, we'll stay as long as you like. There's so much to see and do, it may take quite a while.

"Oh, by the way, Jack will go along to be available to attend to my needs and take care of any emergency that could arise."

Reynolds went on to describe other specifics, ending with, "You have a life-long dream, and I want a final fling doing something I should've done long ago. I want to do it now accompanied by someone who'll enjoy it as much as I.

"Alice, I know this is extremely sudden, but I fervently hope you'll consider the idea. I know there's a lot to think over. Please take your time. If I'm fortunate enough to have you agree, I know it'll take time to plan. That's about it. Whatever you decide, we'll remain good friends."

****

Well now, how does one respond to a lightning bolt? Alice Abernathy's dream coming face-to-face with potential reality would require the same strategy. Dozens of "what ifs" rocketed around her mind with no answers. Among the first was how she would explain such an arrangement to her children.

Alice Abernathy's lifelong penchant for thinking before speaking rescued her–momentarily, at least. Finally, she spoke. "Well, Mister Reynolds–Jeff–there's one thing for sure. This is truly as important and as surprising as it gets. Thank you so much for your ever so kind thoughts, and for not pressing for an answer.

"As you said, there's much to consider. As to what others may think, I share your feelings about them. That aspect will not be a consideration. You have my word that I will think carefully about everything and we'll talk again."

"That's good enough for me." He summoned chauffer Jack who was waiting at a discrete distance. "Jack, please take Missus Abernathy home, then come back for me. I want to sit and enjoy the scenery for a while."

Jack stared briefly. What was this "enjoy the scenery" stuff from his always-on-the-go boss? Shaking he head almost imperceptibly, he led Alice Abernathy to the limo.

****

For a week, Mrs. Alice Abernathy was in full-out "go, no-go" mode. She tried everything to break the stalemate, including making two columns on paper, one "for" and one "against." Half an hour later, she tossed down the pencil.

She may not've been overly concerned about what other people would think, but that didn't include her children. They rapidly became the major item in the "against" column. Awake at 3:00 a.m. on one of several restless-sleep nights, an option occurred to her. She'd inform them together that she was going, and get their

89

reaction. Maybe, just maybe, they'd provide something to help her make a decision.

****

Curiosity brimming over about what could be so important that a "children-only" meeting was being held, Carol Ann, Ellen, and Meredith James sat at the kitchen table. Their mother began by telling them of her life-long dream of which they had no inkling.

After their surprise and questions subsided somewhat, she announced that she finally had an opportunity to realize her dream of an extended European tour. The bigger news was that she planned to take advantage of it.

Their reactions were as expected. Carol Ann first. "Way to go, Mom!" Meredith next. "Well now, tell us more." Ellen smiled.

Before questions could begin again, their mother continued, explaining how she would be able to take such and extended trip, and how the opportunity had come about through her friendship with Jeff Reynolds. *And,* how he would be going along.

KA-BOOM! Carol Ann had no chance to be first this time, her brother Meredith's reaction exploding instantly, ***"He's what! Mom! You can't be serious!"***

There was more–much more–the least of which was, "What can you be thinking! What would dad say! What will *everybody* say!" He turned to his sisters. "Why aren't you two saying anything? *What's the matter with you!* Didn't you hear Mom say she was gonna go to Europe with a *strange man?"*

Carol Ann looked at him and using his nickname, responded, "Merry, it's our *Mom* you're talking to and about. And as for what dad would say, it'd be that he trusted her and if it was going to make her happy, by all means do it. So Merry, just *shut up.* Someday you'll have a dream, and if you're lucky as Mom, you may get it."

Meredith dismissed her with a wave of the hand and continued his arguments for another ten minutes. Finally, he demanded, "What about you, Ellen? Aren't *you* gonna say anything? You just gonna sit there?"

"A couple things, Merry. I agree with Carol Ann about what dad would say. And, I think you should remember that Mom is almost seventy-five years old. In all my life I've never seen her make a wrong choice.

"Besides that, it seems that a highly respected ninety-five year old person has a chance at something very few ever have. Seems to me he deserves what he calls a 'final fling.'"

Red-faced, Meredith rose to leave. "Well, I hope all three of you come to your senses in time."

After her children left, Mrs. Abernathy sat thinking. *(Well, that's about what I expected from Meredith. Sounds like the girls are for me going. As per usual, Ellen, ever the subtle one, did her usual thing—working in that business about my age and making good choices. Then later, without saying anything about my age and deserving a final fling, talking about Jeff's age and how he deserves one. Piece of work, that girl.)*

A virtually untouched lunch sat before her as she continued thinking, catching only an occasional sound byte on the news. What was that last one? Something about the 1915 World War I poem, IN FLANDERS FIELDS wasn't it? She'd read much about the area. It'd be most interesting to visit the actual site.

The switchboard operator answered, "Reynolds International, with whom do you wish to speak?"

****

Among the many conversations with Jeff was one about deciding how many places they should plan to visit. "Oh, just pick

91

a few to start. No need to spend hours on a complete list. It'll be more fun to pick and choose as our interest dictates."

Other items could not be attended to so easily. Neither then nor later was any approval going to come from Meredith. No way! He tried every tactic he could conjure up to make her abandon her trip, going so far as to vociferously brace Jeff Reynolds just outside the gates of his estate.

As a final effort, he voiced his intent to see that his mother could no longer visit with her grandchildren. However, his sisters and wife put a stop to *that* nonsense. Finally, he gave up, vowing never to speak to Carol Ann and Ellen if their mother went through with her plans. Almost in unison they replied, *"Good riddance!"*

****

The Reynolds children, grandchildren and great grandchildren joined Alice's bunch, Jeff, and chauffeur Jack at the airport for the big sendoff amid promises to keep in close touch. Ellen and Carol Ann got Jack aside to swear an *"if-you-value-your-life"* oath to contact them *immediately* should anything, absolutely *anything*, went the slightest bit awry. Carol joined them and added, "And, we mean *immediately*!" Then in unison, *"Understand?"*

To Ellen, *"Yes ma'am!* Turning to Carol Ann, *"Yes, ma'am!"* Smiling they rejoined the group.

****

With few exceptions, every day Alice e-mailed descriptions of the places they visited and sights they saw—so many that the girls had little difficulty keeping track of her travels. After five weeks in England, she and Jeff were in Eastern Europe amazed at the contrast between Buda and Pest across the river. Then it was on to visit Mozart's home town of Salzburg. The music at the opera house was great, too.

On and on it went. They visited Belgium, Amsterdam, and Luxembourg first, then a side trip to Oslo. After that, France and a boat trip down the Seine. Switzerland next, with a trip over the world's highest bridge followed by going back to Germany to visit the Christmas market in Nuremberg, one of the top priorities on Alice's list. During Spring, it was Southern Italy and Malta.

Alice Abernathy's reports seldom concluded without her expressing extreme pleasure in experiencing her life-long dream. Also, about how ecstatic Jeff had been about their final fling. But, any attempt to report their mother's happiness to Meredith fell on deaf ears. At last, they gave up trying.

****

Finally, the final fling was over. At the airport, Carol Ann and Ellen were amazed at how fit their mother and Jeff Reynolds looked. And how happy. Of course, Meredith James Abernathy wasn't there to witness this.

In a joint dinner in EMILE'S *Premier Room*, family members took part in a celebration that lasted well past midnight. After a lengthy recounting of their experiences, Alice Abernathy and Jeff Reynolds stood and thanked everyone for understanding the facts surrounding the final fling of two very good friends.

Jeff was particularly effusive in his praise and thanks to this "incredible lady beside me." He brought down the house with, "And, who'd have guessed all this at my tender age."

No less was Alice's admiration for him, finishing with, "I surely must be one of the luckiest people in the world."

The following week at a rare happenstance meeting with Meredith, his sisters made one last attempt to get him to understand how much it meant to their mother. He remained unalterably resolute in his stand that it was a terrible mistake, and he would never, ever, forgive her.

****

Naturally, the funeral six months later was an "event." Everyone was there. Even the few who didn't know the deceased but had heard of the 'final fling' just had to be there.

Meredith Abernathy attended despite his feelings about the "arrangement" Jeffrey Reynolds and his mother made. After the final rite at the cemetery, he walked over to a group of nearby mourners. They stopped talking and waited for what he could possibly say. Everyone knew what he had said and done.

In the silence he stood for a long moment, removed his hat and cleared his throat. "Everyone here knows how I felt about your trip and what I said and did. I'm here to say *I was wrong!* I want to apologize and thank you from my heart for making a dream come true, Mister Reynolds."

READY IS AS READY DOES

Tom and Martha Carson, both products of hard-working families, agreed it would soon be time for their twin adolescent sons, Mark and Mathew, to begin learning what it's like to work outside the home. However, each time Tom suggested that *now* was an appropriate time, Martha wasn't so sure it was apron-string-cutting time—not sure if they were "quite ready yet."

****

Two days after their latest discussion, Tom saw his chance to prove his point and perhaps overcome Martha's insistence. Cleo Showalter asked him whether he knew of someone who could be hired to clear the trees and brush from a couple acres of woodland. Then, he could get Jay Bans' crew to dig out the stumps and level the land so it could be cultivated.

"No problem, Cleo. Got two healthy and nearly full-grown boys plenty able to do a little brush and tree clearing. Tell you what. I'll contract for the job and see that it gets done on time."

The school year just over, twins Mark and Mathew were anticipating another summer of hanging out at the park in town. This year there was an added attraction—the Snyder twins, Jolene and Janet. Maybe, just maybe…wouldn't that be something!

As expected, the woodland-clearing news and their assignment met with less than a rousing reception from the boys when their father gave them the word at the dinner table. After describing the job, he dropped the other shoe. It was time "two nearly grown men" learned about real work.

Orders were specific. Clear and pile brush, Cut small trees, trim and stack branches. Cut larger trees in preparation for a crew to remove stumps, trim and stack logs. Keep at it till the job is done on time.

Well now, those didn't leave room for stalling, and the twins knew better than to object outright. Both looked toward their mother for support as she previously gave when the subject of their readiness to work arose. This time, she said nothing. OK, maybe she'd talk him out of it tonight.

Mark, the more forward twin, did venture, "If we are gonna do men's work, do we get men's pay?"

"Sorry I didn't mention that. Since I'm the contractor for this job, I'm gonna do what most of them do for new-to-the-job hired hands. Minimum wage. That's part of your learning about work outside the home. We'll see how things go."

Lucky for them, their father couldn't read their thought. *(Minimum wage? Big deal!)*

Next morning, the tone was that of a Last Breakfast. Both woodchoppers assumed their best hangdog expressions. They could tell by their mother's demeanor and the special favorites before them that she lost any argument about them not being ready, only growing boys, dangerous work, etc., etc. At least she was sending them to their doom well fed.

Tom Carson said things about his boys growing into manhood, how good it was to work, and everyone's role in society–other father stuff like that. No sale.

****

As Cleo Showalter gave instructions to the twins about what was to be cleared and where to put the brush and logs, he got the impression they were considerably less than eager. He wasn't too concerned. Knowing Tom Carson as he did, the job would get done on time for Bans' crew to begin on the agreed-upon date.

The beginning of the clearing work and complaints coincided almost perfectly. How in the world could their father expect them to do all this work? Had he not listened to their mother? No one alive could finish this job in such a short time. *Just look at the size of these trees!* And, these chain saws couldn't be more dangerous. These axes, too. Wait'll mother hears about everything!

All that talk about growing up and work being good didn't fool them. Minimum wage was it! Probably gonna get that instead of an allowance. Their dad was gonna make a big profit. Was that fair? Cold lunches, too. How could you work after that?

On and on—whine and gripe, gripe and whine. Rest periods came more often, the piles of cleared brush and trees grew little.

****

After a week, Tom Carson knocked off work early on Saturday so he could visit the clearing ground. He was pretty suspicious, what with all the mumbo-jumbo he heard at the dinner table about how terribly hard and dangerous the work was.

When he got to the site, things were worse than he feared. In one full week, no more than half a day's work for *one* worker was done, let alone for *two* able-bodied hands. Fortunately for everyone, the twins departed before their dad arrived. They escaped a verbal thrashing, and Tom had an opportunity to think over what he was going to do about their lack of effort.

By the time he reached home, he decided punishment might not be the best idea. A tongue lashing might only give him some satisfaction, and restricting privileges couldn't last forever. Besides, neither would get the woodland cleared and only prove Martha right about them not being ready. That didn't mean he was going to allow them to dodge their responsibility. Then, too, there was that contractual arrangement to finish the job on time.

****

As Tom washed up before dinner, a plan suggested itself that might get the boys hopping and Martha off his back. He smiled at his thoughts on the way to the ham, green beans, potatoes and all the trimmings. (*Well, we'll see. I'm pretty sure they can do it, and I'm pretty sure I know how to find out if I'm right and Martha's not.*)

After the clinking of eating utensils died down, Tom addressed the tree-clearing subject. "Pretty hard work is it boys?"

The goldbrickers lunged for the bait like starving sharks. "Yes sir, it surely is," from Mark.

"Never knew that trees were anywhere near so tough to bring down, and the brush is terrible mean to cut up," followed Mathew.

Mark again: "Hot and dusty and you have to be *real* careful with the tools, too." (The latter especially for his mother's benefit).

"Oh *yeah*," from Mathew.

On they went, building their case, each argument getting the backing of the other. Each more strident.

"Terrible hot for this time of year."

"You wouldn't *believe* how much dust you breathe in."

"Bet we almost have a bad accident every hour."

Etc., etc.

Tom kept listening. Martha smiled. Looked as if her husband was beginning to yield to reason–their boys *weren't* ready yet.

Encouraged, the two loafers pulled out all the stops. Using every point they could conjure up, they spun them out in the frenzied fashion of the condemned-hoping-for-a-stay.

****

Tom Carson patiently waited for them to run out of hot air. A gap in their plaintive pleas occurred when they paused briefly to dream up other nightmares of child-labor horror. Finally able to respond, their father remarked, "Well boys, it surely sounds for a fact that the job's a real back-breaker."

After waiting for head-bobbing and affirmative votes to slow, he continued, "I certainly wouldn't want you to keep doing something so all-fired hard and dangerous as this job looks to be."

Martha's hopes rose. It *really* looked as if he were going to back down. The twins clenched their jaws and breathed enough to keep life going–but, quietly, very quietly.

Tom looked around with the even expression of a riverboat gambler who knows he has the rube's money in his pocket. "Yes, I'd hate like the dickens to think I'd gotten you, as boys, into something you're not ready for yet."

The woodchoppers went on instant alert. Was he about to cast aspersions upon their manhood? Their mother "protecting" them until they were "ready" was one thing. But, any such reference from dad was something else.

They glanced at their mother to see whether she caught on to what might be happening. She did and was about to chime in when Tom jiggled the lure. "On the other hand, I'd hate to think I was responsible for you not getting your extra money." Jiggle, jiggle.

What was that! Talk about bombs bursting in air! Rocket's red glare! Did he say *extra* money? What *extra* money? Ten thousand antennae exploded outward, but no one uttered a sound.

Pausing for even greater effect (if that were possible), Tom jiggled the bait again. "I'd been thinking about your pay. Maybe as a little reward for your first time of going out to work, we could've done something like this. My contract with Mister Showalter calls for finishing the first quarter of the job by a certain time, and he pays in full for that quarter if it's done on time and writes a contract for the next quarter. If not, he deducts a certain amount for each day it's late and doesn't write another contract. Well, my thinking was that when you finished on time, we'd divide the money for that quarter between the three of us–an even three-way split."

Two pairs of shoes shuffled in four-part harmony, but no sound came from their owners. All eyes were on empty plates.

Tom prepared to set the hook. "Yes, I think that way would've been good. But, by the looks of how slow things are going at Mister Showalter's woodland, I'll need to hire someone else to finish the job on time. Too bad, though. My contract calls for quite a chunk of cash. Your share of that plus the wages you've already earned would also be quite chunk'a money."

Bingo! Both sharks nailed the bait. Throughout history, many have made abrupt reversals of their original position. None have about-faced faster than the woodchoppers-two.

Suddenly engrossed in silent speculation about how much that "chunk" could be, the precision of Tom Carson's hooking job didn't cross the twins' minds,. Now was no time to think about saving face. *"Wait just a minute!* We didn't say we *couldn't* do it! We just said it was hard,' sang out Mark.

"Yeah, we only said it was hard," from Sir Echo Mathew.

After much more repetition and elaboration of their newly formed job-completing abilities, even Martha was impressed by the speed of the turncoats' turnabout. She was so taken aback that she didn't offer a single counter-argument. Besides, with whom was she to argue? The very troops she so ardently attempted to support deserted her in a body.

Later, she accused husband Tom of questionable tactics, but he only smiled. The one retort she mustered right then was the *"LOOK,"* the one all husbands instantly know means, "I'll deal with you later." This time, "later" would include cold biscuits and thin gravy (no meat) three breakfasts running. Weak coffee, too.

****

The next few days could be called the "Miracle of the Woodland." Dawn to dusk, a furious assault raged against trees and brush with the twins winning every skirmish. Nothing interfered, not even talk of how much money they'd get. In only eight days, one-quarter of the job was done. This feat became the talk of the area. The minister even included it in his sermon.

****

At Saturday dinner, the *boys* that "weren't quite ready yet" proudly announced in several ways and several times that the *men* got the job done. Tom was very proud, of course. Martha didn't say much, but the meals were OK again. Tonight's was especially great. After all, grown men need to keep up their strength.

For the twins, dinner lasted at least a century. Never was food toyed with so diligently. Even Martha had a hard time waiting for the accounting. Tom didn't seem in any hurry. When the meal was over and he finished his coffee, he pushed back his chair, pulled out his wallet, and spoke the words they were dying to hear.

"All right boys. The deal was that if you cleared a quarter of that woodland on time, we'd split the money three ways…if you were ready to do some work away from home." That was for Martha's benefit as she very well knew.

Tom continued, "Mister Showalter stopped by and paid me for the quarter you finished. He admitted he was a little leery about getting it done on time, or at all for that matter. But, he was real high on your work and for doing it on time." He paused, then took the bills from his wallet. "Well it's time to split the money. Now, it's your money to do with at you like, but I'd advise putting aside some of it. That's part of becoming a man."

Around and around he went, putting a bill at each of the three places. It was quite a show, all right. Divvy-up completed, the retelling of their epic effort went on and on. Everyone seemed to sense that this was a significant event in the family's history. The boys proved they were old enough to earn a man's pay for a job well done. Was there more than a touch of pride in Martha's eyes? Perhaps a tiny bit of mist, too?

When things calmed down, Tom *"ahemed"* in his way of stifling uproars and causing folks to listen carefully. "Boys, when we started this, I wasn't absolutely sure you could do it. And, your mother didn't think you were quite ready. Well, you did it, and we're both real proud, aren't we Martha?" She nodded while giving him a "good losers" smile.

****

After Sunday dinner, Tom Carson *"ahemed."* "Boys, everyone's learned you can do a man's work. There's something else you need to learn about being a man and earning a man's pay. You'll be working for a boss who sets the pay and won't split the profit equally. I'm raising your pay to three dollars an hour over the minimum wage. Maybe a bonus if the job's done early."

The twins stared at each other. Finally, Mathew, ever the quiet one, shrugged. "Gonna hafta tell sometime. Might as well be now."

"Tell what, boys? What's to tell?"

"Well, last week we already did what you just said we should. We started a savings account at the bank last week with our regular allowance so we could put some of our pay into it."

Tom Carson smiled broadly. "Why, that's *real* good news. Part'a what growing up's all about. Aren't we proud, Martha?" Again she only nodded.

In a minute, Matthew advised, "There's more."

"More, boys?"

"Mathew ordered, "Tell the rest, Mark."

Mark sucked in a lungful. "Well, we got to talking about getting to be a man and decided on something."

"Go on, go on."

"Well, we made a deal with Mister Showalter last week."

"A deal? A deal to do what?"

"To clean out the rest'a the woodlot. Bargained and got four dollars an hour over minimum and a guaranteed on-time five percent bonus."

Looking down, Martha Carson tried to hide a wide grin, and she did her best to stifle her chuckling. But, her shaking shoulders betrayed her.

Finally, a smile gradually replaced husband Tom's silent stare. Then, "Good luck...*men*."

TUFFY

There were so many people at Bobby Sherman's house that he and his brother George had to sleep on cots in the big upstairs hallway. Bobby didn't know exactly why all those people were there, but it was probably something to do with another brother, Clinton, being sick.

Clint, the biggest of his brothers, the outdoor lover, the semi-pro baseball ballplayer, was in the local hospital and gravely ill. When he first entered the area's small hospital, he didn't feel so bad, and looked about as usual. It was only a little something dragging him down, and the alcoholic-appearing medi-guesser had no tests run at the time, saying it was "probably only a little pneumonia," and a good "rest-up" would be the best medicine.

George kidded Clint about being lazy, and they both joked about the whole thing. George and Clint kidded around a lot. But after a week, Clint was no better, and the kidding slowed to a stop. Daily, George became gloomier–lately, by the hour. Bobby didn't quite understand everything going on, but he became pretty gloomy, too.

****

George and some other family members went to see Clint that dark November afternoon, taking Bobby along. Knowing the hospital had rules not allowing kids less than twelve years old to visit patients, he was nervous about it, but the nurse didn't say a word as she took them to Clint's room. Bobby was surprised to see the number of people standing around outside. The rest of the immediate family was there and some aunts, uncles and cousins.

Bobby's dad and mom led him inside. He thought it kind of spooky in there. The room was dim, and Clint had a thin tent-like sheet all around outside of him making it hard to see him very well.

After some of the others already in the room went to the bedside, Bobby's dad took him over to stand beside his brother, George who was already there. Close up, Bobby could see Clint better. *Holy Toledo!* That fellow in the bed didn't look like the brother who taught him to play catch. Somehow, he was so much *smaller*. All *over*. He must not've looked too good to George, either, judging by his depressed expression.

Bobby couldn't believe how different Clint looked, lying there with that tent thing all around him. His dad said it was to help Clinton breathe better. It also seemed it made it really hard for him to recognize his own little brother. At least Bobby thought that's what it was. Or, maybe it was because there were so many people in the room, what with the family there all the time and so many relatives filing in and out.

Pretty soon, the nurse came back and spoke quietly to Bobby's dad. After another brief visit to the bedside, the family started getting ready to leave. George hung back a bit, and said to Clint it wouldn't be long before they'd be going bird hunting. Bobby didn't hear any reply or even if there were one, but George didn't sounded very convincing.

Everyone trooped out to the parking lot. It began to snow, but the relatives kept standing aside and speaking in solemn tones. Then, Mr. and Mrs. Sherman went over and spoke to them. What his parents said he couldn't hear, but the relatives began leaving.

Bobby's dad returned, and said there was nothing else anyone could do, so the rest of them may as well go. He and Mom would stay and phone should anything change. Looking very sad, George and sisters Ernestine and Mary got into Clint's Ford along with Bobby. Not much was said on the way home. Mary and Ernestine were weeping softly. George stayed stone-silent as he gripped the wheel and concentrated on driving. Bobby wanted to ask if Clinton was really going to be OK because he looked really sick, but everyone was so sad-looking he thought he better keep quiet.

****

When they got home, there were more people there. Relatives and even some neighbors brought in food. Bobby thought there sure was a lot of food, but not very many people were eating. Bobby's cousin Joseph and he ate some, though, and so did the other kids.

After a while, Bobby's mom, who was finally persuaded to come home from the hospital, left her rocker and began helping to clear the table, even though the others kept telling her she didn't need to. But, she didn't stop. Nobody was saying much, and shortly the neighbors left.

Then it was decided where everyone would sleep. George and Bobby were assigned to cots in the upstairs hall. They went up, and not until then did he ask about Clint. George didn't answer, just turned out the light. Bobby didn't think it was a good idea to ask again. He must've been pretty tired. He was dead to the world minutes after his head hit the pillow.

****

In what seemed only a minute, someone was shaking Bobby's shoulder and telling him to wake up. He couldn't believe it was breakfast time. It wasn't. It was only around 2:00 a.m. He blinked against the light and saw his dad.

Finally, Bobby was awake. Could his *dad* have been *crying*? It sure looked like it. Bobby had never seen him cry—didn't even know he could. After a minute, he said, "Boys, I've got some

107

mighty sad news. Your brother Clinton passed away tonight. Went real peaceable in his sleep."

He said more, something about Clint being at rest. Bobby hardly heard. How could Clint be dead? He just saw him! They played catch last summer! George said they'd be going bird hunting pretty soon. How could Clint be dead? *He couldn't be!*

Mr. Sherman just stood for a long moment, rubbing his hands together and acting as if he should say something else. But, then he just turned and went downstairs. There were sounds from others moving around and talking down there. Bobby looked at George, and he stared back. Neither knew why, but they started getting dressed. Then something happened that Bobby never quite figured out. Later, he thought maybe it was because they were tired or tense or something. He just never knew.

****

George and Bobby weren't the only ones sleeping in the upstairs hall. George's toy terror, Tuffy, was there, too. That dog was a caution! For one so tiny, he had some major shortcomings. One was that he had more guts than brains, another an intense hatred for anything faintly resembling a cat, regardless of its size.

Smaller than many barn cats, time after time he took on the biggest and meanest. Naturally, he got slapped silly every time. But even before the claw tracks healed, he went after another cat. The routine was the same. It was *always* bark-bark, claw claw, *yelp-yelp-yelp-yelp!* The fool never learned.

And nosy! That animal had more curiosity than any ten cats he so despised. He was always sticking his nose into something. Once, he nosed in behind a plank in the barn where the meanest-of-the-mean, Flossy, stashed her kittens. Instantly there came a dog-scream and Tuffy shot out in reverse in afterburner mode.

He had cause for retreat. An enraged mama cat was hanging on with needle-sharp claws buried up to the hilt behind each of Tuffy's ears while applying a fang-facial. Simultaneously. she was trying to unzip his front legs with her hind slicers.

At last he shook free and fled, still screaming, far back under the porch. The experience didn't teach him a thing. Only four days later that fool dog went back for an encore. Flossy was only too happy to oblige.

****

Silently, George and Bobby went about getting dressed. Tuffy was using a worn-out ladies coat for a bed and poked his head into the top end of a sleeve that nearly detached from the body of the coat. Snooping farther, he soon had his head between the partly separated lining and the outer sleeve. About half way down toward the other end, he became lodged between the two.

Panic stricken, the more he thrashed about attempting to back out, the more constrictive his entrapment became. During his struggles, the entire sleeve tore totally away from the body of the old coat, making escape even more difficult.

George spoke quietly to his dog. "Shake yourself out'a there, ya dad-blamed idiot." At the sound of his master's voice, Tuffy frantically lunged about, making a mighty effort to escape, but only succeeded in becoming further ensnared. The effect looked for all the world as if the sleeve had a life of its own. First one way, then the other, it bobbed up and down or jerked side to side. As soon as he established any sort of a regular pattern, off he went on some other wild gyrations, becoming more terrified by the second.

George and Bobby took turns trying to corral him, but as soon as they touched him, he became what could only be described as hysterical, probably thinking the cats had him. His actions were so frenzied that they gave up trying to hold and calm him.

As his energy grew more depleted, Tuffy quieted and the sleeve action became more rhythmic, appearing even more life-like. When one brother whispered something, the sleeve swung toward him and paused as if listening intently before answering.

****

A snicker sounded in the silence. The sleeve swung to "look" at Bobby who looked at George, but quickly realized he, himself, was the guilty party. George chuckled, and the sleeve turned and "looked" at him. Both brothers giggled, then looked at each other with shamed faces. What a time to see something funny!

Next, the sleeve swung back and forth between them as if expecting either to speak. George strangled back a laugh-snort. Bobby bit his hand, but couldn't stifle the snickers.

George snorted again, but quieted and put his finger to his lips. Bobby nodded "yes" and tried. There was a pause, but they couldn't keep it in check a second longer. Strings of half-choked-back giggles firecrackered from both.

They kept trying mightily to stop, first biting their hands, then pillows. Nothing worked. George shushed Bobby, and he shushed George. Again it was no use. Each time they got barely under control, the sleeve turned to look at either one and they lost it.

How could they be doing such a thing! Ten minutes after their dad told them about Clinton and here they were laughing and behaving like fools. Bobby didn't know what got into them. He was sure the people downstairs must've heard, but even that didn't slow them, no matter how hard they tried.

****

At long last, Tuffy somehow freed himself, and things stayed quiet for a while. Perhaps they ceased being such jerks at last. Abruptly, George grabbed his pillow and dashed into the walk-in closet at the end of the hall. Bobby sat thinking. Maybe hiding in the closet and smothering the giggles with a pillow was a pretty good idea.

Maybe he should do that, too, except he didn't feel the slightest bit like laughing anymore. Even when thinking of the sleeve, Bobby didn't raise so much as a smile. Matter of fact, he was feeling just awful, so terribly sad and *awful*.

He sat in the chill, not bothering with a blanket. He was surprised George was still laughing. The more he thought about it, the worse he felt about all the laughing. It was really appalling. He just didn't know how they could've done such a thing.

Then he began to get very angry with George. The sounds from the closet were muffled, but Bobby could still hear them. Sitting there in the cold and dim hallway, he simply couldn't understand how George could keep laughing and laughing after what just happened to their brother.

****

As he listened and wondered, Bobby began to think the muffled laughing didn't sound the same. Holding his breath and straining to hear better, it occurred to him George sounded different since he went in there. Maybe it was the pillow. No, it was something else. Suddenly Bobby knew why it no longer sounded as if George were laughing.

IT BE THAT TIME AGIN

THIS HERE'S CLARABELLE CADWALLADER SAYIN' IT BE COFFEEIN' UP TIME OR SUCH. Y'ALL LIKED THEM LAST TALES, DIDJA? 'SPECIAL THEM TWO ABOUT TWINS? BETCHA A BUSHEL YA DIDN'T GUESS EITHER ENDIN'.

AW, C'MON NOW. CERTAIN-SURE? WELL, I RECKON A BLIND HOG'LL NOSE UP AN ACORN OR SO IFFIN HE ROOTS LONG ENOUGH.

AWRIGHT, AWRIGHT! I'LL ALLOW THAT MAYBE, JIST MAYBE Y'ALL'ER A MIDDLIN'-FAIR GUESSER. WE'LL SEE IFFIN THAT'LL KEEP HAPPENIN' DURIN' THE NEXT GO-'ROUND. NOW, GO AHEAD ON'N COME BACK FIT'N READY TO SEE IFFIN Y'ALL'S GUESSIN' IS STILL GOOD.

Y'ALL BACK A'READY? GOOD ON YA! NOW, JIST KEEP READIN'N GUESSIN'. THE FIRST ONE'S REAL SHORT TO GETCHA WARMED UP. REST OF 'EM GO EVER WHICH WAY FROM HERE TO THERE'N THERE TO HERE. GOOD FOLKS AND BAD. FUNNY AND NOT SO MUCH. SEE Y'ALL DOWN THE ROAD.

HANNA WHO?

Ed was almost seventeen. Old enough back then to mull over what he was going to do now that he was a "grown man." There he was, still working in his father's blacksmith shop, when he could be out on his own.

Then, good fortune struck. A friends who "made it" on the "outside" sent word that there was a job for him as a clerk in the coal-company store on the other side of the mountains at Hanna, West Virginia. Paid "three dollars a week plus room and board."

Now on the late-afternoon "local" 30 miles into the 70 mile train trip to Hanna, Ed had to admit that his determination to leave for the "outside" had eroded a bit. The train seemed to crawl along more slowly than ever. And, he was *starved*. The last of the sandwiches he bought from "wore off" hours ago.

With all the stops for passengers at stations closer to Hanna, mostly men, Ed thought, *(Probly miners. Why aren't they living at the coal camp? Oh well, I'll find out when I get there.)* Finally, a couple hours past his usual bed time, he nodded off to be aroused by the conductor calling something about ***"Hanna, West Virginia."***

Stepping down onto the station platform, Ed immediately saw that it wasn't much of a place even for a coal camp. He knew something of them having seen other camps closer to home. They were all about the same, a few scattered houses, some shacks, and a company-owned store where the miners spent most of their pay.

Where was the coal-company store, anyway? The train wheezed out and the others left before he thought to ask anyone.

It was black as pitch except for the railroad signal lights and a dim lantern hanging in front of the locked waiting room. The scent of impending rain was in the air. Certainly was a lonesome place. Home was a million miles away.

Glancing at the dimly lit schedule board again, Ed got the shock of his life. He hadn't noticed it before, but the name on the board didn't say **Hanna, West Virginia**! It said MILLTOWN, WEST VIRGINIA! What in the world was wrong? He was sure the conductor said, "Hanna." Then, he saw the wording beneath was CHANGE TRAINS FOR HANNA, WEST VIRGINIA AND POINTS EAST. Beneath that the schedule showed that the next train to Hanna wasn't due for hours.

Panic neared when a rattling Model T Ford with *TAXI* hand painted on the door pulled up. It's one good headlight blinked off and on and Ed hurried over, trying not to look too apprehensive.

Eyes straining against the darkness inside, he peered at the driver. He must've weighed well over three hundred with another forty pounds of dirt on him. Man, oh man, was he dirty!

Didn't look exactly harmless, but Ed figured he could move faster than the walrus wedged under the steering wheel. Besides, in his situation, he'd have taken his chances with Beelzebub himself. A hoarse voice drawled, "Sorry to be late. Always have lots'a trade from this here late train. The one-ten goin' back, too. Y'all lookin' fer somethin? Wanna go somewhere 'round here? See somebody?"

Teeth close to chattering, Ed replied, "Yessir, I surely am. I'm wanna go to Hanna. Can y'all drive me? I heard it's not far."

The walrus grinned, exhibiting half a dozen remaining teeth. "Ain'tcha a mite young to be goin' to Hanna?"

"Old enough, and I got money to pay. Gonna take me or not?"

"Whoa-back, sonny. Just which Hanna ya wanna go to?"

"Whataya sayin'? There's only *one* Hanna."

"Not so. *Both* sportin' houses 'round here gat a Hanna."

NEVER, *EVER*, AGAIN

Unfortunately, some kids never have a Bestest Friend. There are different levels of friendship. Among them are "acquaintances," "friends" and "good friends." A kid can have many of each, but there's only one "Bestest Friend." They are just that. Bestest Friends can be trusted completely. Once the pledge is made, it's set in concrete.

It often takes considerable time before a relationship matures to the point where two kids become Bestest Friends. Pinkie-swearing makes it for life. One would need to do something pretty dreadful for the other not to ignore or excuse it. Boys could be Bestest Friends as could girls.

****

Billy and his cousin Pat were Bestest Friends. Seldom was the week they didn't spend some time together, summer or winter. Either Billy's folks or Pat's became the parents for both, depending on who was hosting.

Pat often rode his bicycle out to Billy's home from his home in New Kingston. It was ten miles, and Billy thought his cousin was a hero for being able to make it. Sometimes, he rode "double" on the bike's top bar while Pat pedaled them the three miles to Tarryton, another feat Billy much admired. They called his bike "The Red Streak."

After a hard week's play on the farm, they traded residences and wore out the parks and streets around New Kingston. Their relationship was one of brothers, Pat having none and Billy's grown. Two years older, Pat was the leader during their adventures, but Billy could do nearly everything Pat could except one–ride a bicycle. That required two things Billy didn't have. First, a bicycle. Second, funds to acquire one.

Billy made one or two feeble attempts trying to ride The Red Streak, but never could get the hang of it without one on which to practice. If envy was a cardinal sin, then Billy was on the verge. If he could only ride like Pat, one of life's great goals would be realized by the ripe old age of thirteen.

****

Naturally, Billy didn't nag his parents for any luxury such as a bicycle. By some combination of telepathy and acceptance of reality, kids in families of limited resources knew enough not to waste everyone's time begging for the impossible. But, reality doesn't dim the dreams.

Billy racked his brain for a plan to earn money but had no luck. Then the weekly newspaper opened applications for paper routes. *Hot dog!* Here was the answer! Billy's dad gently identified a small problem. True, the paper route paid a fair return on effort, but the farms were so far apart it would take days to deliver the weekly rag–without a bike, that was. Talk about frustration!

Just when the slightest clouds of doubt began forming that he would never succeed in achieving his bicycle fantasy, a miracle happened! Good ol' Bestest Friend Pat came to the rescue with an offer of "help." By delivering papers and selling his old bike, at the end of summer he'd have enough to buy a brand new one. He'd sell Billy The Red Streak.

Immediately, Billy set about to close the deal. Pat said they'd just call it a "Bestest Friends Agreement." How much would he want? When would he need the money? *Exactly* when? Pat stated his terms. He'd "let Billy have" The Red Streak for $40.00. (A fortune!) Bottom line? He'd need the money in eight weeks.

Obviously, parental approval was necessary. When prattling on about the bike and how a deal could be finalized, Billy's dad said nothing, not wanting to shove another road block in front of a dream. Billy's mother was far more inclined to commit road-blocking. However, she relented when his sister pointed out that it would be an excellent way for him to learn never to make bad deals. A kid can always count on older sisters. Always.

****

The first hurdle cleared, now for the harder part. The old saying among Billy's sportier relatives, "Talk's cheap. It takes cash money to buy good whisky," almost immediately took on new meaning. From day one, he felt the pressure of something new, a financial deadline. Eight weeks of working to meet the terms of the "agreement" was not going to be nearly so much fun as eight weeks of the usual summer routine. But, Billy was determined, and two months weren't forever.

He soon learned how outrageously hard it was going to be for a kid to accumulate forty dollars during such local economic misery, but he pushed onward. Working and sweating in the July sun, he dreamed of long rides.

On and on went "Operation Red Streak." After five weeks of bone-tiring labor, scheming, trades, and conniving, Billy's official depository, a pint canning jar, held $21.92. Time was fleeting. A major speed-up was in order. He pulled out all the stops, trying anything and everything. By now, the campaign was running everyone ragged.

****

Shock time! Pat tried to renege on their "Bestest Friends Agreement!" It was something about keeping a spare bike in case

121

of emergencies. Here was Billy's *Bestest Friend* pulling a stunt like this! Sensing his cousin's dismay and reluctance, Pat reneged on his renegging, "That's OK. It don't make no difference. I'll just hafta figure out somethin' else." Good ol' Pat.

****

Another three weeks of furious activity flew by. Almost daily, the pint jar grew heavier. The Red Streak drew ever closer, but would there be time enough? Yes, with any luck at all. But, it was Thursday morning, and Saturday night was the absolute deadline.

Friday night, Billy sat staring at his pint-jar bank. All desperate last minute efforts were exhausted. He thought about checking the results of his grueling summer-long campaign, but already knew the sad total. He hadn't earned one red cent since Tuesday. He was *$3.60* short. Reality had come to call. Might just as well have been $36.00. Or $3,600. Eight weeks of scheming, hard labor, no visits with Pat, and he missed by a *lousy $3.60!*

Fearing disaster, he asked Pat for a one-week extension so he could scrounge up the rest of the money. His Bestest Friend's reply? "A deal's a deal." What in the wide world happened to *"Bestest Friend's Agreement?"* Suddenly, Billy had a very strong suspicion that his cousin made a better deal with Harold Martin, his new summertime pal.

Talk about moping! It was mope-central for Billy on Saturday. So close and yet so far! The consolation prize of $36.40 meant nothing. If he couldn't get a bike, what good was money?

Dad advised, "Better count again to see if it's really short."

What foolishness was this? For eight weeks, he knew at any given *second* exactly what the total was. His dad insisted. Oh well, if he had to prove it to 'im.

He counted again, quickly arriving at $35.00. Then $35.50 and $36.00. Something was wrong–there were some bills left. Should be only coins. Sighing, he counted once more, but it turned out the same! Suddenly hope flickered. He counted furiously. Forty dollars exactly! *How could this be!* He was dumbfounded, but it didn't take long to realize that his dad made the money come out right. Elation got in the way of proper thanks. About the best he managed was inviting his dad to ride the bike, too. Dad seemed real happy. Later Billy learned his father carried a cold lunch to work for days to save the $3.60.

****

Waiting for everyone to get ready for the drive to get The Red Streak demanded almost more patience than a bicycle-crazed-just-turned-13 boy possessed. *Finally*, they arrived so Billy and Pat could complete the "Bestest Friends Agreement."

The car barely rolled to a stop before Billy bounced out and ran to the door. "OK Pat, I got all the money. Let's go get the bike." Out they went to the garage. Now would come the big payoff for the summer's work. Once inside, Pat stuck out his hand. "OK, gimme the money and she's all yours."

"Here ya are, Pat. The whole forty dollars, just like we agreed." Pat counted it twice before reporting, "I jist wantcha to know I could'a sold this bike to Harold for *fifty* dollars."

Pat brought out his brand new bike that he bought only the day before. Said he borrowed the last forty dollars from his dad. It was a beauty, but Billy only had eyes for the one his cousin now rolled out. There she was. *Wow! The Red Streak!* He grabbed the handlebars. A second later, "Wait a minute, Pat. Looks like something's different!"

Pat's reply shattered the "Bestest Friends Agreement." The words also tore to tatters something else, the pinkie-sworn Bestest Friends vow between cousins. "Oh, I forgot to tell ya back when we made the deal that the seat didn't go with it."

Talk about stunned! Billy couldn't say a word. What was going on! His thoughts raced. *(How could he even think of doing such a thing! He's my Bestest Friend!)*

Pat added, "I putcha one on just as good."

(Just as good, my foot! It's nowhere near as good. Why, it's a piece'a junk! Probably sold my good seat to Harold.)

Pat blathered on, trying to explain things. Dazed, Billy didn't make out a word, the ominous seeds of disillusion exploding into full bloom. This couldn't be happening! Not from *Pat.* Not after all the summer's work and sweat! *Not from a Bestest Friend!*

Sounding *proud* of what he did, Pat enthused, "Just lookit how good that seat fits your bike! Wanna try to ride 'er?"

"No, I guess I'll just wait'll I get home."

Billy didn't look at the bicycle any more until they loaded it. Didn't talk to Pat, either, especially as he "explained" about ten times just exactly what the *"deal"* was. He needn't have wasted his breath. His cousin knew exactly what the *"Bestest Friend's Agreement"* was.

****

When they got home, Billy wedged the bike between the barn and a broken-down wagon, then never touched it again. Of course, he thought a lot about what happened. Nothing good. He was burned at Pat, but also at himself. More than angry, he was also *heartsick.* This was his big brother/cousin, *Bestest Friend,* Pat who did this bad thing. *Pat* wouldn't do such a thing! But he had. His *Bestest Friend* slickered him!

In the weeks following, Billy avoided Pat almost totally. His change of behavior was hard to overlook. It was totally quits with Pat. What he did was close to what the Amish call "shunning." Oh, Pat tried to buddy up, pretending not to know what the trouble was.

Billy seeing Harold Martin riding around on *his* bike seat didn't help matters.

At last they had it out. It took all afternoon. Words first. *"No I didn't!" "Yes you did!" Etc.!* Next, shouts. Much more of the same, even louder. Finally, fists. All three confrontations were a first between them, all three ended in a draw. Pat was older and bigger, but Billy was righteous.

****

It's indeed a sad day when betrayed by your Bestest Friend. Billy learned his lesson. The whole "Bestest Friend" thing was a *joke*. He'd never, *ever*, become Bestest Friends with *anyone* again! Nope, never, *ever*, again!

He remained gloomy even after school started in September. Well, he did perk up a little when that new girl, Doreen Coleen McCarthy, was given the seat just behind his in math class. It wasn't long before she asked for help with her lesson. Billy didn't know why. She seemed to be a whiz in the subject.

Then, she needed help in Literature class. That was also odd. He thought she was okey-doke in Lit, too. Soon, they were sitting together at lunch. Got so they talked and kidded around a lot, spending more time together. She was really good fun.

****

Monday morning after the Thanksgiving holiday, Doreen Coleen asked, "William, do Bestest Friends *always* have to be boy and boy or girl and girl? Can a boy and *girl* be Bestest Friends?"

ONLINE PATTY

Calling Harry Olean "shy" was the same as calling the Washington Monument tall. Interacting with him wasn't necessary to determine this. Somehow, one look and you knew it. Perhaps some are born shy, and Harry may've been. But, he had the double-whammy of being raised by the dictionary definition of a dominating mother. His dad escaped her Do-As-I-Say-Or-Die overbearing presence when Harry was three, so Harry was left with no one to share the brunt of her battering.

Beginning in the third month of first grade, Harry Olean's teachers referred him each year for counseling because his shyness interfered with his progress. After one joint session with Mrs. Olean, counselor and teacher agreed that the only thing possible was for them to do the best they could for Harry in the classroom before passing him on to the next grade's teacher/victim.

To the profound relief of teachers and administrators alike, they escaped further pummeling from his mother when Harry graduated. Principal Glen Armon once growled that there was no way he could be found guilty of strangling that "crazy bitch" by any jury in the land.

Math teacher Nelson warned, "Careful Oscar, you're gonna have every dog-owner in the state on your butt for insulting dogs," The counselor quickly put in, "All the crazies, too."

Everyone who knew Harry felt they didn't need all the fingers on one hand to count the times Harry crossed swords with his mother, but it *could* happen. When he protested that he should be given more than fifty dollars from his weekly paycheck at the assembly plant was one time it did. Surprisingly, she increased the amount to one-half of his weekly check, but only on his promise to place half of his half in a joint savings account. "Just in case something should happen to either of us, you understand."

A major eruption occurred anytime Harry inadvertently made reference to a girl. He had the usual 22-year-old male's interest in the opposite sex and slipped up more than once. The latest occurred during the dinner he always prepared. He mentioned sitting at lunch beside Lois Graves, the boss' new secretary. Instantly, Harry kicked himself as a fool.

Lately the barrages far exceeded his expectations, each salvo more demeaning of girls. In spite of his increasingly intense vow not to succumb to her harangues, he always did. As usual, he promised to be more respectful and avoid "those hussies" trying to lay waste to all the hard work she did in raising him. Only after he promised and poured her third glass of wine did she switch topics, often to some other "transgression" of his.

What Harry's mother didn't know was that over the past months he became good friends with fellow-worker, Greg Mason. Hades would've paled to a glow compared to her wrath had she discovered Harry was revealing bits of his life to him.

In addition to a wide variety of experiences, Mason was a good listener. At 41, twice divorced and with a reputation as a ladies' man, he gradually became something of a combination alter-ego and father-figure to Harry.

Mason was responsible for Harry obtaining a computer based on his judgment that the lad needed some form of relief from his wicked-witch mother's constant badgering to maintain absolute control. In the process, he finally extracted a promise from Harry that, for once, he'd stand up for his rights.

When Henry brought the computer home the scene turned instantly ugly. First, it was his lack of regard for her feelings by buying a laptop without discussing it with her. To make matters worse, he paid for it and the internet-server contract from part of his pay. "If you could do that, then you should be putting more money into the joint savings account!"

Finally, for the first time in either's life, she was forced into stunned and grudging acquiescence to her "rebellious" son. The very same son she "...tried so hard to raise with proper respect." The best she could get from him was an agreement to not "...do those dirty things on the computer" she saw on TV.

Harry was computer-literate of course. Computers were an integral part of his high school education, so social networking was no mystery. But, aside from sneaking a peek at school now and then, there was no opportunity to fully participate. Two such sites were the very first things he logged into. It was past 1:00 a.m. before he forced himself into bed.

****

Greg Mason greeted Harry at work next day with, "From the looks of your bloodshot eyeballs you got going on your new computer. First tell me, mother give you much of a battle?"

"Nothing I couldn't handle."

"My oh my! Aren't we the new big man about the house! Since you're the master of the manse, tell me how many sweet young things you hooked up with during your first ten minutes. Any hot prospects?"

"Aw, nothing like that. A couple were pretty friendly, but I'm not so good along that line. Don't know what to say."

"Harry, you gotta get with the program. Gotta learn the game. I'll help you along. For starters, you don't need to do it all on social networks to hook up with girls. You could check out some of those outfits that arrange meetings, but I doubt you're ready for that. Besides, some of them charge an arm and a leg.

"There's lots of other ways. Tell you what. I'll give you some sites where you can meet babes—where you can e-mail direct and don't need to do all that profiling first—don't have to tell much at first except what you're looking for."

"Hey, Greg! Thanks a bunch! I think that'd be better than what I tried. Can you give me some today? I could try them tonight."

"Will do, kid. I'll do it at lunch."

****

Next morning, Harry could hardly wait to tell Mason about last evening's surfing. "Greg! You wouldn't believe it, but I was e-mailing nine girls last night! Three of them really friendly. I'm gonna contact them first tonight. I really appreciate it, Greg. You're a great friend."

Mason smiled at the boyish enthusiasm. *(How could a kid his age be so green? That bitch mother's had some hold on 'im.)* "Told you so, didn't I? First thing you know, one of 'em will be propositioning you."

"Aw Greg, it was nothing like that. It was just friendly talk. That's all it was."

"Never can tell. How's mom taking the new you? She been checking out your computer?"

"She's been pouting a lot. Doesn't know how to fool around with the computer. She's learned how to turn it on, I guess. I never leave it on—never, but it was on last night when I sat down."

"Mom know you're hooking up with girls?"

"No way! She keeps asking what I'm doing on it, but I just say I'm googling something."

Two days later, Harry came to work all agog. "Greg, last night one of the girls asked me for a picture! I told her I'd send one, but, Greg, I don't have a good one."

"Not to worry. We'll drop by the Insty-Pic booth at the drug store and get you all fixed up. By the way, did she say she'd send you hers?"

"Oh, she already did." He fished it from his pocket and handed it to Mason.

"Harry she's a *looker!* I gotta warn you, though. Sometimes you get a picture of somebody else. She say how old she was?"

"Yeah, twenty-eight, but she said she likes younger men."

"What else do you know about 'er?"

"Oh, lots." Harry proceeded to relate all he knew, adding, "She calls herself 'Online Patty,' but of course I know that's not her real name. I'm not completely stupid. It's just that with mother, I never had much chance to get to know things like other guys do. Greg, you don't know how much I thank you for wising me up."

"Think nothing of it, kid. We all gotta learn. You're just a little late, that's all. It's good to see you're gettin' with it."

****

In the ensuing weeks, the e-mails between Harry and Online Patty became ever so much more personal and intimate. Hers progressed from implying they might meet someday to suggesting it outright in her most recent e-mail.

Harry told Mason of this and how he didn't know what to do, Greg advised, "Careful kid, don't get trapped into anything messy or illegal. What name did you say she used? Where did you find her on the web? Maybe I better check things out."

"Meaning what?"

"Well, I know about these things. I can soon find out if she's just a tease or on the level. Don't wanna see you get dragged in over your head. Just gimme the site and I can do the rest."

"Greg, you're a real friend. I'm sure she's on the level, but I'm also sure your advice is good. It always is."

****

While Harry waited for Mason's advice about meeting Online Patty, it wasn't long before he began to see a marked decrease in the length of her e-mails. Nor were there any more references to a meeting. He asked Mason what he thought the matter was.

"Don't know, kid. These things come and go. Stop e-mailing her for a while. That might work."

Harry took the advice and stopped. Strangely, she stopped also. Mason encouraged him to continue his hold-out, counseling, "I'll keep checking her out. Sometimes these things take a while."

Another three days passed, and Harry could stand it no longer. In a lengthy e-mail, he asked what was wrong and apologized if he did something to upset her. He was surprised she resounded so quickly. Then he sat, immobile, in total shock.

Dear Ready Harry–

I have put off writing because I didn't want to hurt your feelings, and I didn't know exactly how to say this. But, I know I must tell you that it is best we don't e-mail any longer. To be honest, I've met someone else, and we are meeting soon. He's a bit older, but he sounds kind and always answers my e-mails right away.

I will always remember our e-mails.

Online Patty

****

Passing by Harry's room at 1:45 a.m., his mother saw the light under the door. "Harry, are you *still* on that computer! Turn it off and go to bed! *Right now!* You'll be half asleep at work tomorrow, and won't that be fine! Lose your job over that contraption and then what'll we do? *Hear me, Harry?"*

Startled, he jostled the table and the screen lit up. It hadn't been a bad dream, the message was still there. His mother demanded again, *"Go to bed!"*

****

A mind-jumbled Harry Olean stumbled to his work station the next day having slept no more than two hours. Greg Mason came over. "Great suffering horned frogs, Harry! You look like you've been dragged through a knothole–rode hard and put away wet. How'd you ever get in such a sorry shape?"

Without answering, Harry pulled a dog-eared copy of Online Patty's e-mail from his pocket and handed it to Mason. He read it slowly and handed it back without comment. Finally, Harry questioned, "Well?"

"Well what?"

"Well, you said not to e-mail her, and I didn't. Now look what's happened! When I quit, she found somebody else!"

"That's crap, and you know it. It's lucky you found her out now. Just think what could'a happened if you got real serious, then she pulled a stunt like this."

"But Greg, you said you'd e-mail her and let me know if she was up to anything. You haven't said a word."

"I also told you sometimes these things take a while. Anyhow, now you know. Like I said, it's better to find out now."

"But Greg...."

"There's the bell. Time to go to work."

"But Greg...."

"Kid, whataya want from me? I told you sometimes they don't pan out. If you just gotta, we'll talk during lunch."

133

****

Harry waited in the lunchroom until it was time to go back to work. At afternoon break, he couldn't locate Mason, either. During the remainder of the afternoon, his questions about Mason became doubts. What had he done to make Greg act like this? He was the one who always said what to do. Why hadn't he warned him? Maybe he was wrong all along about Greg. He trusted him for advice, and now look what happened!

After work, Harry still couldn't locate Mason, so he walked to his car and waited. Fuming, doubts flickered closer to full flame.

Greg Mason arrived, and Harry's flames exploded. Mason let the kid yell on and on about getting bad advice. *"How could you do such a thing! You're the only person in the world I trusted! You know me, Greg. You know I don't know much about women. But you knew Online Patty was the only girl I ever had a chance with! Now, since I didn't e-mail her like you said not to, she's found somebody else!"* On and on it went.

On the way to their cars, other workers got an earful, one commenting, "Looks like Mason's gettin' it good. Knowin' him, it's probly about a woman."

Occasionally, Mason attempted to reason with Harry, but to no avail. Harry raged on until finally his target had enough. "Kid, if you can manage to *SHUT UP* long enough to listen just one minute, I'll tell you a thing or two. First, I know what your mother's done to you, and I've tried to be your friend. But, you gotta start listening to yourself. You're a big boy now. Start acting like one. It's time for you to *GROW UP!*

"Something else you gotta learn is that stuff just happens sometimes. Nothing you can do about it."

Harry interrupted with another volley, ending with, "What's that supposed to mean! You about to give me some more of your *good advice*?"

Mason was angry-calm. "Nope. This time you're on your own. I hoped I wouldn't have to do this. But, since you think I'm such a bastard, I'm gonna do it, anyway. Better yet, read for yourself. He handed Harry an e-mail copy.

****

Mr. OneAndOnly–

I can hardly wait till Saturday when I finally get to meet you. I hope you are feeling the same and won't be too disappointed. I must confess that photo I sent was made a couple years ago, but I haven't changed much.

Don't forget the directions. When you get to Petoskey, the pier is right downtown. You can't miss it. There are benches, and I'll wait there for you.

I know you said you were sorry about your friend Harry and all that, but his e-mails told me he was a little too immature. Besides, things just happen. I hope he will understand that.

So long for now. See you Saturday.

Online Patty

****

Scarcely believing his eyes, Harry read it a second time, then a third. Abruptly, he crushed it into a ball, slammed in onto the ground, spun and ran the two miles home. Mason retrieved the crumpled e-mail, smoothed it as best he could and stuck into his jacket pocket.

Ignoring his mother's questions, Harry dashed upstairs, went into his room and slammed shut the door. For the first time ever, he didn't prepare dinner. In fact, he ate nothing at all. And for once, his mother had sense enough to remain still. The fury exhibited on her son's face probably helped her make that decision.

****

135

When Detective Mark Ritter arrived, he had no problem identifying the shooter. That morning, astonished co-workers saw the whole thing. In the parking lot, Harry Olean fired into Greg Mason until the bullets ran out, then stood over him clicking an empty gun.

Before shocked onlookers could react, he calmly walked into an adjoining wooded area. Ritter immediately instructed the desk sergeant to put out an all-points, "armed-and-dangerous," pick up order for Harry Olean.

While completing an inventory of the late Gregory Mason's belongings, the detective came across the precipitating e-mail, read it and called his partner over. "Mel, take a look at this. Think it could have anything to do with this killing? Everybody here says the vic and the perp were buddy-buddy. Think a woman could'a got between 'em?"

Mel read and observed, "Could be a motive, all right. See the date on it? Day after tomorrow he was supposed to meet the sender. If there is anything to the woman thing, you reckon there's any chance the vic could'a told the perp about this? If he did, think he might go after her too?"

"By golly, Mel! You're smater'n dirt, after all. If we don't nail this Harry Whosit by this afternoon, maybe we better notify the local law up there to be on the lookout."

"What about asking them to alert the woman? She ought'a know what's gone down."

"Small problem—nobody knows who she is or her real name. We could e-mail 'er, I guess, but she might not get it in time."

"There *is* that photo from his wallet, but it could be anybody. Maybe Mason's kid, she looks young enough. Y'know Mel, I'm thinking the best way is for somebody to go up there to work with the locals in trying to find either the perp or her—or both."

"A twofer. Save one and nail one. That'd be something!"

136

****

While local police set in motion procedures to apprehend Harry Olean, Detectives Mark Ritter and Melvin Kelly took up positions on Petoskey's pier–Kelly as a pretend fisherman, Ritter a Hawaiian-shirted, plaid-shorted, sandal-shod, tourist.

By 9:00, early-morning walkers were on their way to coffee shops. Two boats docked and away went the passengers to the up-scale shops two block away. The only person remaining the entire morning was a late-fortyish lady who arose from a bench for an occasional walking-break from reading her book. On one of her trips, she smiled and spoke to Ritter, but kept walking.

A trip later, she paused. "So nice to be out here, isn't it?"

Ritter eyed her. Something was trying to click, and Ritter grabbed on. She looked twice the age of the one in the e-mailed photo he had, but there was something of a resemblance. "Could you by any chance be waiting to meet someone this morning? Could you be On Line Patty?"

Smiling broadly, she answered at once. "That I am, and I'm guessing you might be *the* Mister One And Only looking for me."

Before Ritter could respond, Detective Kelly rushed up from his "fishing" spot. "Mark! I just got a cell from the Chief! That Harry Olean character we came up here to warn somebody about– somebody usin' the name'a 'On Line Patty?' Well, we don't hafta hang around. They just found 'im up in Riverside Park. Hanged himself. Just think–a murder and a suicide could'a happened all over somebody neither of 'em ever saw. Don't reckon that Patty person'll ever know."

"STOP PRAYIN', DADDY!"

All the Ledbetters were more than happy to welcome another family of them into what local residents in New Plymouth termed the "Ledbetter Colony." So many of the same name moved to town and settled in the same area that one of the long-time locals observed, "Those first few hillbillies were the scouting party. When they found a place to live and a job, they whistled in the rest of 'em."

At first, the townsfolk may've been a bit wary about the growing southern contingent. But, they soon discovered that the migrants were a hard-working, keep-your-nose-out'a-everbody's-business bunch. This acceptance was probably helped along when the straight-laced city fathers figured how much more tax revenue would be generated.

Then too, it became obvious that not only did the outsiders have the same names, they were all of the same religious belief, faithfully attending the small strictly-fundamentalist church just outside of town. Further, the Ledbetter kids tacked on a "ma'am" or "sir' onto their "Yes" or "No" when addressed by an adult.

For months, relatives in New Plymouth encouraged Buford and Mabelene Ledbetter to move north and join them, but there was no reason to do so. They were perfectly happy where they were. Fickle fate sometimes intervenes.

****

Deep in Appalachia, Buford and Mabelene Ledbetter observed traditions in place for generations. He spent his workday far down in a coal mine, she with the continuous chores of raising six kids—now minus the two older boys who also worked in the mine and beginning families of their own.

There were two "breaks" in the long-continuing household routine. The first was shopping for goods and groceries at the company store. Coal miner's wages were above average, and most everything was available at the company-owned commissary (the "company store" of songs and stories).

True, there was never much cash around, but the company extended credit to be paid in full each two weeks or so at the "first of the half," or the "last of the half" (could be near the middle or last of the month on payday, but the "halfs" matched payday regardless of where they fell on the calendar).

The second weekly break was Sunday service at the coal camp church. Not believing in having a full-time minister, various members preached the sermons. As a church Elder, Buford Ledbetter was often called upon to perform this function. In addition to his fire-and-brimstone delivery, he was noted for the volume and length of his prayers. Members often commented that his faith must be awfully strong.

Yes, there was no reason for Buford and his family to move way up north to New Plymouth. Then, circumstances changed dramatically, seemingly overnight. During mid-afternoon, the emergency siren at the tipple over the mine shaft began wailing. Instantly, everyone dropped whatever they were doing and rushed to the site. As usual, no information was available beyond that of the superintendent announcing that there had been a "slight accident" and the miners would be coming up "soon."

"Soon" proved to be well past dark. As the grim-faced miners appeared, it was obvious that not an entire shift was present. The "slight accident" claimed the lives of seven. The story immediately spread that safety violations, so long ignored, were ignored at least one day too long. A section of one tunnel collapsed, and there was no chance anyone survived.

After the national 24/7 news channels went on to something else and the federal mine-safety inspectors departed, the company prepared to resume operations. One little problem. The miners demanded that safety must be improved. There was no response and the miners went on strike.

The coal company locked them out, claiming they violated the labor agreement. Not only that, they'd no longer be extending credit at the company store. The reason? If they weren't working, how could they pay up each payday? The solution? Just go on back to mining and everything would work out. No sale.

Weeks passed, and the miners were in a desperate situation. All the help they could give each other was exhausted. Buford Ledbetter's prayers became louder, longer, and much more often for the Lord to provide. They didn't want much—just a little food. More time passed, and Buford overheard one member remark after a lengthy service that maybe Elder Ledbetter's faith wasn't quite as strong as they thought.

In the following day's mail, another letter from relatives up north arrived with the latest suggestion that Buford and Mabelene move the family there. They talked it over all day, and at the supper table, he sadly declared that the only thing they could do was pack up and go.

****

Pooling their resources, the Ledbetter Colony arranged housing for the latest arrivals. Sooner than he could've hoped, Buford had a job, the kids were in school, and Mabelene had the household organized.

An added bonus was the nearby church whose membership was of the same belief as the one back home. Within a month, Buford's reputation for his passionate prayers was reestablished, helped along by his entreaties for rain. In the midst of the worst drought in New Plymouth history, he became the acknowledged leader of those praying for rain-relief.

In addition to praying several times at each service, Buford did so before departing for work in the morning and after supper. In the absence of results, he stepped up his campaign, moving from indoors, first onto the porch, then into the yard. From there, he delivered his most fervent morning and evening prayers. Buford explained to Mabelene that he was nearer to his intended listener. The same reasoning was responsible for the increased volume of his pleas.

****

As the drought wore on into late June, Buford's efforts did not go unnoticed. Ledbetter relatives understood his zeal and offered encouragement. However, some others didn't share the same appreciation. Buford and Mabelene lived on the perimeter of the Ledbetter Colony, their side-yard adjoining Nelson's Poultry Farm. The Nelson's soon became *considerably* less than enchanted about the strident, twice-daily, outdoor prayers arising just beyond the high board fence separating the two properties.

June melted into July, July into August, and Hershel Nelson had enough. "Those Ledbetters are a decent enough bunch, but there's a limit. We're churchgoers too, but by Jupiter there's a limit, I say! I'm goin' over there and speak to them about the racket! Scaring the daylights out'a the hens is what it's doin'. Surprised they keep on laying eggs.

"On top'a that, the days are getting shorter. Pretty soon, he'll be out there after dark. No telling how much louder he's gonna get.

I've talked to those two Ledbetters I know, and they haven't done a cotton-pickin' thing about 'im. Time I put a stop to it!" Etc., etc.

Wife Jenny dissuaded him the first few times he made the threat, but it became increasingly difficult to sell a variation of her usual, "Now Hersh, those are good folks trying to do the right thing. Don't go off half-cocked. It'll surely rain pretty soon and that'll take care of the praying problem."

But, it didn't rain.

In late August, on the way to collect eggs just after next door's morning prayer session, Hershel Nelson had a brainstorm. Aloud, he exclaimed, *"Ah-hah!* They want it to rain, I'll make it rain! Good people or not, this twice-a-day holy-hoo-haw's gotta stop!"

****

The Nelsons were known for more than the high-quality brown eggs from their free-range Plymouth Rock and Rhode Island Red hens. Known even on national sports talk shows, they were the parents of twin sons likely to be chosen in the first round of next year's major-league baseball draft.

Dan, a pitcher, was reputed to possess the strongest arm since Hercules. Dave, an outfielder, had the keenest batting eye since Cyclops to go along with a copy of his brother's pitching arm. New Plymouth High hadn't lost a baseball game in four years. Recruiters and scouts from far and wide watched the boys at every game for the past year.

Dad Nelson was also recruiting. While their mother was at choir practice, he called his sons aside. "Boys, I have a super-secret mission for us. It's so secret that if you ever breathe a *single word* to your mother, you'll never get another red cent of an allowance again...*ever*. Also, you'll be grounded till you're seventy-five. I'll come back and getcha if you squeal. Top'a that, I'll pass the word to baseball scouts that both'a you've been takin' arm-juicin' pills for years. I mean mouths shut...*forever*! Got it!"

Laughing, both swore allegiance and silence. Hershel ordered, "Get your stuff and warm up. Don't wanna screw up an arm that's gonna pay for my retirement." Ten minutes later, he led them around back to two half-filled baskets alongside the high board fence separating the Nelsons and Ledbetters.

****

Agnes Mae, June Alene, and Bo Ledbetter, Buford and Mabelene's youngest children, were getting a last just-before-dark playtime in their side yard, and their father was just beginning his evening praying-for-rain session. Cloudy skies made rain seem more promising than usual.

Suddenly, an egg splattered within inches of June Alene! Before she could react, another exploded between the other two kids, followed by a veritable egg shower.

Nine-year-old Agnes Mae instantly dashed around the corner to the front yard where her dad had the volume turned waaay up on his prayer. *"Daddy, Daddy! Stop prayin'!* **Stop Prayin'!** Somethin's gone awful bad *wrong!"*

At the first shriek of his daughter, Buford rushed toward the side yard, meeting her on the way. *"What'n creation's the matter, child? What's the matter!"*

"Daddy, somethin's gone awful bad wrong with your prayin'! It's not rainin' *rain*, it's rainin' *eggs!"*

"WHERE'S *MY* FIFTEEN SECONDS?"

Once again, Quincy Eberhart Smythe suffered the daily disappointment. Neither the mail nor his e-mail brought notification whether his entry, HAS-BEENS ANONYMOUS, received an award at the annual Universal Book Competition. There certainly was plenty of time to have heard by now. Even if he didn't win a medal of any kind, just an honorable mention would mean so much. After nine attempts, he was positive this year he'd get *something*. Well, maybe tomorrow.

Three "tomorrows" later, there was still nothing. Second noontime Martini in hand, he sat on the tiny balcony of his "gulf view" apartment the rental agency highlighted in their ad. For the umpteenth time, Quincy griped, "*Some gulf view!* Might be if a person was atop a fifty foot ladder on the roof. Aside from the park across the street, the only "view" is the run-down fire-traps on each side of this one." He slugged down another gulp and added, "Oh well, with my mucked-up vision, what do I care?"

Finishing the Martini, he considered the empty glass. Again aloud, he remarked, "What the hey, bartender, I'll have another." What he mixed was more like "another" times two. No sense in wasting an olive, either. Drink half gone, he sat thinking and analyzed himself, something he'd been doing a lot lately.

(Quince, you eighty-two-year old clown, once more in the same place as usual. Tried everything and amounted to nothing. By now even a bonehead like you should've learned he's never gonna

amount to a lead dime. Maybe this time you'll finally get it that you'll never be anything more than a bit in the terabyte of life.) He was proud of the analogy. *(Maybe I'll try it in another book that will amount to nothing. No chance, though. Too old.)*

Only his typed manuscript of HAS-BEENS ANONYMOUS remained after shipping his very last Print-On-Demand 10-copy order to the Competition. He picked it up, thinking ruefully. *(Talk about has-beens! I oughta know about 'em. No, I'm wrong. At least they're has-beens. To be a has-been you gotta have first been something. I'm no has-been, I'm just a never-was. That's me, a never-was!)*

The afternoon sun awakened him. *(Crap! Forgot the lotion again. Gonna look fried. So what, who cares? Nobody's gonna see me, anyhow.)*

He went inside to check for e-mails again. *(Still nothing. Not time here for another, but it's five o'clock somewhere.)* He mixed while commenting aloud, "There's been more'n enough time. If I was gonna hear, I would'a by now."

Later, Quincy managed a restless two hours of sleep, but was awake again just after midnight. In case there'd somehow been a delay, he opened his e-mails. Nothing from the Universal Book Competition. Nothing from anyone, not even any spam. He leaned back and chuckled sardonically, "At last, I've been recognized as something by spammers—recognized as the world's biggest nobody. Not even worth one lousy come-on."

Before continuing, he squinted for a long moment at the blank IN-BOX on the 27-inch monitor he was forced to use since that old-man's eye thing half-blinded him.

Abed again, he griped, "Didn't someone say everyone's due fifteen minutes of fame? Where's mine? Fifteen *minutes!* I'd settle for fifteen *seconds!*" There was more before he dropped off.

****

In the morning fog, Quincy sat on his balcony while sipping coffee and thinking about last night's conversation with himself leading to today's firm decision. *(Yessir, I'm exactly right. Even people always chasing rainbows are entitled to at least fifteen seconds of fame. Me for instance. I was so sure Has-Beens Anonymous was finally gonna do it for me. But, you gotta face it, Quincy old man—three year's work is down the crapper. Would'a had it done sooner if I could see more'n inch-high words and a four-word line. Well, no matter now, I got my fifteen seconds all figured out and we start tomorrow morning.)*

****

Quincy sat on a bench in the small park across the street and waited. He knew it might take some time, maybe even hours, but sooner or later, a fire truck would have to come along. There was plenty of business for them practically every day. On down the street in that ratty neighborhood, a suspected arsonist was on the prowl. In the unlikely event a firebug didn't strike today, there was almost always an ambulance racing down this main drag.

He was prepared to wait all right, having brought along a lunch sandwich and coffee. Two hours later, he heard the sirens. *(This is my lucky day. The park's jammed and I'm ready.)*

Calmly, he picked up his thick manuscript of HAS-BEENS ANONYMOUS, walked to the sidewalk and waited. With his extremely limited vision, he could only make out approaching vehicles for a couple hundred feet. But, even with lousy vision, he was able to discern bright flashing lights farther away. He was pretty sure he saw some. And, his hearing was adequate. The raucous sirens were getting louder. The fire truck was much closer.

Now, it *was almost there!* Erstwhile Author Quincy Eberhart Smythe folded his arms over *HAS-BEENS ANONYMOUS* and stepped forward into the street. Unflinching, he turned to face the

147

speeding fire truck much in the manner as the Chinese student facing a tank in Tiananmen Square during a failed revolution. At last, his 15 seconds of fame had arrived.

The sirens were almost upon him. In spite of his absolute resolve not to, he closed his eyes and tensed for the impact. But, there was none. Not only that, the sirens were growing weaker and then stopped. Only later, Quincy learned that the fire truck turned left a block down the street to battle a blaze three blocks farther on.

Furious, Quincy damned his eyes and strode back to his bench to await a speeding ambulance. Noon came but no ambulance. An hour later, he ate his sandwich. By 3:00, he had enough waiting.

During his wait, he realized that he hadn't heard a single scream from those in the park he was counting on during his 15 seconds of fame. Damning all non-screamers, he retreated to his small walk-up and giant Martini. No e-mail, two gulps downed and still furious, he raged, ***"Damned unthinking deadheads!"*** Another gulp, then, *"I'll fix 'em! That's what I'll do!"*

****

Next morning, Quincy walked briskly to the commuter train station three blocks distant. This time, he wouldn't have to rely on a fire truck or ambulance. Commuter trains ran on a strict schedule. Arriving, he was surprised that so few passengers were waiting for the 8:38. *(Well, lots of office workers have already left.)* He sat and waited for the usual announcement of the train's arrival in 10 minutes. Another 15 passed and still no announcement. Again, he listened to his talking watch–9:04. Clearly, the 8:38 was very late.

No matter how long it took, Quincy swore he'd be ready. This time, there'd be no slip-ups. Even he could see a locomotive, and they didn't make left turns. Also, there'd be a bigger audience. In addition to those preparing to board, drivers and their passengers waiting at the downed crossing gates would also see everything.

With *HAS-BEENS ANONYMOUS,* Quincy rose and strolled up and down the boarding platform. He passed a security guard eyeing him, but smiled and kept moving. During the third round-trip the guard stepped forward. "You've been here quite a long time. Something I can help you with?"

"Oh, no thank you, I'm waiting for the eight-thirty-eight, but it seems to be running late today."

"Mister, don'tcha watch the news? Been on for a week. Today's the day the time switched to eastern standard. There's an hour difference from yesterday. The eight-thirty-eight was right on time. The next down-towner don't stop till twelve-twenty."

****

Martini time again! And again. And again. No e-mail from the International Book Competition again. Quincy looked out the window and suddenly realized he'd overlooked the obvious site for getting his 15 seconds of fame. It was right there in the park across the street all the time.

****

Next morning, dressed in his best and carrying the two-inch-thick typed *HAS-BEENS ANONYMOUS* manuscript, Quincy walked across into the park. It was Saturday, and by late morning, it was packed. Just ahead was the six-story circular tower in which viewers could climb to the observation platform atop it.

Stopping often for a breather, he struggled up the long circular stairs to the crowded platform. Everything was perfect. Not a cloud in the sky, no wind, temperature just right. Crowded with spectators. Why had he never thought of this place before?

Quincy moved to the safety rail and paused to drink in the exhilarating moment. He had a sense of total relaxation as if this were the moment for which he labored all his life. He could now smile at the thought of all his failed efforts to achieve some of the fame that tomato-can artist said everyone deserved.

****

Finally, the number of viewers dwindled to a few well out of sight, and "author" Quincy Smythe made ready for his 15 seconds. Gripping his manuscript of HAS-BEEN ANONYMOUS in one hand, he gripped the chest-high railing topping the plastic see-through panels in preparation for his journey. One mighty vault would do it.

Re-gripping the railing, he propelled himself upward with every ounce of strength he could muster. Alas, he neglected to factor in the difference in ages between his once 16 years and his current 82. His "one mighty vault" lifted him approximately six inches. Fuming, he dropped his manuscript and grabbed the railing with both hands. This time he elevated almost a foot.

Cussing, he backed up and crouched for take-off. A deep breath and he was off. Off, that is, for two strides before old legs and poor vision sent him sprawling over his discarded manuscript.

Startled, two tourists who came onto the platform just then rushed to assist Quincy to his feet. Thinking they were attempting to restrain him from his leap to fame, he yanked his arms free and glared at them. *(Idiots!)*

Puzzled, one responded, "Sorry, fella, just trying to help."

Quincy continued glaring, his opportunity gone. *(These knotheads are sure to butt in again if I go ahead.)* He wheeled and stormed out through the entryway door and back down the stairs.

One flight down, Quincy remembered his missing manuscript. *(Hell with it—just one more reminder I can't get anything right. Gonna zip back across the street to my lousy digs—figure a sure-fire way for later today. Wish I had gin for martinis.)*

****

Quincy's Good Samaritans followed him inside and watched him until he exited the tower six flights below, then went back outside onto the viewing platform. One picked up the *HAS-BEENS ANONYMOUS* manuscript, read the short preface, and inspected the covers again.

Over the sounds of screaming sirens of several approaching emergency vehicles, he remarked, "Must'a been that grumpy old dude's. Say, look at the title! Looks like the very same one they were talkin' about on the TV news this morning. Somethin' about it bein' a masterpiece and the author gettin' some kind'a great big award and lots'a money from a book contest. Whataya s'pose he was doin' with this?"

HEY Y'ALL! BREAK TIME!

THIS HERE'S CLARABELLE THAT'S COME CALLLIN'. HOW'S GUESSIN' GOIN'? SAY Y'ALL GOT SOME OF 'EM? HOW MANY DIDJA? WELL NOW, THAT BE COMIN' RIGHT ALONG PURTY FAIR.

SPEAKIN'A GUESSIN', BETCHA CAIN'T NEVER GUESS WHO I RUN INTO LATELY. RECKON Y'ALL'D BE S'PRISED TO FIND OUT IT BE JUDGE HAROLD HAND. REAL FRIENDLY LIKE, TOO. NOTHIN' LIKE WHEN HE BE SIITIN' UP THERE DOIN' HIS JUDGIN' BACK YONDER IN THE FIRST TALE. WE BEEN HITTIN' IT OFF SOME BETTERIN' MIDDLIN'.

WELL ANYWAY, HURRY ON BACK. LOTS MORE GOOD STUFF ON DOWN THE ROAD. GOTTA GO. SOMEBODY'S KNOCKIN' ON MY FRONT DOOR.

Sorry I'm a little late. Happy to hear y'all had a good Breakin' time. Right happy to hear yer pinin' smartly to go ahead on readin' n guessin'.

Meant to ask y'all, what about that Quincy Smythe? You 'member 'im don'tcha? That writer guy that couldn't never get the hang'a doin' hissef in?

Never could figger iffin he got the prize or them 'mergency vehicles down on the street was there to scrape 'em up. Gotta speak to Mister D. D. Huddle 'bout leavin' a string hangin' thataway.

Happy readin'.

THE "NECESSARY CAN"

Ten-year-old Carl Wilson just loved airplanes and flying. His fondest dream was to become a pilot. Model plane after model plane was built. Book after book read. Web site after Web site scoured. Carl was a romantic at heart. Jets were fun, but he also wanted to experience an old-time open-cockpit flight, the kind he learned of in his extensive study of aviation history.

Of course he was aware that the originals no longer existed except in museums. But, he also knew that pilots in current reproductions were appearing at air shows and small private airports. Some sold rides and performed stunts. The only problem was, none were appearing close to the rural area where he lived.

The following summer, a miracle dropped from the blue, so to speak. An item in the weekly paper announced that renowned pilot, "Ace" Hawkins, would be doing stunts over the area on Saturday. Afterward, he'd land in the pasture behind Wellman's Point and take people for rides. Apparently, he was between air shows and picking up a buck any way he could.

Nothing more than a gas station at a crossroads, Wellman's Point was just east of the local town about four miles from Carl's farm home. *Wow!* Here was his chance! He grabbed the paper and started begging. Then, his sister, Arlene, of all people, also said she'd like to take a ride–a second miracle! Then a third, the biggest of all. His parents said they could do it!

****

Saturday morning, Carl and Arlene sat in the yard observing Ace Hawkins doing his stuff. Seeing loop-the-loops, barrel rolls, spins and other stunts, their stomachs churned and shadows of doubts arose. When older brother Forrest said the pilot did stunts with everyone who went for a ride, Carl croaked, "Aw, that's not so," fervently hoping it wasn't. Arlene stopped watching and went inside. Forrest kept it up.

Around noon, Ace began flying smoothly over the farm with passengers, and Forrest stopped the scare tactics. Carl's stomach stopped churning, but his enthusiasm definitely suffered a blow.

From Carl's demeanor, his dad sensed some hesitancy on his part. "Getting cold feet, are ya, son?"

Proving he'd rather lie and die than appear a coward to his dad, Carl piped up, "No sir, not a bit." (Liar, liar, pants on fire.)

Old helpful Forrest was quick to put in his two cents worth. "Not much, he's not. He and Alene are both shakin' like a leaf. Haven't had a bite'a food for fear'a gettin' sick." Of course the latter was true, but Forrest needn't have blabbed.

Things were quiet during the ride to Wellman's Point, Forrest's vivid descriptions of how sick they were going to be ringing in their ears. Arriving, they were surprised at the big crowd. Carl kept his thoughts to himself about what Forrest might say at the large turnout. *("Just look at that crowd. Probably came to watch you chicken out...or crash and burn to fritters.")* Good old Forrest. You could always count on him.

****

As if the possibility of imminent death weren't enough, the added burden of a secret scheme was raising Carl's anxieties. His best buddy for years was his big white collie dog, Old Charlie. He could always depend on Carl to sneak out a treat from dinner or side with him in his on-going war with cats.

Concerned whether Charlie would recognize him when he waved from the plane, the day before take-off, Carl devised a mad plan to make sure he would. Doing what seemed a good idea at the time, he hacked off and hid a chunk of raw beef from Sunday's roast-to-be.

His mother would've whacked him good had she known! And, what if she discovered the details of his plot? He dared not contemplate the grounded-for-life consequence–among several other probables.

He was going to ask Ace to fly over the farm so he could throw his surprise treat right into Charlie's jaws. Carl was certain he'd recognize at once from where it came. Wrapped in plastic and in a jacket pocket, the meat-missile was ready for launch.

The self-assignment didn't appear too difficult. Carl planned to sit on the right side of the seat behind the pilot so his meat-throwing arm was free. When the right moment came, he'd distract Arlene some way and throw his brisket-bomb to Charlie.

****

So few people were signing up to fly, Carl and Arlene were second in line. That seemed odd. Nervous, Carl could just hear his brother saying most of them were there only to watch Arlene's and his final minutes. However, when he got a close look at pilot and plane, his apprehension was replaced by the previous excitement.

From his shiny riding boots to leather helmet with goggles, Ace Hawkins borrowed a page from the past and dressed in the style matching the plane's ancestry. Also featured were such accessories as a chest replete with mega-store toy-department-medals and Hollywood's flying ace's long white silk scarf. By golly, things would be hunky-dory with this splendid specimen at the controls.

159

The plane was a bright red two-winged copy of post World War I, mid-1920's, models. It had the two open cockpits like most of those in Carl's books. It looked to him like a heavenly scarlet cloud sent to waft them gently skyward.

While Carl's dad paid the fares, Ace asked if they wanted to fly any particular place. Carl began describing the way to the farm and was surprised when Ace broke in, "Oh, you mean where the white dog is? I been flyin' passengers right over 'im. Climb right up and off we go."

Ace gave a few instructions beginning with, "Buckle your seat belt up tight and keep it buckled so ya don't fall out."

Shades of Forrest! Was Ace going to "stunt" them after all? It didn't help much when he added, "I know you're not gonna get sick, but if ya do, there's a big empty tomato can in your cockpit for each of ya. We call it our *necessary can*."

Withdrawing nearly all of the precious little left in his "brave" account, Carl blustered to himself. *(No need to bother with sayin' that. I won't have any use for it.)* Talk about whistling past the graveyard! He stole a glance at Arlene. She didn't seem quite so nervous as before, appearing less pallid–looking only about seventy-five percent as ashen now.

Having no doubt dealt with newbies plenty of times, Ace did some pluck-pumping. "Go ahead, jump right on up. You're gonna have a nice smooth ride and lots'a fun. Soon's we land (comforting prediction), you can tell all your buddies you've been up and saw your dog when you flew over your farm."

Smart fellow, Ace. Reminding him of Charlie prompted Carl's return to his grand plan. He felt OK again and eager to get on with it. With that lucky stroke about Ace knowing just where to fly, could anything go wrong? *Oh yeah!* First, he learned the pilot sat *behind* the side-by-side seat for passengers, not in front as Carl thought. He couldn't believe it! In those World War I books and movies, the gunner sat *behind* the pilot. How could Ace see to fly?

Carl hesitated, and Arlene scrambled up into the right-hand side, his meat-throwing side. The plan started to appear less and less possible. There would be more problems. Several.

****

They buckled up, and Ace hollered, ***"CONTACT!"*** His assistant standing in front of the propeller responded, ***"CONTACT,"*** and spun it. They had to try a second time before the engine coughed into life. *Wow!* Was there ever a lot of *noise!* And *vibration!* This was nothing like jets!

After a short taxi to the very end of the runway (pasture), Ace revved 'er up (louder noise, increased shaking), and they began rolling–slowly. About halfway to the fence at the far end of the field, Carl developed a major uncertainty. There was no way in creation this poking-along thing was gonna get into the air!

He hadn't really let down his weight all the way, and now strained upward against the seat belt to give them all the lift he could. *Too late! They were going to hit the fence!* Carl shut his eyes, but quickly opened them (barely), curious about the details of their impending demise.

Here came the fence! Just before impact, he felt a change. They weren't ricocheting off so many bumps. This must be it, the calm just before the crash! Eye-closing time again. With a slight shudder, they were floating. *(Good-bye cruel world!)* Carl sneaked a sideways peek. *(Funny, heaven looks just like farms.)* Then he realized the fence was behind them.

Wow! That was some kind'a Wheeeee-O! Nothin' to it! He unclenched his teeth and relaxed a little. *(Just wait'll I tell Cousin Glenn about how easy it was. Nothin' to it!)*

Pretty soon, Ace began pounding on the side of the plane, hollering, and pointing out places for them to look. Next, he circled over town and headed for the farm.

****

Carl began rethinking his plan. It wouldn't really be necessary for him to so-obviously *throw* the meat. Arlene might see. He could just toss it out, and gravity would do the rest. No need to worry about hitting Charlie squarely in the chops. His nose for meat was so good, anything within a half-acre was close enough.

That left only the pilot to consider, and chances were he'd be so busy flying he wouldn't see Charlie's treat-toss. What if he did? Once it was tossed, what could Ace do? Things might get a trifle tacky later, but the mad meat-tosser was willing to take the chance. Things were looking up.

****

Only minutes after settling down for the ride over the farm, Carl saw a tiny white animal. Couldn't be Charlie–too small. And, no way they already flew all the way to the farm. Behind them, Ace was pounding and hollering something about going down lower and circling.

Suddenly, their scarlet cloud hurtled earthward. *This was it!* They were either gonna die or go into those stunts Forrest talked about. Carl felt the need to grip his "necessary can" with both hands. They might be going down but it suddenly seemed something might be about to come up.

Abruptly, Ace leveled off, and Carl's insides regrouped. Ace then banked the plane so Carl could better pick out everything in his yard. In a second, he caught sight of Charlie again who sprang up at the noise of the low-flying plane. His buddy was so funny that Carl momentarily forgot his plan. Then, realizing it was now or never, he readied for action.

Everything was about right. Ace circled, and again banked sharply so Carl could see, and Arlene didn't seem to be interested in too much except staring straight ahead as if willing the propeller not to fall off. Carl fished Charlie's treat from his jacket pocket. On the next pass, he'd do the deed.

They climbed over Mullums' farm, circled, and dropped low for another pass. Just as Carl got his nerves and muscles in gear, good ol' Ace double-crossed him and banked the opposite way so Arlene could look down. Carl could've told him *that* was wasted effort. Now, what was he to do? No problem, he'd just wait until Ace made the next pass.

****

Carl should not've counted his toss before Ace's next pass. Former friend Ace completely triple-crossed him by leveling off and continuing on toward Wellman's Point. The flight was about over. Now, what was he gonna do with the raw meat? Couldn't put it back in his pocket, the wrapping was gone and it was getting ever more oozy.

If he tossed it now, Ace was certain to see. In level flight, it might even miss his windshield and smack him in the kisser. And Arlene, more relaxed now that they were heading home, was sure to rat him out. What to do? *What to do!*

Then it hit him! Distracting his sister by pointing to her left as if there were something very interesting to see over there, he sneaked Charlie's meat treat into his "necessary can." Sometimes the best solutions are the simplest.

****

Soon after, their sterling pilot attacked the ground. To say they landed hard is a major injustice to fact. To this day, Carl cannot say with complete certainty whether they flew the last 50 feet or fell.

As they climbed down, Ace told them they were good fliers and real sports, probably for not getting sick in his airplane.

The big adventure was over. Carl swaggered to the car, a veteran flier, surer than ever he was destined to be a pilot. Arlene didn't feel disposed to express a desire for further flight.

****

Carl didn't achieve his early dream of becoming a pilot, but *did* obtain a position often requiring transcontinental air travel. At 35,000 feet over the Atlantic, enjoying first-class accommodations on Boeing's finest, he sometimes reminisced about Ace's flight. Each time, it ended the same–contemplating the reaction of the next passenger upon inspecting the "necessary can."

"AW, EVERYBODY KNOWS THAT STUFF"

A mid the dregs of Sidney Morrison's final pre-adolescent summer-break from school, he found himself with an advanced case of sixes and sevens. Every form of adventure and activity had worn threadbare. His hanging-out pals, Gerald Jones and Skinny Elson, were traveling with family. Mom and sisters were visiting a cousin's, and his dad's yearly vacation was history. Minding the house was all there was for Sid until school began.

There were only two highlights he could count on. One was the arrival of the mail. A second, Martha Jane McGill biking by on the road out front on her daily round trip to her aunt's. She followed her schedule all summer, but as August neared, Sid began to observe that she was making more trips and riding past more slowly. He also noticed a change in her attire—more appropriate for the August heat.

In mid-month, he found a reason to be in front of the house at Martha Jane's morning and afternoon ride-by. Now and then she stopped on the return trip for some chitchat. Pretty soon, her bike trips surpassed the mail as the top event of the day.

****

Occasionally, a rainy day or work detail caused cancellation of Martha Jane's trip. Then, house-sitter Sid was stuck with nothing to do but spend the dreary morning waiting for Lem Pearson to ram the mail into the box across the road.

It was just such a day when the *package* arrived in the mail. A small package. A package just about the right size to hold a book. An *unmarked* package with no return address or anything. A package addressed to Sid's sister, Glenda. Hmmmm.

He examined it thoroughly, but could find no hint of the contents. The more he looked, the deeper the mystery. Who'd be sending Glenda anything? An *unmarked* package at that. Surely she would've mentioned something about it before she left with Mom. Come to think of it, her customary warning that he better not be a mail nib-nose was emphasized more than usual. Hmmmm.

After examining the package another five times to see whether it was properly sealed, Sid decided it probably was and dutifully put it on the table with the rest of the magazines and stuff addressed to his sister. Gone, but certainly not forgotten.

For two days, the coals of his curiosity smoldered before erupting in flames. Mail-Inspector Sid decided he couldn't fully trust his earlier findings concerning the security of the package's contents. After Martha Jane's first trip, he went to Glenda's mail, retrieved the mystery package and adjourned to his room for reassessment of his earlier conclusion.

His curiosity was intense, all right. On that particular morning Martha Jane smiled and called out that she'd see him later! Any other time he would've nailed his shoes to the spot and waited for her return trip. Instead, he was passing up promised delights for maybe an old book. That's curiosity!

Turning the package over and over, Sid felt and shook it. Still no clues. Sure looked suspicious. Maybe someone sent something harmful to Glenda. Since he was charged with the safety of those receiving U.S. mail, perhaps he better give it one final inspection. Maybe in better light, he could see for sure it was OK. Of course he could, so he took it to the kitchen—lots of light down there.

166

Would anyone believe it! After looking closely a few more times, a defect in the packaging became obvious. One of the seams was partially open! How could the sender be so careless! Another look validated his first. A seam was coming unstuck! Right there, just above the steam coming from the teakettle.

Determined to take additional precautions against a shipper so sloppy and inept as to send a parcel so easily undone by a little moisture, Sid tested the other seam. Sure as shootin', it virtually sprang open! Well now, since the sender demonstrated such gross negligence, shouldn't an authorized inspector examine the contents to see whether exercising his further responsibilities was in order? Of course!

Tipping the package, Sid found his speculation as to its contents to be correct. A book slid out easily with only moderate shaking. He looked at the title. *SHOCK TIME!*

****

Sid read the book's title again, then turned it over. There was an expansion of what the title promised. His neck tingled as his eyes raced over the purple prose. Great day in the morning! From behind him came the sounds of a teakettle in desperate trouble. Some fool let it boil dry.

Shaken into action, the neglectful party shut off the stove and flew to the safety of his room. No sooner was the door slammed and locked than he remembered the empty wrapping on the kitchen table. No time to hesitate! His dad would be home from work in another couple hours. It was three-at-a-time down the stairs and back with the damning evidence.

Once again secreted behind a locked door, Sid dared to sneak another peek. Nothing changed. He still held the serpent in his hand. There in all its decadence was a S - E -X book. (Ssshhh!)

Curiosity fueling courage, Sid lifted the cover and flipped to the table of contents. *"Oh my gosh!"* And those chapter titles! His eyes nearly popped out.

Whatever could Glenda want with such a book! Other girls might read this stuff, but not *his* sister. S*he'd* never read a thing like this! Somebody sent it to her by mistake. Then he saw the letter placed inside the cover.

Dear Glenda, *(Oh my Lord, it wasn't a mistake!)*

Thank you for your order. Please be advised that this textbook contains the very latest scientific information regarding the sexual and reproductive functions of the human female. It is written so that both interested laymen and students can fully understand these important functions.

Should you have questions about any of the chapters or plates contained herein, please do not hesitate to forward them to the authors whose addresses are printed inside the back cover.

Once again, thank you for having the foresight to have ordered this fine volume. We are certain it will be of assistance in your preparation for medical school.

Sid's thoughts raced. *(I never knew Glenda wanted to be a doctor. Even so, why'd she want this kind'a book? The publisher even signed the letter. Hard to believe he'd do that.)*

****

Could anyone think for a minute that Sid had the unmitigated gall to look further into the pages of this shortcut to eternal perdition? A greased slide down the primrose path? A non-stop ticket to the fiery pit? *Betcher sweet life!*

The book fell open to the middle. There in complete detail was a diagram of some *very* interesting non-male internal apparatus with a detailed explanation beneath it using what he partially overheard the girls on the school bus discussing. It used the *"V" word! Holy Smokes!* This was far, worse than he could've ever possibly imagined!

Sid fast-forwarded through most of the pages, pausing only for attempts to re-read each shocking revelation. Calming down enough to return to the front, he was about halfway down the first page of the introduction when the squeak of the kitchen screen door penetrated his tumbling mind. If hair could scream, this was indeed the time. He held his breath and tried for transparency. No luck.

Several questions shot to mind. Chief among them, had Glenda and Mom come home early and caught him in the act? No answers presented themselves in the stillness. Sweeping his brief foray into federal crime under the bed, wrapping and all, he tiptoed to the door, eased it open and listened. His dad must've left work early. He was speaking to their dog.

Slithering down the stairs, Sid tried his hand at "mosey" on the way to the kitchen. It must've succeeded because his dad didn't seem to detect any of his son's guilty secrets. He was on the verge of asking why his dad was home already when he saw the time. If anything, Dad was a few minutes later than usual. Time flies when you're crime-committing and sneak-peeking.

His dad may not've noticed anything when Sid came in, but he could hardly miss all the flibbertigibbet behavior during the evening. Finally it was time to retire. Curiosity and guilt at their peaks, Sid waited for the sound of soft snoring before daring to begin the organized study of his new curriculum.

In spite of his keen interest in the subject matter, he dropped off after 125 pages. His dreams were replete with colorful visions of events having no previous place in his subconscious prior to the evening's reading.

****

When Sid awakened, it was broad daylight, his dad was at work and, the bed resembled Hatfield's barn after the tornado. It took him a moment to sort out things. First item of which he became fully aware was the book that he was clutching as if it were the last life preserver on the Titanic.

Plunging onward, he accumulated more information, and a sense of euphoria washed over him. He was getting keys to "grown up" status. Equally contributing was the realization that he was one step ahead of his buddies, Gerald Jones and Skinny Elson.

An hour later, someone tapped on the front door. Sid jumped, but quickly recovered. He was now better at being "cool" and "mosey." Lots of things would be smoother, since he was in the process of joining the grown-up club. His breath held steady as the tapping sounded again. It was probably only Mr. Gibbner from next door asking to borrow the lawnmower. *WRONG!* There stood Martha Jane McGill!

****

Sid often heard that it's not always wise to wish for something too much or you might get it, then what'll you do? In a time-frozen instant, he knew truer words were never spoken. Opening the front door to Martha Jane may not've been number one on his fantasy list, but he'd be hard put to name anything else.

He always knew exactly what he'd say. Only a few of several snappy possibilities he rehearsed for just such a moment included, "Why, hello there, Martha Jane. Nice day, isn't it? Would you like to take a walk?"

Those were before the *book*. Now he knew far too much to go with the weather and walking. There *must* be something better! But what? Stricken dumb, his recent elation plunged downward on its way to crash and burn.

His tongue benumbed, a granite grin remained transfixed as the goddess on the other side of the screen asked, "Sidney, I do believe the chain's come off my bike. I wonder if you could please help me with it."

"Why, hello, Martha Jane. Nice day isn't it?"

She smiled prettily and repeated her question. Without answering, he went to work on the crippled steed. A good stunt— his total bicycle-repairing experience was limited to helping a friend tighten a handlebar. (More specifically, he held a wrench.)

After wrestling the dumb thing around for a while, Martha Jane voiced the opinion that it might be a good idea to push here and pull there. Presto! It flopped back in place as if by magic. Later that day, he wondered how she knew just what to do.

Martha Jane tested the chain job and found it OK. Afterward, there wasn't much left to talk about, but she made an effort. Try as he might, Sid couldn't remember a single thing she said. He'd only mumbled answers to her questions and comments, and couldn't maintain eye contact.

After all he read about those differences between "males" and "females," how was a fellow supposed to look at someone who'd been a kind-of buddy on a bike one day and a "female" the next?

Martha Jane kept trying, conversing about this and that, every once in a while asking why Sidney was so quiet or whether anything was wrong. The way she kept at it made his ears redden and suspect she knew very well what might be the matter. The more she talked, the more he froze. Here was his big chance, and he was flubbing it.

Martha Jane gave up and rode off. Sid's chagrin was complete. With such a miserable performance, he'd never, *ever,* get to know her better. Plummeting back to reality from his recent venture into adulthood, he retired to tend his wounds.

After imbibing a gallon or three of bitter humiliation and self-pity, not to mention a quart of lemonade and a big slab of chocolate cake, a ray of sunshine peeked through. Perhaps something could be salvaged from the morning catastrophe, after all.

The encounter with Martha Jane may've been disastrous, but he still had some ammo with which to blast Gerald and Skinny when they got home. He knew stuff from the book they'd never even dreamed of! Thinking about the possibility, his spirits rose.

They'd been buddies for over a year, and nothing this detailed was ever discussed. Surely it would've been had they known anything. *(Just wait'll I see that know-it-all Gerald. I won't tell 'im everything right off—make 'im sit up and beg. Skinny, too.)*

Sid wouldn't have long to wait. Gerald would be home in four days, and Skinny just before school started. Meantime, he carefully (*very* carefully) reread the book, meticulously inspected it for signs his sister might detect, re-sealed it with brain-surgeon care and placed it at the proper chronological spot in the rest of her mail. Recovery from the mental nosedive with Martha Jane was progressing. Things were definitely looking better and better.

His mood kept spiraling up-up-and-away, fueled first by Glenda's return and not a word of suspicion about the package. Then, there was Gerald's return and the great coup-to-be. What a day it'd be when he dropped his new found knowledge on him!

****

Next day, the sun and Sid, both radiant, rose simultaneously without a cloud in either's sky. Sid zipped through chores while rehearsing dialogue with Gerald, trying on ways to drag out the pleasure as long as possible. After one final expression of awe from Mom about how quickly his assigned tasks were completed, she gave the green light to take off for the Jones'.

Sprinting from his yard toward Gerald's, Sid saw Martha Jane pedaling his way. He *knew* things were too good to last. There was no way out. He could only stop and wait for the rain of scorn to follow. Clouds suddenly obliterated his sun.

Braced for the worst, it took Sid a minute to realize that the witness to his embarrassment braked to a stop and was saying something sounding not at all demeaning. "Why, hello there. I've missed seeing you the past two days. Been away?"

Fighting the urge to turn and look for the person to whom she was speaking, he managed a reply. It must've seemed appropriate because she continued, "I have to hurry to Aunt Ruth's to help her with some cleaning, but I should be back by two or two-thirty. Maybe we could talk then."

Zap! Zing! Zippo! Was the world his oyster or what! Talk about being on a roll! Life didn't get any better! He watched her peddle from sight as his sun blazed forth again in all its splendor.

The usual pal insults finished, Gerald and Sid began an exchange of what occurred in the two weeks of their separation. Sid waited patiently while Gerald recited events such as the record fish he caught, how vicious bears raided the camp every night, the time they almost drowned in a storm, and the hold-up man they helped capture. Other boring stuff like that.

Sid feigned interest. He could wait. The more Gerald tried to puff up his measly episodes, the harder he'd land on his nose when he got bomb-shelled out of his socks. Relishing his pending rise to fame, Sid could afford to indulge his old friend. Besides, now there would be great lies to tell about Martha Jane and him in addition to the book info.

As Gerald finally wound down recounting his litany of dull experiences, Sid began to set up his pal for the kill by leading him through the field to Spence's orchard. Next, he spent some time swearing him to secrecy using every blood-vow he could muster.

Then came the teasers. On and on they went until Gerald was practically frothing at the mouth over Sid's racy hints of lurid disclosures to come. His begging had no shame. *Glory Hallelujah!* It was even better than Sid could've hoped. His day had come! It

173

was well worth all the anxiety and depression. Was he at the absolute apex of glory or what!

When Gerald's entreaties reached the level of pre-teen apoplexy, Sid decided it was time. Everything went as planned for about five sentences. Then with one short swift response, Gerald hacked out Sid's heart and spirit, leaving a spirit-shattering void.

"Aw, everybody knows that stuff," he scoffed, "Is *that* all you got to tell me?" Then he hammered the final nail into any remaining of Sid's self-esteem. "Don't mean to tell me you're just now findin' out about all that!"

Silence erupted as Sid's personal sun abruptly plunged from sight. Once more he soared to the heights only to pitch ego-first into a bottomless abyss. Struggling up through the depths, all he could manage to rejoin was, "Course not, Gerald Stupidhead, but you never said anything. So, I figured you didn't know what everybody else did." (Sounded pretty lame to Sid, too.)

Gerald wasn't through with his heart-hollowing. "Well, for your information, *my* folks told *me* all about that stuff last spring. I thought all parents did," Gerald Jones (of the know-it-all Jones') gloated. With one swipe, he branded all non-enlightened parents and their ill-informed offspring as ignoramuses.

After some additional phonied-up excuses for having presumed to instruct an expert in anatomical and sexual matters, Sid told Gerald there were chores to do and shuffled off homeward. What he really had to do was make another raid on the cake and lemonade before again sinking completely from sight.

****

Sid lay low, mired in his dank foggy psychological cellar except for weak and futile ego-rehabilitation efforts. No matter how sunny it was outside, his weather report was always gloom, gloomier, and gloomiest.

He could avoid Gerald and Skinny right now, but it would be tougher sledding in a couple days. School would start, and without question, Gerald would blab his head off all over the place about the greenhorn in their midst–probably even to the girls. There'd be no end to the whispering and tee-heeing.

Sid walked all the way on opening day to avoid the school-bus bunch. Once there, he avoided even the fringes of the milling students. Looked as if they were really having fun in the morning sun. Not him. His sky would forever remain dark.

Just before the first bell, Sid hurried toward the restroom. It'd be a good place to mope and it was unlikely anyone would be there. But, someone was. Sid rounded the obligatory divider-screen inside the door shielding those entering from the interior, running squarely into Skinny Elson. "Hey there Sid! I been lookin' all over for ya," he grinned.

(Sure you were. Just couldn't wait to kick a pal when he's down could ya!)

"I would'a come over last night, but we didn't get home till way late."

"Yeah, yeah, Skinny, so what." *(Too bad you had to wait till this morning.)*

Just wait'll I tell you! I found out some stuff you'll 'bout bust to hear!"

Skinny didn't try to set up Sid, just plunged right in. For a minute Sid couldn't believe his ears! It sounded like an echo, an echo of his own opening to Gerald!

He listened intently to be absolutely certain his hearing hadn't tricked him. It hadn't! In a minute, Skinny slowed enough in his display of newly acquired knowledge for Sid to echo another statement he heard recently. "Aw, everybody knows that stuff," he drawled, turning to walk out into the glorious sunshine.

ROGER RETARD

When his wife, Mary Beth, noticed "something's not quite right" about Roger, their newborn son, Jim Henderson refused to believe anything could be wrong with any son of his. After all, he was the product of a long line of strong and smart ancestors.

When the pediatrician gently informed him that his son was a "special needs" child, he refused to believe it and changed physicians. After the second diagnosis was the same, Henderson damned the entire medical profession as a "...bunch'a quacks out for a buck."

Roger neither walked nor talked by the age of two, but his father said many kids waited that long. He continued to deny the obvious more vociferously than ever during the next three years. Even when he tried to teach Roger anything requiring a response beyond a smile and failed, the adamant denials continued.

Reality *finally* forced its way through the denial fog when he tried to teach the boy to play catch. No matter how hard he tried, he simply couldn't react correctly to instructions or master the physical act of receiving and returning the ball. Desperate to please his father, he ran to pick up and carry it back to him, resulting in a harsh scolding.

The remainder of that fateful Saturday afternoon, Jim Henderson sat morosely staring at, but not seeing, the TV screen. Wife Mary Beth asked what was wrong, but got only a mumbled reply. In the days following, she began to see his increasingly negative attitude toward Roger. No longer did he speak of things he and his son might do together. No longer did he make any attempt to teach him anything. Soon, he began ignoring hm altogether except to administer scalding scoldings.

In a matter of months, Jim Henderson's non-engagement demeanor disintegrated into outright hostile rejection, the first step to negative physical reactions to Roger's attempts to interact with him. Pushing his son away became shoving. Shoving led to more aggressive actions that emphasized his total rejection of the son he now referred to as "Roger Retard." Whippings followed.

When Roger was twelve, a domestic confrontation between the Hendersons relating to Roger's treatment lasted most of an afternoon and marked the beginning of years of physical abuse of his wife whenever she tried to intercede on her son's behalf. It was also the last time Roger would share the family's living areas. Jim Henderson's rejection of the boy had become so great that he was confined to the basement. "I'll not have that *thing* around where I hafta look at it."

From that day forward, Roger Henderson only saw his dad when he came to the basement to beat him with a belt for an imagined infraction of one of a multitude of rules. Then, before turning off the single light bulb and TV, he scattered Roger's most prized possession–his collection of photos and books about sailing ships–all about the basement.

Returning upstairs, he often continued to use his belt on his wife for imagined complicity in Roger's rule-breaking. "You can teach a damn dog a thing or two, but not *Roger Retard*. Gets it from you, that's why. "

****

Roger figured he didn't mind living in the basement too much. He could watch his favorites, cartoon and animal channels. He couldn't keep a live animal with him, but he could still pet his favorite stuffed toy, Elmer-dog,

Roger could also arrange his many books and pictures of sailing ships in exact order, a passion since childhood. Each morning for 24 years, he meticulously organized them on his only table. When his dad was away, Mom sneaked him out to the library so he could read books about ships.

Strangely, the one thing Roger could do pretty well was read. He remembered that Daddy said if he could do that, he should be able to do other stuff, too. But, the man they took him to a long time ago said why he could read and not do other stuff was because of something not easy to pronounce or remember very well. Sounded like some kind'a sandwich–some kind'a burger or something.

Nope, Roger figured the basement wasn't too bad most of the time. But, when he wasn't allowed to use the light bulb or turn on the TV, it was very hard to see his ship pictures with only the light coming in the little window way up by the ceiling.

Another thing was that when the light was off, the monsters could come out from behind the furnace. But, having the light and TV off was way better than when Daddy took off his belt.

One more thing that Roger figured wasn't too good about living in the basement was that he had to be real careful to not fall down on the wobbly steps, especially the second one from the top. He could remember this now, because Mom always reminded him when she knocked on the door with his food. Other times, too, like when he could come upstairs to eat when Daddy wasn't home for lunch, and when she could take him to the library.

He rang the little bell his Mom gave him to ring when he needed something real bad or finished eating. But, if he made a mistake and rang the bell when Daddy was home, he'd come down to the basement real fast and take off his belt. Then, he'd say maybe this would teach *"Roger Retard"* to remember a thing or two. After he used his belt, he shut off the light bulb and TV again. Lots of times, he took Elmer-dog upstairs, too. When Daddy left for work next day, Mom gave Elmer-dog back and turned on things.

****

Lots and lots of times—lots and lots—he heard Mom asking Daddy real nice to please let their son come upstairs and live. Or, Mom asked Daddy to stop calling him "Roger Retard." This caused lots of loud talking. Sometimes, he could hear Daddy tell Mom to pack up and get out and take Roger Retard with her. This was *real* scary! But she never did.

Roger remembered that once it sounded like Daddy had done something bad to Mom. Sounded like she was crying. Really *hard!* That was real bad! *Real bad!* After Daddy left for work, he asked Mom what happened, but she always said it was nothing and not to worry about it, but it kept happening. Maybe it was because Daddy was way bigger. He was bigger than Daddy now, but he didn't have a belt like Daddy did.

****

Roger was hungry. Mom hadn't knocked on the door to say breakfast was ready. He couldn't understand it. She was never late. After waiting and waiting, he shook his bell. Finally, she came to the door and looked down. He couldn't see very well, but Mom looked awful! Real *awful!* He hurried up the stairs faster than he was supposed to go.

He was right! She *did* look really bad, and he asked her what was wrong. This time, she didn't say it was nothing and to forget it. But, she still didn't say what was really wrong. Just said she'd get him something to eat and left the door standing open. Pretty soon, she came back with two doughnuts and some milk. He ate them, but it wasn't very much for breakfast. What could be wrong? He worried about it all morning.

At lunchtime, he heard the usual knock to let him know his food was ready. Wasn't much this time, either. What could be wrong? He worried about Mom all afternoon.

Dinner was a little better, but not much. Roger thought about ringing his bell, but he wasn't supposed to do that unless something was really, *really*, bad. He didn't ring it, but it was really hard to go to sleep that night.

****

Things got no better. The next evening, Daddy's shouting was so loud that Roger could hear every word. He couldn't hear what Mom was saying, though, but Daddy said he didn't give a damn if she had enough and said she was going to leave. She better not try it or else.

They must've gone into another room because he couldn't hear as well now. Then he heard Mom scream. *That was Mom!* He dashed up the stairs and tried to open the door, something he never did before. It was locked!

Back down the steps he raced two and three steps at a time. Grabbing his bell, he rang and rang, but nobody came for a long time. Then Daddy opened the door and said you damn retard, if you don't wanna get belted so hard you'll never sit down again you better stop ringin' that damn bell.

At breakfast, Mom looked worse than the day before, but she *still* didn't say what happened. Later, Mom knocked and told him to come into the kitchen. After he ate, she told him to listen carefully. Then, she said Daddy had done bad things to her and told her if she left, he'd do worse things. Then, Mom said for him to go downstairs and pack his things in the boxes stored down there. She said Daddy had been doing such bad things for so long that they were going to live with Aunt Jane for a while till she could figure out something.

When she told him that Daddy had been doing such bad things, Roger began to get very angry. The more she said, the angrier he became. How could Daddy keep doing such bad things to Mom!

Finally, she patted his hand and said to go and start getting his things together, but be quiet after Daddy came home and don't do anything to make him come down to the basement. They had to keep everything looking the same as usual that evening. Aunt Jane would come by after Daddy went to work tomorrow and take them away. Mom said everything would be lots better and they'd be very happy. She talked a lot about them being happy at last.

As Roger packed his books and pictures, his anger flamed even higher. After dinner and then all evening, it built up, fed by his frustration that he couldn't do anything to help Mom. If only he could do something so Daddy wouldn't do bad things to Mom. He pounded his fist on his cot.

When Mom knocked and brought his food that evening, she smiled and put a finger to her lips. He smiled back and said nothing. He knew what she meant, all right. Seeing her bruises and still swollen face, it was hard to keep from asking if she was OK, but he didn't. Still angry, he watched TV but didn't pay much attention. Soon, his anger began to boil again. Really *boil*.

Suddenly, he heard loud talking from upstairs. It sounded real close to the door. That was odd. Mom said they'd act like nothing was going on. He inched his way up to the door. Daddy was yelling that if he ever found out she was gonna leave, she'd be really sorry. Then, Roger heard slapping sounds and Mom start to cry. *Hard* slapping! *Harder!* She was crying funny sounds. Awful sounding sounds.

Roger tried the door, but it was locked. He tried again. And again. It was no use. He stood and listened. The loud talking had stopped, but Mom was still making those funny sounds. After a while, it wasn't quite so loud. Soon, it almost stopped. There was more yelling from Daddy after what sounded like somebody falling real hard.

Roger waited and waited for more sounds, but none came and he finally started back down the dim stairway. Halfway down, he stopped and turned to look up at the rickety second step from the top…looked a long time, then went up to inspect it very closely.

Back downstairs, he began ringing his bell furiously. No one came to the door, so he rang it even longer and harder. This time, the door flew open.

****

At headquarters, Watch Commander Captain Jeremy Wichter sat talking with the two investigating detectives. "Now, let me see if I got the info on your preliminary report straight. Second step from the top came off. Found it lying down at the bottom. Right?"

"Right."

"Vic took a head-over-heeler all the way down. Right?"

"Right."

"Head got caved in when he hit bottom. Right?"

"Right, Captain. Landed smack-dab on it. "

"Straight up accident. Right?"

"Right."

The captain put the remainder of the report aside. "OK. Let's talk about things you might want to put in your full report. For example, was it poorly lighted? And. why was the vic going to the basement?"

"Dark enough so that we had to use flashlights to check it out. Why was he going down? Missus was so weak she could hardly talk, but she got out that he was probably gonna beat on his son living down there for ringing his bell too much. Had this little bell to ring only in emergencies.

"Seems the vic treated him like crap all his life. Grown man, but not many marbles in the upstairs."

"How's the Missus doing? For sure, is she in the clear for involvement in the deed?"

"She's in the hospital and doing OK. No way she's involved. She was so beat up that she was barely able to do a nine-one-one."

"That it for her?

"That's it."

"What about the second step coming all the way off? Anything look fishy about that?"

"At first, it looked smelly that all those rows of nails could come loose all at once letting it tip off forward and fly off when somebody stepped on the edge, but the whole stairway was shakier than a dog crapin' razor blades. Wouldn't have taken hardly anything for any other step to go, too."

"And the son livin' in the basement?"

"Like I said, slower than slow, Cap. *Really* slow. He was pretty upset about his mom. His aunt had come over and got him calmed down by telling him his mom was gonna be all right. Even so, he couldn't add a thing to the aunt's questions or ours about anything that happened."

"Nothing at all?"

"Nope. Mostly he only shrugged his shoulders or shook his head like he didn't understand. During the rest of the investigation, he just sat hugging a stuffed poodle and smiling a lot."

1122 POPLAR DRIVE

Near closing time, Eddie Joe sat nursing a stale beer and staring at nothing. This wasn't news to bartender Bill Johnson. The scene was repeated almost nightly. He came down the bar. "Well Eddie Joe, 'bout time to put another one to bed."

"Yeah."

"Good day today?"

"Nothin' ever changes, Bill. She lives to bitch and whine at me. Starts in with the same old crap, then tacks on whatever she's thought up durin' the day. Must be tough for 'er to hafta wait till I get home from work so she can start in.

"Tonight, it was why don't I ask for a raise. Said everybody else that'd been workin' at the plant as long as me got one. Said she'd been talkin' to that nib-nose Millie Page, and her man got one. And that old gossip-mouth Alene Guilford's man got one too. Total crap, Bill. Neither one did. I asked 'em. Either she's lyin' or they are. Guess which.

"On top'a that, she's spendin' money like a sailor on leave after a year at sea. Should'a seen the outfit she come home with! Farmers could use it to scare off the crows. Said she needed it to wear at some fancy-pansy to-do those other old hags cooked up. Ain't bad enough she bought it, but she gripes that they got better lookin' duds 'cause their men make more money. 'Nother lie.

"That's not the half of it, Bill. It's all the other stuff. Stuff like why she ever married me in the first place. And, why don't I have the get up and go like other men. Why don't I do this, and why don't I do that. Why don't I take more interest in her. Never stops. On and on it goes. Top'a her lungs, too."

"None'a my business Eddie Joe, but ever consider leaving?"

"Don't think I wouldn't if I could! She knows I would. Warns me if I try, she'll take me for what little I got and every red cent I'd ever get. She'd do it, too. Beginnin' to think it might be worth it. What a day that'd be, gettin' rid of 'er for good! What a day!"

Before drawing Eddie Joe a "last-call" beer, Bill walked to the other end of the long bar to collect the tab from the only other customer who then passed a few quiet words with the bartender before leaving.

Over coffee, once again Edna Mae was complaining to her friend, Millie Page. "I tell you, Millie, I'm absolutely determined to make something of that foot-dragging husband of mine. Why I ever married him I'll never know. Maybe it was that all my friends were getting married. That, and Mama always whining about me still living at home. She said she knew he was no bargain, but women can change a man. Said just look at dad. Some change!"

"Edna Mae, ever think about divorce?"

"Now you know my religion doesn't allow divorce, but it most certainly does not say I can't change him into something besides a slovenly beer-bum.

"Know what he said last night! Saw my new hat and said I should be thinking about buying a new head to go with it! Can you imagine! I slave away around here and all I get is nasty cracks about spending money and trying to fix up a little.

"He dresses like a slob. Thinks blue jeans are dressing up. Never gets a haircut till he could tuck it into his belt. Practically have to drag him to a barbershop. Not only that, he embarrasses me right in front of the barber. Wants to know why you should tip somebody for just doing their job. In restaurants, too.

"He accuses me of nagging him all the time. Well, if I don't try to get him a little more civilized, who would? And, you know what else? He's been at that job for eleven years and it's been three since he got a raise. Know what he says? 'All in good time, all in good time.' Well, it's a *good time* now."

Another half hour of Edna Mae's complaints and Millie had to go. She left, promising to help any way she could.

****

Eddie Joe left the bar to go on home to face the diatribe he knew was waiting. Not even an all-evening beer-buzz deadened his expectation of the inevitable. As he rounded the corner, a figure stepped from the shadows, startling him.

"Easy, easy, no need to fear. I only want to talk."

Recognizing the man from the bar, Eddie Joe relaxed enough to respond, "Talk? Talk about what? I saw you talkin' to Bill. Something about that?"

"Not really. I couldn't help overhearing you talking to him about a problem you might be having."

"Problem?"

"At home."

Eddie Joe tensed again, his thoughts racing. *(What's this guy after? The few bucks in my pocket? Is this a stick-up after all? Some kind'a touch, maybe?)*

"Your wifey problem, buddy. If you were just BS-ing the bartender, I'll move on. If not , maybe I can help."

Still wary, Eddie Joe hesitated. "Well...."

With, "Sorry I butted in," the stranger turned to go, but paused when Eddie Joe, realizing the man wasn't a threat, waved a hand. "Hold on a second. You caught me a little off guard. Go on talkin'. I wasn't BSin' the bartender. You said you can help do somethin' 'bout my problem? What kind'a help?"

"Can't answer that out here. Takes some time. Besides, from what I could overhear, you're going to have plenty to handle when you get home without giving her more ammo by being late again."

"Say I wanna hear more. When and where?"

"Well, if you're really interested, how about two nights from now? I have a little business to attend to tomorrow. I'd guess you go to that bar quite a bit. How about there? And, that bartender is the nosy-talky type. So, don't act like you know me. I'll take care of things. If you're not there, I'll know you don't want to hear what I have to say."

"Why do we hafta be so secret?"

"Just an old habit of mine. Not much for anyone nosing in. If you don't want to meet up, it's perfectly OK. You can probably work out things with your wife."

Eddie Joe responded quickly that if there were any way to get her to lighten up, he certainly wanted to hear it. But, he had one more question. "Sounds like you might'a helped other guys with bitchy wives. How'd that workout?"

"No one I helped ever complained. Is it a go or no-go?"

"Reckon it won't hurt to talk some more."

****

Millie Page ran into Edna Mae at the grocery. "Edna Mae! You get the program yet for the Self Awareness Club? Looks like something you might use to help with your husband problem."

Pausing only long enough for a 10-minute blast at Eddie Joe and to buy eggs, Edna Mae rushed home to get her mail. She was delighted! Sure enough, the program *did* look as if it could help in her efforts to reform her husband into something more respectable. Noted psychologist and author Sebastian Xavier Moffet III would be discussing his newest book, *Behavior Modification Applied To Spousal Relationships*. Afterward, he would lead the ladies in the art of what the book recommended as the most successful ways to moderate their own and their spouse's behavior. *Glory be!* Here was the answer to changing her nothing husband from nothing into something. She could hardly wait.

****

Eddie Joe assumed his usual stool at the end of the bar. Bill the bartender was busy and had no chance to talk. Near the end of his third tired beer, the stranger from two days previously entered and took a stool halfway down the bar.

Later when others seated between them departed, he moved several stools closer to Eddie Joe and remarked, "Say, aren't you the fellow I saw in here a couple nights ago? He picked up his drink and moved next to Eddie Joe. "I'm ducking out on my old lady, too. Buy you a beer?"

After the standard introductory chatter, the man suggested, "Why don't we move over to a booth? More comfortable." Eddie Joe picked up his mug and followed.

Once seated and both with fresh beer and drink, the stranger looked across. "Well, I guess you're wanting to know what I was talking about out in the street night before last."

"That's why I'm here."

"First, let me ask, are you still as upset with your wife?"

"*Oh yeah!* You should'a heard her tonight when…."

The stranger interrupted, "OK, OK! I get the picture. You figured anything yet to do about her?"

"*Do?* What'n blazes can I *do!* Can't leave. The old battleaxe'll take every cent and bleed me dry for the rest'a my life! She only lives for the pleasure'a bedevilin' me'n makin' my life more miserable every bless-ed day!" He banged down his mug so hard that his beer sloshed onto the table.

"Easy, easy, big fella. Don't waste your beer. Sounds like you might want to do something about your problem. That so?"

"You got that right! But...say, she put you up to somethin'? Yeah, that's it! She's tryin' to set me up!"

Eddie Joe started to jump up, but the stranger waved him back down. "Hey, take a breath! I'm only here to help. If you don't want any, I'll go right now." He began to rise.

"All right, all right! Sorry, I'm on the prod most'a the time 'cause'a that bitch. You said maybe you could help. How?"

"Well, let me ask a couple questions. First, just how much would you like the problem solved?"

"More'n you could think."

"I don't mean *temporarily*. How much would you like it solved *permanently*?"

"Permanently?"

"Permanently."

Eddie Joe abruptly put down his beer. *"Great suffering Jehosiphat!* You mean...."

"I don't *mean* anything. Just answer the question. *'Yes,'* and I keep talking. *'No,'* and I go and we both forget we ever met."

"I don't know you. You could be a cop wearin' a wire."

"Want to go to the john with me so I can strip and let you see for yourself? Shall I go ahead or not?"

"Just to be sure you're suggestin' what I think ya are, could you tell me a little more?"

"Eddie Joe, let's quit all this beating around the bush. You know very well what I'm talking about. If not, your wife is right about you being dense. C'mon, you know what's going on here. Do we talk or not?"

"This is comin' on so awful fast. Can't say doin' away with 'er ain't crossed my mind, but I'd never have the balls. Probly wouldn't get away with it, anyhow."

"That mean you want to talk some more?"

Eddie Joe took a long swallow and stared at the stranger for several seconds. "OK, but I'm only listenin, not agreein'. Probly couldn't afford you anyhow. Just how much is it?"

"Depends."

"Depends?"

"Depends on how you want the problem solved. Accidents are more. Disappearing without a trace is more. Torture first is more. Cheapest way is a quick in-and-out of the house making it look like a burglary gone bad. In that case, though, something of value has to come up missing to make it look legitimate."

"How much altogether for the quickest way?"

"Five down and ten after."

"I ain't got that kind'a money!"

"How much could you raise?"

"Well, I been sneakin' a little aside. Got about thirty-five hundred. Would that work?"

"For starters, maybe. You have anything of value? If things were set up as a burglary, there's a chance that could work out."

"Only thing I got in the whole world worth anything is my stamp collection. Been collectin' since I was a kid."

"Well...could be hard to move. How much is it worth?"

"Close to seven grand. Had it appraised last year."

"Anything else?"

"Just a gold lodge ring. Don't know what it'd bring."

"Should be worth something if it's gold. Anything else?"

"Nothin' I know of."

"Well, it sounds like the stamps might make up some of the difference. How do you feel about making an arrangement to get your problem solved?"

191

"I…I don't know. My life's a livin' Hell, all right, but…can I think about it? Would it be a burglary like you said? When do I hafta have the money? I…I just don't know."

"The cash could maybe work for the up front, and maybe the stamps and ring for the rest. You can think about it, but I'm leaving town in a couple days or so. Why not have a beer right here tomorrow night?"

"I guess that'll be OK."

"Fine. By the way, the charges work differently in this kind of deal. If you decide to go ahead, bring the thirty five along with the stamps and ring with you. We'll work out the details then."

****

Sebastian Xavier Moffet's lecture at the no-husbands-allowed Afternoon Self-Awareness Club, began with the participant session called "Clearing the Air" during which each lady would voice her thoughts, and/or complaints about their spouses. Doing so served as a "getting it off your chest" cleansing.

This "cleansing" was the preface to stating the degree of their dissatisfaction or discomfort in their marriages and to what extent this had progressed. When a participant finished, Moffet would go into detail concerning how to best modify the situation.

He added, "If you do not wish to participate, please feel free to abstain or even leave, and everyone will understand." There was some nervous shuffling about, but no one left.

After some hesitancy, the first two ladies "cleared the air," and the remainder followed rather quickly. Most were fairly well satisfied with their husbands aside from minor disagreements or dislikes, saying they responded reasonably to suggestions about changing this or that. Even two women who were more than a little irked with their husbands were not to the point of expressing a desire to abandon the relationship.

192

As promised, Psychologist Moffet offered advice about modifying their husband's and/or their own behavior. His humorous style created a relaxed atmosphere which was helpful in gaining a participant's acceptance of his advice.

The group's mood became a bit more serious when the last participant's turn came. Edna Mae proceeded almost stridently in her recitation of the many behaviors her husband needed to modify. For starters, dragging him into a store to get something respectable to cover his dumpy overweight frame was like pulling teeth from a gangrenous crocodile.

Yes, he made pretty good money despite his lack of an education, but he was so tight with it that moths flew out every time he opened his wallet. And, the way he complained every time she bought a little something to dress up her new outfit, he complained like he was being tortured.

And, he could hardly wait to finish gobbling the good dinner she fixed so he could go down to the bar and swill beer all night.

"*And...And...And....*" On and on she went as if she couldn't stop, each time punctuating his transgressions by describing how he refused to change despite her many well-intentioned efforts.

She continued so long that Moffet broke in, "I think we have a pretty good picture of your situation. Now, perhaps you'd like to relate your thoughts about continuing your marital relationship."

"I'd divorce him in a second but for my religion. I can't leave–got no place to go. And, I know him. He'd try to cut me out of every cent I had coming." She glanced at the others, most of whom were looking down. "I'm sorry for going on so long, but I'm at my wits end. I just hope this seminar can help."

Moffet thought for a moment, then responded, "I believe we have a case here that requires more than what may be appropriate in this forum. Edna Mae, if you wish, I can offer some suggestions during the social hour which follows at this point." There was an almost audible sigh of relief that the final somewhat embarrassing club-member's turn ended.

The advice he offered Edna Mae was the usual: Seek professional help. She and her husband should get counseling, etc. She left for refreshments more frustrated than ever, and if it were possible, angrier with her husband after hearing how well the other women had husbands willing to change.

Coffee in hand, she stood alone by the wall, looking isolated. As she was about to leave, another attendee wandered over. "I'm Mica Miller. I just wanted to say I can sympathize with you in your situation and think you're very courageous to have talked about it so frankly."

Edna Mae knew she wasn't a member, but non-members could buy a ticket to attend special programs. Apparently, she was well off, judging from the attire and jewelry.

Edna Mae smiled tiredly. "Why, thank you. I appreciate that a lot. I guess I rattled on way too long, but it just seemed to keep coming out. When you're stuck like I am, it's hard to hold it in."

"Edna Mae, I couldn't agree more. I know exactly what you're going through."

"You do?"

"Oh yes. You may wonder why I didn't take part today. Well, for two reasons. First, I don't have a husband any more. Second, I had one once that was even worse than yours."

"He must've been *really* bad."

"Much worse than the one you described."

"How'd you change him? I'd try about anything."

"I didn't say I *changed* him. But, I was able to do something about the problem."

"I don't understand."

"There's no way you could know this, but a cousin of mine is something of an expert in these matters."

194

"He helped you? How?"

"It would be much better if he told you himself. It just so happens that he's in town for a few days. I don't want to meddle, but I might be able to arrange for you to meet him."

"Is he a psychologist? Does he charge much?"

"He's not a psychologist as such, but *is* a recognized expert in his field. There's usually a fee, but I think that's something you'll need to talk about with him. There's no fee if he decides he can't take your case. Would you like to speak with him?"

"The fix I'm in with this loser, I'll try most anything. Go ahead. When and where can I meet him?"

"He may be free now. I'll phone."

****

In the rear booth of the coffee shop down the block from the meeting, Mica Miller introduced her cousin to Edna Mae, then added, "You two have some talking to do, and I must run."

Mica's cousin wasn't one for small talk. "I understand you have a problem you may need some help with."

"It's my husband. I made a terrible mistake marrying him, thinking I could change some of his bad points, but he's gotten worse and worse. I never thought I could say this about anybody, but I just can't stand the ground he walks on."

"Sounds like a problem, all right. Can't you just leave him?"

"Can't—my religion. Besides, he'd make my life a bigger Hell on earth than it is already. You don't know him. I do. He'd stop at nothing. Mica said you're an expert in these things. Just what is it you do? Can you help me change him?"

"Well now, *changing* him is not exactly what I do. I'm more in the field of just making problems go away."

"Away? Where to? How long? I wouldn't think it'd help much for just a little while."

"No ma'am. My solutions are more of a permanent nature."

"How in the world could you convince him to stay away?"

"Oh, he'd stay away. Permanently. Guaranteed. Permanent."

"For sure permanent?"

"Lady, didn't Cousin Mica tell you anything at all about how I work? How I make certain the problem goes and stays away?"

"She only said you helped people solve their problems and were an expert."

"Listen to me! I make problems go away. Don'tcha get it?"

"*Oh my Lord!* I think I *do* get it. You...."

"*Now*, I think you're getting it. Like to hear more or do you want to go on with your problem?"

Edna Mae gasped and started to rise. Halfway to her feet, she paused, then sat back down. "Maybe it wouldn't hurt to find out a little more."

"You already know enough. What it boils down to is what choice you're going to make–solve your problems or go on living with it. Which is it going to be?"

"Never in my life did I ever think I'd be sitting here, and...."

The man rose. I guess you've made your choice. Good luck the rest of your life with your beloved."

"Oh, please wait! This is all so sudden that my head is spinning. Just give me a minute...*please.*"

He sat. Finally, Edna Mae asked, "You do this all the time? Solve problems, I mean."

"Only in special cases where it's really needed."

"Everywhere?"

"Come on, lady. You want to talk turkey or do an interview? I can help. You need help. Simple as that. Do I go on?"

"Well, I do really *despise* my husband, and I don't see how I can stand much more. When you say "permanent" how do you make it that way? Like an accident?"

196

"Could be. There are several ways."

"Not that I'm agreeing to anything, but what do you charge for making a problem go away?"

"Depends."

"Depends?"

"Depends on how you want the problem solved. Accidents are more. Disappearing without a trace costs more. Cheapest way is making it look like a burglary gone bad. But, something of value has to come up missing to make it look good."

"Mica said you charged a fee. Just what *do* you charge? "I'm not agreeing to anything, but how much is the burglary thing?"

"Five thousand down and ten after the problem goes away."

"*Oh my!* I couldn't afford nearly that much. Not that I'm agreeing to anything."

"Of course not. But, say you *were* agreeing, how much *could* you afford?"

"Well, over the years, I've managed to squirrel away about four thousand from my skinflint husband. With that and what I could borrow against credit cards would be about six thousand altogether. But, there's no way I could get one penny more. So, there's no way I could agree to anything…even if I wanted to."

"If we were to come to an agreement, there may be a way you could come up with more. Remember, I said something of value has to be taken to make the robbery-gone-wrong look good. Do you have anything of value?"

"The only things I can think of are my engagement ring and some earrings. Old penny pincher said he paid four thousand."

"They might work."

Edna Mae didn't respond. After a long pause, he inquired, "Well, what's your choice? Going to fix your problem or not?"

"The whole idea is so sudden. But…do I have to decide this very minute. Can I think about it a little while?"

"All right. I'll be here two days from now. If you don't show, I'll know your answer. If it's a go, bring the money and jewelry with you. Payment works differently in a deal like this."

****

Eddie Joe set his beer aside and pushed the plastic bag holding the cash and stamp collection across the table. "There it is. What we agreed to. You can count it and look at the stamps."

"Oh, I don't think that'll be necessary. I think you're smart enough not to try any funny business." He pocketed the money and continued. "Let's get on with the details we need to talk about so I can fix your problem."

After Eddie Joe furnished all the information the problem-solver wanted, he responded with instructions for Eddie Joe, then commented, "I guess that's about all I need, but there's just one more thing."

"One more thing?"

"What's the address, Eddie Joe? That might come in handy."

"Oh yeah. It's 1122 Poplar Drive."

****

Edna Mae was a few minutes late getting to the coffee shop, but the man was still in the rear booth. Obviously quite nervous, she hesitated when the waitress came for her order, and he ordered coffee for her. "Calm down lady, calm down. This won't take a minute and you can be on your way."

Still nearly speechless, she managed, "I've got what you said right here. Want it now?"

"In a minute. First, I need some information."

They finished and she handed him a small bag. "It's all there. That's what we agreed on."

He pocketed the bag. "There's just one more thing."

"One more thing? It's all there just like we agreed."

He smiled. "That's good. But, it would probably useful if you told me the address."

"Oh, of course. It's 1122 Poplar Drive."

****

Fifty miles from town, Maryanne Keller a.k.a. Mica Miller, reached into a small bag, pulled out a diamond ring, and placed it on her finger. Holding it up to her husband, she commented, "Really nice stone. Looks good on my finger. Just fits, too."

"You know our rules, Babe. Convert to cash as soon as possible so we don't leave any evidence around. You want a ring, buy one from your half. By the way, I already called Jess about the stamp collection. Says it sounds like a good hit."

"That's good. Dick, are we lucky or what? You overhearing that husband in the bar and me those two women at the grocery. This was great fun–a double-header–but, there's one thing I would've really liked to have done."

"And that is?"

"Be a fly on the wall so I could be there when Eddie Joe and Edna Mae figured it out. They can't go to the police, and neither one will ever get a good night's sleep for fear of what the other one might be up to."

HEY, Y'ALL! IT BE BREAKIN' TIME!

HOWDY. CLARABELLE AGIN. HOW'DJA LIKE THEM TALES? BET THEM TWO FOLKS THAT HIRED THE SAME GUY TO POLISH OFF THE OTHER ONE HAFTA BE GITTIN' PURTY SLEEPY BY NOW. THINK THEY BE BAD? JIST WAIT TILL Y'ALL SEE WAT A LAWYER WAS UP TO IN ONE'A THE TALES COMIN' UP.

ANYWAY, TAKE A BIT'A TIME TO DO WHATCHA GOTTA, THEN C'MON BACK AN KEEP ON READIN' SO'S TO KEEP HAVIN' THEM REAL GOOD FEELIN'S FROM GOOD READIN'N GUESSIN'.

WELL NOW, I SEE Y'ALL DONE TAKEN MY INVITE TO C'MON BACK'N KEEP ON WITH THE READIN'. GOOD ATCHA. REAL GOOD.

I'D BE BEHOLDIN' IFFIN Y'ALL KIN SEE YER WAY TO 'SCUSE ME FER LEAVIN' KIND'A EARLY. I GOT SOME LAW-BOOK STUFF'N SUCH TO TALK OVER. MAYBE WE KIN TALK SOME MORE AT ONE ANOTHER MORE LATER. THANK YA KINDLY, BLESS Y'ALL'S HEART.

ICE CREAM

Reggie Nelson just *loved* old-fashioned homemade ice cream made with *pure* cream, sugar, pure vanilla and small amounts of wholesome additives. Put the works in a two-gallon upright wooden cylinder, pack ice and salt around it, and turn the crank until pure magic happens.

And the taste! It wasn't a *taste*, it was a *heavenly experience*. Open the dictionary to "delicious," and there would surely be a picture of old fashioned homemade ice cream.

Yep, Reggie just loved it so much that, although only barely fourteen, he became renowned for his capacity Last year, he finished second only to Earl Woggoman, the undefeated champion in the annual ice-cream-eating contest at the area farmers' Fall Ice Cream Social.

This year, a month before the Social, anticipation began running high. Most everyone predicted that this time, there'd be a new champion. Next Saturday night would be it for ol' Earl and put a stop to his bragging about his ice-cream-eating prowess.

Reggie was caught up in the moment and vowed to eat very little during the day of the contest. By golly he'd end the incessant needling he got from Woggoman all year.

****

Five years previously, the Mullums family was able to accumulate enough "scratch" (funds) to buy, for little more than a song, the run-down Claywell farm just across the county line from the Nelsons. After one of the many foreclosures of the time, the bank was happy to finally dump it.

One meeting with the Mullums and it was obvious that they were a lot more "hillbillier" than the few other hill country families that were able to migrate to the Midwest looking for a better way of life. In a short time, the Nelsons and the Mullums' became good friends, even if the newcomers were more than a bit off the track local-standards wise.

Mr. Ebenezer Mullums rarely ventured very far from his bed. During summers, he might get as far as the front porch swing once in a while, but that was about the extent of it. Eb labored hard all his life and "retired" years earlier at the ripe old age of 34. "Cricky back, don'tcha know. 'Sides, don't figger a man wuz put on this here earth to be no slave."

Evidently, "woman" was not included in this reasoning, because his retirement left all the management and operational functions of both household and farm to his wife, Matty. With help from their boys with the heavier farm chores, she proved well up to the joint tasks. Although scrawny and only fourth-grade educated, she was wiry and resourceful. Split about fifty-fifty between rawhide leather and solid brass, folks said.

Matty's attire was, politely put, "functional." An all-seasons felt hat topped earth-tone hair. Following on down, a blue cotton work shirt was trapped in place by bib "overhalls." All but her knee-high boots were fighting a downhill battle for survival.

During the week, it was not uncommon to see her slopping hogs or in the field driving the hay wagon, and then on Saturdays doing the marketing in town. As a consequence of her dual chores, she sometimes suffered from what a talk-show psychologist might now call "role confusion." It was difficult to keep up appearances as a proper homemaker-type lady and still tend to the farm work.

Part of her bafflement may've resulted from some of the comments she occasionally overheard about her garb. She was surprised at their stupidity and reacted accordingly. Take the one about her wearing gum (rubber) boots to the store. "A'body'd be a danged fool to change boots'n go to town when they knowd they'd be back home 'for long walkin' in the ho-do again."

She was also puzzled by the many recommendations made by the local storekeeper for the several brands of cologne he stocked. "Can't understand why he's always tryin' to sell me that stinky terlet water. What'n tarnation would the likes'a me need with such dang-nabbed foolishness?"

Eb usually responded to her dilemma as sympathetically with something like, "Didja fetch my chawin' tebaccy from town?"

****

The Mullums had their full share of children and then some. Enough so that they sometimes seemed to lose track of the exact number. All of them had gone their own way except Erlena Fay, Ogbert, and Millard.

Ogbert was the biggest and strongest and did most of the heavy lifting around the farm. He was a good ol' boy working his way up toward qualifying as half-bright. The neighborhood story was that Matty and Eb intended to name him "Egbert," but Eb didn't write so well, and his "E" was deciphered as an "0" on the official birth certificate, and "Ogbert" it remained.

Millard was of course named after President Millard Fillmore, daddy Eb's political idol. Millard didn't do a lot but sit around and smile. Many surmised that he was about ten face cards shy of a full deck. In a joint celebration, he and the school parted company on his 16th birthday. "Main trouble with schools is, they's always after ya to know somethin'," was his chief complaint.

Erlena Fay so shy that very few of the neighbors knew for sure whether she was still at home–so seldom did they catch a glimpse of her. Hers became one of the most important chores on the farm.

****

The Mullums fared reasonably well as farmers during the great economic depression era of the 1930's. In addition to the regular crops, Matty had better than average success with a moneymaking enterprise–raising hogs–which she called "mortgage lifters."

Matty wasn't just a lucky bumpkin who stumbled into a hog trough and surfaced with an apronful of dollars. She always kept an eye out for other "mortgage lifters."

Another idea she hit upon was separating the cream from cows' milk. More money was paid for cream from which to make butter than was paid for whole milk. The skim milk could be fed to the "mortgage lifters," thereby ready for butchering faster. Matty scraped up every penny of spare cash and bought a mechanical devise for separating the cream from the whole milk.

****

One crisp late fall day, Mrs. Nelson and son Reggie went to visit the Mullums just after evening milking time. It was also pretty obvious that they'd butchered a hog that same day. As they walked into the yard, Matty waved part of a hog liver at them in welcome as she flopped it onto a cutting block.

"Hi-dee, Miz Sally! And Hi-dee, Reggie." Matty's voice sounded like a tin wagon being dragged upside down over a concrete sidewalk.

"Glad to see ya," Matty continued. "Come over'n let's gab. I'll be through cuttin' up this here mortgage lifter's liver in a minute.

"Jist looky there–purty thang, hain't it? Nothin' like a milk-slopped hog fer good liver."

Reggie was squeamish, but his mother didn't bat an eye. "Fine looking liver, Matty, doesn't look a bit flukey."

Reggie's face nearly betrayed his thought (*EE-YECH!*)

Matty Mullums reiterated, "Nosiree Bob. Nothin' like a milk slopped hog fer good liver."

It seemed to Reggie that they'd exhausted this topic, and he was happy when she and his mother started talking about whatever it was they were there for. Pretty soon, they must've wanted to discuss something they didn't want him to hear, because Matty asked, "Reggie, like to go see separatin' the cream from the milk?"

Reggie thought it was a dandy idea. Seeing the separation program would be OK, but what he really wanted was to see Erlena Fay in action. Matty often bragged that the separator contraption was her daughter's pride and joy. She spent hours seeing to it being spic and span and in apple-pie working order. She might need a little help with the heavy lifting, but her overall devotion to milk-person duty prompted Matty to consider her Chief of Separations.

****

Anyone seeing a cream separator, and especially if they cleaned one, has a fair notion of where the special effects men for science fiction movies could get their scariest ideas. The thing stood nearly as tall as a grown man and had a big squashed-globe looking tank on the top with an opening to receive whole milk. A couple of spouts stuck out its middle, and a super-sized crank was attached for the necessary human-powering. Gallons of raw milk were poured into the top, and it flowed around, up, down, over and through assorted funnels, tubes, and plumbing when the crank was turned. Centrifugal force and other laws of physics were exercised so cream flowed from one spout and skim milk from the other.

Internally, it contained about a hundred of the aforementioned funnels, tubes and mysterious fixtures, all of which had to be meticulously washed and sterilized each time it was used. Maybe Erlena Fay wasn't so shy after all–maybe tending the monster took so much time (twice daily, seven days a week) that there was little left for anything else.

****

Upon entering the small separator-shed, it appeared that the Mullums had a strong new hired hand doing the cranking, one muscular enough to rapidly spin the separator's crank. But it was only Erlena Fay, who certainly didn't look as though she needed any help. She wasn't even breathing rapidly.

At first, Reggie thought she was showing off for a minute, but the crank kept spinning at the same speed. Even though Erlena Fay was a trifle stocky, she still didn't look able to keep up such a speedy pace. But, she had so much practice that she developed a rhythm and wrist-snap enabling her to keep cranking without excess effort. Reggie also noticed her contented smile. Here was a person truly happy in her work.

****

For Matty Mullums, every nickel counted. Each drop of cream wrung from whole milk counted. Great care was taken so the cream emerging from the separator wouldn't overflow its small catch-can–exactly like regular milk can, but less than half as big. One person was assigned to prevent just such a catastrophe–Erlena Fay's brother, Ogbert, in this case. It was his responsibility to have an empty can close by with the lid off so it could be quickly placed under the stream of cream before the first catch-can spilled over. As a catch-can became nearly full, he'd slide it to one side. Then, all in one motion with his free hand slide an empty one under the cream stream. Next, he'd put a lid on the filled can. After these operations, he'd refill the milk reservoir on top of the separator.

The proper sequence would seem a fairly simple one. But, being by nature more distraction prone than most folks, Ogbert had to screw down his concentration in order to follow the routine exactly. Eventually, he mastered keeping clear of possible disruptions endangering the continuity and rarely spilled a drop. He was proud of his work. Besides, spillage resulted in a frightful loss-of-profit lecture from his mother.

****

As Reggie entered, Ogbert looked up and echoed Matty's greeting. "Well, Hi-Dee Reggie-boy!" Next, "Come to see the butcherin' or the seperatin'? If ya come to see the butcherin' ya oughta go lookit them livers Ma's slicin' up."

"No, I only want to see how to separate the milk and cream."

"Well now, ain't that jist plain dandy. You kin stand over there'n watch all ya wanna."

Reggie's entrance must've caused Ogbert to get out of synch. In attempting to work and talk simultaneously, he forgot to put a lid on the filled cream catch-can.

A crisis consists of several components, each of which must come into play in correct sequence for the event to occur. Reggie was about to witness one of those times when everything came together in absolutely perfect alignment. The various parts of this particular crisis included Ogbert, the lidless cream can, Erlena Fay, and a gray-and-black tiger-striped barn cat.

Sensing a rare opportunity, the cat hopped up, somehow managed a delicate balance on the rim of the cream can, and began slurping madly away. Erlena Fay, never once pausing in her cranking, shrieked, *"OGBERT! THE CAT'S IN THE CREAM!"* (Not entirely accurate, but close.)

Ogbert spun with every intention of knocking the offending feline into kingdom come. The cat, being no fool, knew no amount of cream would be worth all nine of his lives. Desperately shifting to full blast-off mode, he tried his level best to become a meteor. Sadly, the precarious nature of his balancing act undid him, and he did the cat version of a sprawling half gainer into three gallons of cream. *Now*, Erlena Fay was correct–the cat *was* in the cream.

Outraged by this maneuver, Ogbert shoved up his shirtsleeve and reached into the can for the thrashing animal. *"I'll getcha,* ya *no good low down dirty damn* **CREAM STEALIN' ROBBER!"** He wasn't known for an extensive vocabulary.

Fishing around, Ogbert grabbed the slippery cat and yanked him out. With appropriate references to the cat's ancestry, he wound up to launch the creamy-rich, semi-drowned cat into orbit.

At that precise moment, Reggie's mother and Mrs. Matty Mullums, keeper of the family fortune, arrived. Instantly sizing up the situation, and seeing hard earned profits about to fly away, she shouted, *"WAIT, OGBERT, WAIT! DON'T THROW 'IM"* Rushing over, she seized the cream-soused cat by the neck in a grip used to hold a sizable pig still while someone punched steel rings through its nose to keep it from rooting in the dirt.

Even in his panic-stricken state, the cat must've sensed there'd be no escape. Holding the lightly cream-colored, struggling, gagging, sneezing animal at arm's length, she thriftily stripped the excess cream from head to tail-tip into the open cream can. Then, she repeated the procedure for each leg, body to paw. At least some of the profits were salvaged.

Handing the dazed, drowned-rat-looking cat back to Ogbert, she commanded, "Now throw 'im, son!"

He grabbed the cat (faintly tiger-striped again) and started to oblige. Luckily for the cat, he was still so slick that when Ogbert drew back to let him fly, he squirted straight backwards out of the intended hurler's grip and through the open back door of the shed.

Ogbert followed through with his delivery anyhow, but it just wasn't the same without the cat.

Erlena Fay did not miss a stroke in her cranking. Aside from a brief admonition to Ogbert, Matty didn't miss ten words in her conversation with Reggie's mother. The cat disappeared for a week and never went near the milk shed again.

Not much was said on the way home. That is, aside from Reggie's mother warning him not to "talk around" what he saw and that no other farmers would do such a thing.

****

Saturday night, all was in readiness for the ice-cream eating contest. To assure an ample supply, different farmers prepared a container of it, the names of the donors prominently displayed. When one container was empty, another was opened. The judge tasted and declared the cream used was especially rich. Applause.

One by one, contestants ate his limit and withdrew to the joshing of the audience. Finally, only Earl Woggoman and Reggie Nelson remained. The crowd was delighted. Woggoman was about to meet his match. And dethroned by a kid, too.

There came a slight break in the action, the other contestants having consumed so much ice cream that only one unopened container remained. As the judge began opening it Reggie suddenly withdrew despite the crowd's urging to continue.

A gloating Earl Woggoman stood, waved his hand high and demanded another bowl. The crowd's silence voiced its opinion.

Abruptly, Reggie went to the judge's table and carried the extra portion to Earl Woggoman. Noisy admiration rang out at this gesture of sportsmanship as Reggie handed the reigning champion the ice cream prepared by Mrs. Matty Mullums.

THE SCORE'S THE THING

O n the way to the special meeting of the school board, Jimmy Brjqloj sat wondering how many times he heard the same thing from his mom. "Now James, always remember that you're just as good as any of them, no matter who they are or what they are." He sometimes thought that if this were so, why did she need to keep saying it, but he didn't think it wise to ask. He could remember several specific times she said it, including the first one.

****

When he was old enough, his mother began taking him to the playground every few days. After a couple weeks, he noticed that more than half of the other kids left soon after he arrived. On the way home, he asked his mother why so many did so. Her response was that it was probably their nap time. Curious, he questioned that so many kids still had to take afternoon naps, since most of them were almost ready for school.

On his next playground visit, he asked one of the early deportees why he had to take a nap every day. The kid responded, "Whatcha talkin' about? I don't take a nap every day. Think I'm a sissy? Mom says there's some it's better off not bein' around."

"Whataya mean?"

"If you're too dumb to know, ask your mom."

On the way home, Jimmy did just that. She waited so long to reply that he was about to ask again. That's when he heard for the first time, "Pay those imbeciles no mind. Always remember that you're just as good as any of them, no matter who they are or what they are, and don't forget it." He never forgot how she voiced the phrase, either. It was the same way tonight.

****

Jimmy reminisced further. When he came home from his first day at school and related how the seats were assigned, there was a lot of pretty loud talking behind closed doors between his parents. He couldn't make out most of it, but it sounded as if Dad were trying everything to get Mom not to go down to "that miserable school" and raise the roof.

He didn't know what the big deal was. All he said was that he was given the last seat on the end row, and no one had the one in front of him. Then, the teacher said the one next to him was to be used for her extra books she needed for some of the stuff she taught. He thought that was kind'a funny. He couldn't remember when saw a book aside from Dad's collection of old ones they used way back before computers.

Finally, Mom and Dad came back into the living room. It stayed so quiet that Jimmy couldn't keep his curiosity in check any longer. What was the matter, anyway? After a bit, Dad looked over at Mom and said, "Might as well get it over with and tell him what to expect. He's gonna hear it the rest'a his life. Might as well give him the bad news now. Dangit Jnolia, the boy only hasta look around to see he's not like the others. Can hardly believe he hasn't said something about it already."

"Exbna, of course he can plainly see he's not like any of the others, but by the questions he asks, I don't think he fully realizes how cruel the others can be about it."

"All the more reason we should talk to him about it now. We've done everything possible to keep him sheltered from what the others are bound to do, but we just can't keep it up."

"I suppose you're right, but we need to talk about the right time to do it."

****

Jimmy's parents needn't have been concerned about choosing the "right times." The others at school did it for them and the "right time" came almost immediately. It didn't take Jimmy long to recognize what was going on.

He first noticed it when the teacher almost never called on him no matter how long or how often he held up his hand to answer her question. Never praised him for having the right answer when she did. Also, when being placed last in line to wash up before lunch.

Lots of stuff from the other kids, too. Like always being chosen the very last to play on one of the playground teams. This was in spite of him being very good at playing the games. Better than anyone else, usually. And never being invited to birthday parties or be in any school plays. Lots'a other stuff.

****

Oh yeah, there'd been so many times in elementary school making him know he was different that he couldn't remember them all. But, he had no trouble remembering the exact time that he heard the word, "colored," used by the others.

That night, it didn't help when his Mom and Dad tried to help things by telling no matter how bad things were now, they were better than before. "Just think about it, son. Today, you can go to a regular school." Didn't help at all. And, it didn't help when for once, Mom forgot to remind him that he was a good as anyone else.

****

Jimmy recalled that by the time he reached high school, he heard, the word, "colored," and other disparaging remarks so often that he ceased to mention them to his parents. Also stopped reacting to them. Doing so only caused more insulting rejoinders.

During his sophomore year, a major incident in which he became involved occurred when the parents of Mqrets Wora learned that she sat beside him at lunch on several occasions. Not only had they stormed into the superintendent's office, demanding action be taken to prevent this happening again, they aroused their friends into signing a protest petition demanding more "protection" for their kids during lunch hour.

While all this was bubbling and boiling, the head athletic coach chanced to be walking alongside a practice field and saw Jimmy working out...by himself, of course. Stopping to observe, the coach was astonished at the physical prowess of the boy. He was imitating some of the practice routine of the regular team. Not only did he run with gazelle speed, he completed the entire drill faster and better than any of the team's star athletes. The coach continued to watch Jimmy, amazement growing by the second. *Wow!* Here was every coach's dream, a path straight to a championship, maybe more. But, there was this one little problem.

****

Fueled by his championship dream, Coach Nxwwr began to carry out a plan. First, he arranged a quiet meeting in his office with Jimmy's parents. He explained that he wanted very much to ask their son to become a team member, but wanted to know what they thought of the idea. Also, whether they thought he could handle what was bound to be a huge negative community reaction. And, could they?

Both parents stated that the community could go hang, but worried that their son could be harmed. After much discussion, Dad said to Mom, "Well, you've always told him he was just as good as anybody, whoever they were. With all the guff he's had to go through, he's gotten to be a really tough kid. Looks to me like here's a chance to prove to him that what you've been saying is true. We can handle the community crap and so can he." Mom hesitated, but agreed.

Next, the coach talked with Jimmy. After his enthusiastic response to becoming a team member, he added, "After all the stuff I've heard about me being *different*, I can handle any BS coming my way. How you gonna handle things with the team? And, with the community? And the school board? They'll be after you too."

"We'll do it together. You'll help us win and I'll take care of the team and the rest."

****

Before the next practice, the coach assembled the players in the classroom next to his office and locked the door. "Gentlemen, how many of you would like to be members of a championship team, maybe more than just one?" The resounding response rattled the windows.

"Well, I believe I may have found someone who can help you do just that. But, there are a few things that must be done as well as keep practicing and playing as hard as you have." Rapt attention.

"To see whether I'm right, at today's practice this new player will participate. If he's as good as I think he can be, we'll decide if all of you want him to be part of the team. I must tell you that he's a little different from you and some may find it hard to have him as a teammate. If there are those who don't want him as a teammate, they may want to turn in their equipment. But, I believe that once you see what he can do, you'll think twice about doing that.

"One final thing. Whatever is decided, you must agree, *right now,* not to say one word of this meeting or anything about the new player until after the next game. Do you agree?"

219

If there was any hesitancy, rampant curiosity stamped it out. The answer was unanimous. The coach asked them to repeat their vow, and they did.

"Good. Now, let's get on out to the field for practice."

****

As per the coach's instructions, Jimmy Brjqloj didn't come trotting out to practice until the team assembled for warm-up drills. When they saw who it was, chattered speculations ceased instantly as the players began the drills. Two were only grimly going through the motions. But, when Jimmy executed each exercise better than any other player, silence blossomed into enthusiastic outbursts.

In the sprints, the newcomer finished ten yards ahead of the next fastest. He handled the ball with more agility and accuracy. In the strength exercise, he was so much stronger than the former best that the coach had him repeat it. Most amazing of all, without ever having practiced with the team, after the drills ended he excelled at completing plays during the regular practice.

****

After practice, the coach again met with the players to discuss the importance of maintaining total secrecy about plans to play Jimmy in the coming week's game. "Yeah, I know there's gonna be some Holy Kadoodle raised, but when the crowd sees what he can do, I'm hoping the fuss will soon die down.

"Like I said earlier, those who don't wanna play alongside Jimmy can turn in your stuff. OK, now all those who wanna have him as a teammate go on over to the locker room and shower. Those who don't just stay here for a minute or two." All but two trooped out.

While one hung his head and remained silent, the other felt he must explain. "Coach, it ain't that I'm against playing with a colored on the team, but my folks'll skin me alive just for thinkin' about it."

"I understand. Tell you what. After they see the game and how good the team's gonna be, maybe things'll die down. You'll be welcome to come back if your folks change their minds."

"Thanks, coach. I doubt they ever will, but thanks anyway."

****

Even the most rabid fan didn't think the team stood a chance against the many-times-champion opponent. When the locals scored quickly, the veteran viewers knew it was luck and only a matter of time before the lads would be steam-rollered into oblivion. But, as the game progressed, it looked more and more as if the impossible was possible.

Who was that number 32, anyway? He wasn't listed in the program. Covered head to toe with that new-type headgear, uniforms, and gloves for getting a better grip, there was no way to identify any player.

Lightning fast, no opponent got by number 32. And score! He had as many points as the other team combined. As it continued to mount, the outcome became clear. When the team took the between-quarters break, the crowd stood as one, the cheering echoing. Then, number 32 removed his headgear.

****

Grave-side silence instantly replaced thunderous applause. Slowly, a murmur of astonishment morphed into muttering disbelief. Soon, expressions of shock, dismay, and rage blended into what began to resemble a near-primal indefinable growl. For a moment, it appeared that a few of the more aggressive might charge onto the playing area, but stopped when Jimmy's teammates surrounded him and assumed defensive stances. The stands began clearing, and a shouted *"N0 COLORED HERE"* became a chant. In minutes, only a handful of fans remained.

****

Outside in the parking lot, small groups milled about, the conversation in each of a very similar tone.

"How in the entire universe could such a thing happen!"

"Never should'a let that kind come into our town in the first place. Ya let one in and ya see what happens."

"Never should'a let that colored kid into our school. That's whatcha get for hirin' a woman superintendent. A man would'a never allowed it."

"Oughta get rid of 'er."

"That coach, too. Oughta be thrown off the planet.."

A voice from the far side of the area rang out. *"WHAT'RE WE GONNA DO ABOUT THIS!"* Answering his own question, he continued, *"WE GOTTA DEMAND A SPECIAL MEETIN' OF THE SCHOOL BOARD. GET RID'A THAT COLORED KID AND THE COACH, TOO!"*

Like vultures to the carcass, the crowd flocked to the shouter. He climbed atop his vehicle and continued the harangue. Soon, by unanimous agreement, he became the crowd's choice to demand a special school board meeting.

****

As they rode to the special meeting, Jimmy inwardly expressed surprise that Dad immediately agreed with Mom that all three of them attend. "That crowd of bigots is not going to intimidate us. We've been intimidated too long."

Obviously, Jimmy wasn't the only one surprised that he and his parents were there. Heads held high and Dad leading the way, they took aisle seats near the front, unmindful of those sitting nearby moving to other seats.

222

Hostility fouled the air. On the defensive, the lady superintendent vowed she had no knowledge of the coach's plans. The anti-female bunch then hammered her for not knowing.

The coach refused to express regret for his decision to play Jimmy, saying he was hired to win, and by Jupiter, he found a way to bring a championship to this school after 35 winless seasons. And winning wasn't the only thing for which he was hired. He was also responsible for helping to develop wholesome attitudes. His manner clearly said "In spite of the garbage being taught at home." Also, "Take this job and shove it!"

On and on it went, every member of the crowd seemingly of the same mind. The coach and superintendent must go. Further, rules should be passed relative to playing kids different from all the others. Who knows what damage it might result if they didn't?

Jimmy and his parents sat stoically. Once Dad started to speak, but Mom put her hand on his sleeve. When it appeared that the board was about to entertain a motion to please the assemblage, Nqrste Vvrbd rose and asked, "May I say a few words?"

Vvrhd was the most respected man in the entire community. Their greatest hero-athlete, during his career he won countless contests. Of course he could speak.

"Thank you. I have only a few brief words. In the previous thirty-five years, I have traveled extensively while competing in various athletic contests. Doing so, I learned that, in another galaxy on the planet called "earth," about three hundred years ago, they had the same sort of situation you now have. I also learned that if you can score, it doesn't make any difference what color you are. My question to you about Jimmy is, if he can score and bring you the championship *for which you are starved*, what difference does it make if he's orange and not green like the rest of us?"

THIRD TIME'S *NOT* THE CHARM!

Another search for a full-time minister at the Second Faith And Redemption Church Of The Holy Savior And Blessed Redeemer was about to begin. This time, it would *not* be conducted by the same entrenched committee also responsible for naming the church when it was established in 2002.

Peacemakers amidst the membership fervently hoped and prayed that a different committee's recommendation wouldn't become as contentious as during the church-naming process. After much *very* spirited deliberation and many tie votes by the full membership of 38, the current name was finally adopted. The major item of contention was whether the use of the term "Second" was misleading, since there wasn't a "First" anywhere.

Approval came only after Alex Messingale was persuaded to change his vote and join the "ayes" after it was successfully argued that using "Second" in the name would indicate to viewers of the hand-painted sign in front of their small rented meeting house that this new church was part of a larger religious denomination.

Alex's defection was not without consequences. For quite a while, his former "best friends" shopped somewhere other than Messingales's Meats and Treats.

****

The more assertive members joined the peacemakers in also desperately desiring a better outcome than those from the previous search. The minister chosen then obviously shared one of the entire congregation's highest priorities, that of attracting younger members to bolster an aging membership.

Preacher Percival Paxton soon succeeded beyond their dreams. Youthful, handsome, and energetic, the high school set seemed almost magnetically drawn to him. After only four months, more than two dozen recruits joined the congregation.

Lowering the average age wasn't his only accomplishment. Motivational sermons and classes stirred older members into action. In addition to its regular activities, the ladies sewing circle organized a drive to collect clothing and other items for the needy, ran bake sales, and knitted caps for the newborn in Africa.

In almost no time, the membership grew in size to well over a hundred, so much larger that new quarters had to be found. The men were now busily remodeling the kitchen and other areas to accommodate social gatherings and innovative programs.

Ah yes, Preacher Paxton was just the ticket, all right. The search committee had done an outstanding job. Even those who had privately expressed doubts were impressed and forced to agree. But, as things transpired, their earlier uncertainties were vindicated.

Nearly perfect in all areas, the following year it was discovered that Preacher Paxton had this *one little flaw*. He ran off with a high-school senior, leaving his wife of eleven years behind.

Well, maybe not just this *one* little flaw. Proving once again that too many times the barn is locked after the horse goes missing, outraged search committeeman Everett Engle determined to learn more about the abdicating cleric.

A second little flaw soon surfaced. Not only had Paxton sped away with the teen-ager, abandoning his current wife, apparently he neglected to obtain a divorce from his first and second before wedding the third. And, oh yes, his real name was Charles Kimble Mansdel, the one on the bigamy warrant seven states away.

****

As might be expected, the search committee received substantial flack for not conducting a more rigorous investigation into "Percival Paxton's" background. Accompanying this was an equal amount of immediate apprehension about no longer having a full-time minister.

Polite inferences that perhaps it was now time for a new search committee to have a go were shortly replaced by increasingly direct ones. On the occasion of the departure of every last one of the recently-joining young members, the growing demand for a newly constituted search committee came to the church Elders in writing. Anonymously, of course.

At a tumultuous special meeting of the entire congregation, the search committee unanimously expressed their disappointment in fellow members for their lack of appreciation. Then they stood, resigned *en masse*, and left the building.

Hiding satisfaction and smiles, those remaining proceeded at once to install an already selected committee which approved previously prepared wording for the new "minister-wanted" ad to be widely distributed. The ad included a very specific statement advising respondents that they would be subject to intense vetting. This time, there would be no slip-ups. *Absolutely* none whatsoever.

Twelve Sundays later, six applicants had preached trial sermons following probing background checks and a lengthy interview. After much deliberation, The Reverend Marion Sanders was selected to be recommended as the church's next minister.

The new search committee was particularly impressed by conversations with two references provided by Sanders. One was by a Deacon, the other an Elder, both members of the church where he was the current minister. In addition to their high praise, each expressed great disappointment that he was leaving, but understood his desire to return to the mid-west from Arizona.

The committee proudly announced their choice to the congregation. After an all-afternoon meeting during which committee members elaborated upon their many efforts, the full membership voted to accept its recommendation.

****

Less than a year later, it appeared that the second search committee had done a great job. Remarkably in such a short time, Reverend Sanders was accepted and greatly admired, not only by his congregation but throughout the community. His weekly radio hour became a hit, resulting in church membership increasingly dramatically. Individuals of all ages joined and participated in the reverend's novel programs.

Mrs. Sanders was also a find. In short order, she plunged into several community self-help programs. The word was that she might well receive the town's "Volunteer of the Year." award.

There was another much appreciated benefit as a result of the increased size of the congregation. With the additional weekly offering, along with various donations and inheritances, church Elders no longer had to worry about having enough cash to meet operating costs. In fact, one or two more years like this one and they could begin thinking about planning their own building.

Though it took a while for members of the previous search committee to come around, eventually they also had to admit that this couple was the real deal. Two of them even agreed to sit in on his yearly evaluation session. It didn't look like much of a job. Few among them could remember when the total membership was as united as it was in its oft-voiced positive view of Reverend and Mrs. Sanders.

****

Ah yes, this time the new minister was the *real* real deal, all right. Everyone said so. Well, maybe there was this *one little flaw*.

228

When the evaluation committee met, The Reverend Marion Sanders was nowhere to be found. Not only that, no one had seen him for several days. Nor had Mrs. Sanders been seen about town. Oh well, there was probably an easy explanation.

What wouldn't be so easily explained was the sudden disappearance of the entire cash surplus of one hunderd forty-seven thousand dollars and 17 cents. Neither was one signature on the check made out to Sanders. As the duly authorized treasurer for the church, Mrs. Sanders' name was on the first signature line and that was in order. However, on the second line, the signature of member Jody Nelson, authorized counter-signer for the church, was forged.

There were more inexplicable examples. For instance, how had the search committee failed to discover one very important fact? The so-called "Deacon" and "Elder," supposedly officials at Sanders' former church, who supplied such glowing testimonials, were actually two cousin-accomplices.

The search committee wasn't the only group experiencing hind-sight clarity. How had so many members failed to connect the dots when viewing a popular exposé-type TV channel which featured a story about an Arizona church whose membership was victimized in the exact same fashion? Although the absconders used different names, even a *slightly* more alert audience should've easily recognized the "minister's" unique speech patterns, regardless of the use of hair coloring and simple disguises.

****

Naturally, the squall generated when preacher Percival Paxton ran off with a teenage sexpot exploded into a genuinely perfect storm when the Sanders flew the coop with the cash. Instantly, the armistice between the old and new search-committee backers shattered, replaced with constant snippy salvos of recriminations from both sides.

Soon however, the problem of "what's next" had to be faced. Obviously, the congregation already demonstrated its ineptness in choosing search committees. After seemingly incessant meetings and peacemaking efforts, a solution was offered about how to organize yet another search committee to find yet another replacement reverend.

"Holy moley kajoly! Not another search committee! We're gonna run out'a names pretty soon," moaned a member.

Yes, there must be one, but this time it wouldn't be responsible for identifying potential ministers. This go-around, the congregation would employ the services of a national placement agency to do the job. From those identified by it after its screening process, the new search committee would only make recommendations regarding which candidates on the list to invite to preach a trial sermon once resumes were checked again.

The long-festering animosity between the previous two committees and their followers would also be addressed. To promote harmony, three members of each side would comprise the new one. After extensive hemming and hawing, backing and filling, both sides reluctantly agreed.

****

During the ensuing weeks, several candidates came, preached their trial sermon and failed to satisfy the membership. The organization identifying them was beginning to have doubts whether any would *ever* be acceptable. Then lucky-lightning struck on consecutive Sundays.

****

Half way through his sermon, the congregation saw that this young man had it all. Enthusiasm, personality, knowledge, delivery–no mistake about it, he had it all! They were ready to select The Reverend Jason Beachom right then, but would have to

230

wait one more week. Another candidate had already been invited to deliver a sermon next Sunday.

The lightning strike on that second Sunday didn't happen without a preceding thunderclap. The Reverend Mardo Anders was a *woman!* A *woman!* No one said anything about inviting a *woman* to preach. A *woman* right up there in the pulpit! *The idea!* Funny first name, too. What kind'a name was *"Mardo!"*

Only later did the congregation learn that well-to-do Sylvia Langaford, the only woman on the search committee, made something perfectly clear. It would be only too easy to change her will, removing the church as the chief benefactor, should *one hint* of the reverend's gender be disclosed before she arrived.

Well, there was nothing to do about it now. After all, there *was* that Scripture about taking in strangers. With flinty expressions and arms folded, they sat back and prepared to pretend to listen. There wasn't any Scripture about how long you had to let the stranger stay, was there? She'd be on her way soon enough. They'd speak to the search committee later.

Now it was lightning's turn. About ten minutes into the sermon, expressions softened, arms unfolded, and members leaned forward. This *person* was great! "Mesmerized" may've been a bit strong, but close. The "Get rid of 'er right after the benediction" thoughts were being replaced by, "How in creation are we gonna choose between this one and last Sunday's?"

****

Yep, you guessed it. The grease was soon sizzling on the griddle. Almost before the service ended, sides were forming as to which of the last two candidates should become the minister. Although roughly conforming to those who supported either the first or second search committee, there was some switching between *pro-Beachom* and *pro-Anders* backers.

While not saying it publically, those voting for the young man privately prattled that those ladies changing sides were doing so just to vote for a *woman*. When an older male member dared to express this openly, the smoldering who-should-be-hired opinions flared into an open conflagration.

Two days later, the voting began. After the first couple or three, it was patently obvious that the congregation was so evenly split that the outcome of any more votes would remain the same. The impasse was so solidified that even the usual peacemakers felt any further attempts at resolving it right then would be futile at best and only further divide the membership.

Finally it happened. Four days later, followers of the original search committee who were supporting the young man let their plans be known. They were in the process of going their own way and forming a new church across town.

Oh, they'd worship the same way as always, but with the minister *they* wanted. But, there'd be one big difference. T*heir* church would *not* be known as The *Second* Faith And Redemption Church Of The Holy Savior And Blessed Redeemer. *Theirs* would be The *Third* Faith And Redemption Church of The Holy Savior And Blessed Redeemer.

****

After such a lengthy no-decision period, the director of the national placement agency charged with identifying candidates and negotiating contracts was becoming increasingly concerned whether *any* of their referrals would be chosen. His letter of inquiry followed. The manager immediately forwarded a copy of the committee's response to the two minister-candidates. Each put down breakfast coffee to prepare a letter to be sent directly to the screening committee.

Dear Brothers and Sisters in Christ,

A copy of a letter written by your membership's screening committee to the placement agency has been forwarded here. To say its contents detailing the friction now rampant in your congregation was a shock is to vastly understate the reaction. Please accept the sincerest of apologies for being instrumental in causing the contention and possible extremely negative actions resulting from the division over selecting a minister.

An explanation is clearly in order. We kept the information confidential that we were aware of each other for two reasons.

First, we did not want it to appear that our candidacy was some kind of game with a winner and loser.

Second, we plan for one of us to take an 18-month sabbatical from the ministry to complete an advanced degree in theology. Whichever one not chosen by your congregation would pursue this educational goal and seek a nearby pastorate upon graduation. Both of us would then remain at our posts indefinitely. The placement agency was advised of our intentions.

Please, we beg of you, please forgive us and accept our sincere heartfelt apologies. And please make every attempt to restore a harmonious relationship among all your members. Our prayers are with you.

One final note. Please remove both our names from any further consideration.

Yours in Christ,

Reverend Jason Beachom
Reverend Mardo Beachom
(*Formerly*: Mardo *Anders*)

233

GREAT FUN

After attending her first, Fredrica Hanover swore she'd never, *ever*, attend another sloppily sentimental, boring, high school class reunion. She hadn't, either, always tossing the announcements into the round file a moment after they hit her desk. But this year was different. About to do the usual, her eye fell upon the first name on the much shorter list of this year's surviving classmates. It was that of Charles Andrews.

Fredrica stopped in mid-toss, her thoughts flashing back to him and to their years at school. *(My word! Charlie Andrews! Lost all track of him years ago. Didn't know he was still alive and kicking. Weren't we quite an item at Harrison High, though! Wonder how things might've.... Oh, well.*

Wonder if he ever did any of those fool things we had such great fun talking about doing when we grew up and got rich. Wonder what.... Oh well, life moves on.)

Instead of discarding this one as she did the previous 12 five-year class reunion announcements, Fredrica placed this one back on her desk. *(Maybe I could stand going just once. We'll see.)*

****

Harrison High seniors Fredrica Hanover and Charles Andrews had a "kind'a buddies" relationship beginning in grade school. Classmates were not surprised when it developed into something considerably more late in their junior year.

As seniors, after their usual Saturday movie date a few months before graduation, the two sat in the Hanover's porch swing talking about this and that when Fredrica suddenly changed the subject. "Charles, I think it's time we have our *now what* discussion."

Charlie wasn't stupid. He knew full well what she meant. Matter of fact, he already gave it considerable thought. But, he tried keeping it light. "*Charles?* You called me *'Charles'* instead of *'Charlie?'* It must be serious."

"I know we're both the biggest kidders on earth, but don't try to get into that *Chuckie-Freddie* mode. This is serious and you know it. We've known for a while this buddy-buddy, how-we're gonna-get rich-when-we-grow-up game has been great fun, and the just-kissy-kissy game wouldn't last forever. So what's it gonna be after graduation? Great fun all this time, but see ya later alligator?"

"Freddie, how's this storyline strike ya? Handsome charming fella takes pity on poor downtrodden damsel and cuts her a break. After college, he weds her in the most elaborate ceremony in history and showers her the rest of her life with goodies far beyond her wildest dreams. Whataya think?"

"Charlie, I said this is serious!"

A long pause. Then, "Fredrica, I couldn't be more serious. Question is, what's downtrodden damsel think of the story?"

Another long pause. Then, "Downtrodden damsel thinks it could win a Nobel Prize for literature."

That settled it. That is, until after a world war and Charlie's military service. A spat over almost nothing occurred on their way to obtain a marriage license. This escalated into handsome fella and downtrodden damsel exhibiting a heels-dug-in side light years removed from their long-lived, back and forth, "gotcha" rejoinders. Stupid stubbornness. Stubbornness resulting in on-the-rebound marriages to someone else within a few months.

****

In spite of her self-admonitions to "stop being an old fool," Fredrica found herself thinking more and more about the reunion and what she might wear in the unlikely event she attended. A few days later, she decided she'd go, but she had to have a new outfit. Grades more important than style to Fredrica, she was never one to follow teen-age trends while in high school. As a result, she took considerable good-natured kidding about being tagged "Frumpy Freddie" wearing "garage-sale-leftovers". This time it would be different. *(By golly, I'll show 'em what real style is. Don't care what it costs. And I must be sure to make a hair appointment for the Saturday of the reunion. Show 'em some style.)*

Once again, Fredrica mentally slapped her cheek, then said aloud, "Grow up! You're acting like a sophomore. And why? No one there'll notice or give a hoot. And, you can't be doing it thinking Charlie might be there. Grow up! This is now, that was then...two lifetimes ago."

But, as the date for the reunion neared, Fredrica found she was reminiscing more about the past. And about Charles Andrews. *(Wonder if he really ever did any of those things we had such great fun talking about? Let's see, what were his most outrageous? I guess the one where he was going to write a world-wide best-seller, win a Nobel Prize for literature, and then play the starring role in the movie. Oh yeah, we had great fun playing that silly game...played it all the way from fifth grade on. Tried to outdo each other with the zaniest prediction. Wonder if he....")*

****

Charles Andrews didn't care much for class reunions, either. At the last one, he discovered that Marty Clanset, his best buddy in high school, stepped off a curb in England, forgetting that traffic flowed on the left side of the street. Sayonara, Marty. After viewing the survivor's list for the previous reunion, Charlie remarked, "So many have bought the farm, the next one will likely be a duet."

When he got the invitation to this one, he scanned the list of survivors and was about to pitch it when a name leapt from the page, the married name he learned of before losing track of her decades ago–Fredrica Coburn.

Charlie sat thinking of his first great love. *(What a peach she was! Not often you see that much beauty with so many smarts. And funny! She invented that screwball how-we're-gonna-get-rich-when-we-grow-up game in grade school. Lotta fun trying to outdo each other.)* More reverie and he abruptly sat upright in his easy chair. *(So much for long ago. But, you gotta wonder what....)*

Sunday dinner at his oldest daughter Frederica's house was a ritual with Charlie. She mentioned that she saw a news article about his class reunion and asked whether he intended to attend.

"Nope. Nothing new. Samo-samo. Besides, it's a couple weeks away. There may not be enough members left by then to hold it."

She insisted, stressing that, "It'll be great fun," adding, "We'll have to do something about that suit, though...show the rest a thing or two about Charles Andrews, Esquire." All she could get was a reluctant promise to think about it.

Later that night, Charlie thought about his daughter's predictions of "great fun." and finally lost the arguments with himself for not attending. *(Besides, maybe Freddie...)*

****

The moment after Fredrica Coburn registered and walked into the meet-and-greet room at the Chandler Arms, she spotted Lou Ambers. It may've been their sixty-fifth high school reunion and Lou was now fat and bald, but there was no mistaking that foghorn voice and his "sense of humor" as he looked at her name tag.

"Fredrica! Good Golly Ned! Thoughtcha was long since dead! Great to see ya!"

"I see you're as funny and full of bull as ever, Lou. It's good to be here. How are you, anyway?"

"Still vertical, Freddie, still vertical." After a few "remember whens," Ambers enthused, "Say, there's somebody else here that don't often come to these things. C'mon, I'll take ya to see 'im." Despite her protest that she was fully capable of finding her own way around, he took her by the arm and towed her along.

Even as they approached, there was no mistaking the identity of the man facing away from them. The same shoulder-slope and the traces of the odd swirl of hair said it all. Fredrica politely attempted to pull away from Ambers, but he tightened his hold on her arm, and turned the gentleman to face them.

The word came out almost a whisper. *"Freddie."*

Before she could respond, the loquacious Ambers foghorned, "Hey Charlie! Lookit what I broughtcha! It's Freddie, your old flame. Betcher surprised. Bet you two got a lot to talk about. Go ahead. Say hello."

Neither responded, and Ambers laughed. "Just look at 'em! They're surprised all right. Go on say somethin'."

This time, Fredrica wasn't polite about freeing herself. Jerking away, she asked, "Lou, would you do me a big favor?"

"Anything, Freddie. Anything your heart desires."

"Go out and play in the traffic."

"But, I...Oh, I get it. Don't hafta have brick outhouse fall on me. You two wanna talk about things. OK, away I go." He left, only to be seen pointing them out to other classmates.

Fredrica turned to Charles. "May I have this dance?"

"The band's not playing yet Fredrica."

"No, but as long as we're going to be the main attraction, we may as well make the spectacle a big one. Come on." She took his arm and steered him toward the chairs circling the room.

Charlie was first to speak. "Well, Freddie, who'd'a thunk it. Eighty-odd years later and here we are."

"You're slipping, Charlie. It's the sixty-fifth class reunion."

"But, it's eighty-some since kindergarten. Gotcha, Freddie."

"And, you know I'll getcha back. You're right, though. Who'd'a' thunk it?" Several classmates interrupted with the usual greetings and questions. More than one of the women complimented Fredrica on her ensemble. Elsa Morningside was especially demonstrative, greeting her with, "Great stars and garters, Freddie! What the ugly-duckling of style has grown into!"

During a break, Fredrica declared, "OK Charlie, I can be as nosy as well as any other old fud here. What's been going on with you the last half-century or so? You a widower?"

"Yes, for several years. Are you?"

"No Charlie, I'm not."

"Oh? Your husband here?"

"He passed away about twelve years ago."

"But..."

"Gotcha, Chuckie-boy. You asked if I were a *widower*. I'm not. I'm a *widow*."

"I give up."

Before Charlie could begin to recount his past, more classmate greetings interrupted. Then, Fredrica remarked, "Enough of you trying to avoid the subject," then ordered," "Start talking. By the looks of that suit, you got rich like you said you would."

"No you don't. Ladies first. Tell me about your life for the past many years. Judging by that spiffy outfit, you're very well fixed. Doing anything like those wild things we planned in our when-we-grow-and-get-rich game in school have anything to do with it?"

"This old thing? Just something I threw together. As to your 'well fixed' question, how else could it have happened? For your information, during these past years, I've done several of those wild things that could account for it."

"Tell me more. Tell me all."

"There's not enough time to tell you *all* of them. I'll just tell about a few of the biggest. You may remember that I planned to swim down the length of the Mississippi. Well, of course I didn't. All sorts of regulations, you know.

"But, after all the pre-swim publicity, I was invited to the White House. The President was so impressed that he appointed me honorary Ambassador to Ireland. You may've heard.

"While I was over there, I modified some of the country's old recipes which were then adopted by the biggest restaurant chain in Ireland. As a result, I started a string of bakeries around the world.

"With the money I made from the bakeries, I started a university in India. My other endowments in this country have permitted two major universities to grant a thousand scholarships.

"Charlie, I've done so many of the things we talked about that it's really hard to pick out the biggest. I just know by that fancy suit you must've also done some great things to make out so well. Tell me about them."

"Well, you're right. I have been lucky enough to have had some interesting and rewarding experiences. But, not all were fully realized. For example, you may've heard that I *did* win the Nobel Prize for literature, but didn't get to play the lead role in the movie of my last book because I was delayed during my Mount Everest climb, leading the evacuation a village just ahead of a landslide.

"Like you, I developed a world-wide business, and a while back, I organized a foundation for developing universities. You spoke of your university contributions. Perhaps you've heard of

241

those named for me over in Norway and Sweden…Charles University? Other stuff like that, Freddie."

"Isn't it great, Charlie…us getting to realize so many of the things we planned?"

"Certainly is, Freddie. I see it's time to dine. C'mon."

****

Dinner and speeches over, Fredrica and Charles skipped the dancing and continued chatting. All too soon, the band began playing the old sentimental stuff. It was obvious that the sixty-fifth class reunion was about over.

Charlie rose. "My driver will have the limo parked right up close. Because of my fake knees, I have a little trouble getting about. I need to go out a bit before the others so I get to my limo ahead of the crowd."

"I understand fully, Charlie. My limo will probably be parked close to the front, also. We'll walk out together."

To the strains of *Good Night Sweetheart,* the "last dance" standard of long ago, Freddie and Charlie departed, holding hands. As they walked slowly down the front walk, each seemed to be about to pause and speak, but Fredrica only noted, "Looks as though both our limos are where we thought."

In the continuing silence, they walked on until Charlie announced, "Well, here are at our limos."

He turned toward her. "Freddie, I want you to know that this has been a very special night and great fun. Now that we know we live in nearby cities, maybe we can keep in touch."

"I was thinking that very same thing about keeping in touch. *And* that playing our game again *was* great fun! *And*, that I gotcha good, Chuckie boy!"

"Didn't!"

"Did!"

Charles Andrews drew silent for a bit. Then, "Frederica, in tonight's version of our old game, we both know neither one could have possibly done *all* of those things during one lifetime. But, some of the good stuff we got done might be worth talking about."

Frederica turned to him. "Charlie, for once in your life, you've said it exactly right."

A hug and their secret four-handed hand squeeze, then former bank teller Charles Andrews climbed into the nearest mini-bus, the one with **SHADY REST RETIREMENT** on its side and AFFORDABLE ASSISTED LIVING beneath. And, former secretary Fredrica Coburn entered the mini-bus behind it, the one with MERRY MEADOWS MANOR on its side.

VOICES

On the way home, Stanley Smitter was relaxed and ecstatic. There was no way on earth the police or anyone else would locate the evidence. And, he meant *ALL* the evidence as well as that back-stabber. Stanley smiled as he thought about his now-former partner. *(Wonder how that scheming clown'll get along with that other one who thought he was way smarter than me. I caught on right away what game he was up to. Didn't fool me one little bit!)*

He smiled again at the stupidity of fools who went off their rocker and did a job in a fit of passion or dope-heads looking for coke or meth money. Only those capable of meticulous planning could properly take care of business. *(I guess it takes all kinds. Oh well, home first, then the office.)*

****

As usual when turning into his driveway in up-scale suburban Maple Crest, the first thing Stanley saw was the 100-year-old maple in the rear lawn and garden area. The old snag was a continuing source of friction between him and wife Edith Ann.

Hit by lightning countless times, the ancient warrior was no more than a split top-to-bottom, 40-foot-high, half-gone eyesore. Stanley was offended every day by this one exception to the perfectly manicured grounds. This was nothing new. He hated that thing from the day they moved in almost 20 years ago. An insult to nature even then, it got worse every year.

Furthermore, Edith's reason for objecting to removing the ungodly thing was equally offensive. She wanted it left as a home for all those rat-squirrels that nested in it. "Foul little beasts," was the kindest term he used. Sitting in the Benz for a few moments staring at that blot on the landscape, he decided now was as good a time as any to have it out over getting rid of the monstrosity.

As luck would have it, Edith Anne was away for the morning. *(Probably out with other money-burning wives planning another charity event for the Lost Leopards of the Arctic or some other foolishness. Wonder what it's gonna cost me this time.)* He brightened at a second thought. *(Hey! Why not call a tree guy and get an estimate on taking down that awful ugliness out back?)*

Cold coffee and an orange juice later, Stanley glanced at his watch. *(Where the devil's the tree guy! Probably why he's hacking down trees for a living—doesn't understand the value of time.)* He went to the door and looked out. A black sedan passed slowly along, turned around and passed by again. He smiled. If his planning had been done by anyone else, it might well be a police car instead of some lost fool looking for an address.

On the fourth pass, *Kelly's Tree Service* drove in. At the door Kelly himself presented his city-issued identification and apologized, "Sorry Mister Smitter. Would'a been here sooner, but I had a little trouble findin' the place. Said you wanted an estimate on takin' down a tree?"

After closely inspecting the ID, Stanley led him around to the rear. "Don't guess I need to point out which one."

"Not hard to tell. Man, that's a really old one. Got any idea how old?"

"Not a clue. Only know it's been there much too long. How much and how soon?"

Kelly walked around the tree and named a price, adding, "Shouldn't take too long. Got a hole clean through it. It's still pretty healthy for such an old one. But, it'll only take no more'n half a day to get it down and hauled away, roots and all." He took out his schedule book. "We can do the job two weeks from today. Fillin' in the hole and puttin' down sod'll take another three hours. Wanna go ahead?"

"You sure that's your best price? Really sure?" *(Gotta watch these guys. They're all out to screw ya.)*

"Mister, if I priced it any lower, my kids wouldn't have any hot dogs in their buns."

"Well...OK, but, my wife's gonna raise a barrel of hell about the squirrels up there."

"Get that all the time. Just tell 'er you're doin' 'em a favor. Next time lightning strikes, it'll fry 'em. Besides, the little buggers'll find another tree in about ten minutes."

"Hey, good idea about the lightning! See you in two weeks."

****

On the way to his office, Attorney Stanley Smitter passed two black and white patrol cars and smiled. *(If they only knew.)*

Two blocks later, the cell sounded. It was Marie, head secretary at Smitter and Wells. "Mister Smitter, will you be in soon? Mister Wells hasn't come in and his wife is very worried. She said he was out of town yesterday and called last night saying he'd be a little late. But, he didn't come home, and she can't reach him. Do you know where he is?"

"Relax Marie. I'm sure he was just held up. I'll be there in a few minutes. We'll find him." *(Oh yeah, we'll find the incompetent sucker. I would've won that Brown vs. Smalley case if he hadn't screwed up the deposition so badly. Lucky for me I caught on so quick that he was trying to take over the practice I've worked so hard to build.)*

247

To his surprise when he arrived, a Detective McCord was waiting to see him. "Mister Smitter, we don't usually get on missing persons reports this early, but Wells' wife is climbing all over the chief. Is there anything you can tell me about where Mister Wells is? Anything at all."

"Detective, I'm as much at a loss as everyone else. All I know is that he had business upstate. A nasty divorce settlement. Done any checking up there?"

"I just got the case. I'm sure we'll check everything. Do you have any reason to think he may have just taken off? Money troubles, maybe? Wife troubles, maybe?"

"Far as I know, not a speck of anything going on with him." *(Keep on with your idiotic questions. Don't think for a minute I'm not onto you. You're out to get old Stanley. You'll just be one more that didn't.)*

The detective departed after a few more routine questions with a promise from Stanley to phone if he thought of anything to add. On the way out, he passed a stringer from TV Channel 14, *All The News All The Time*. Apparently Mrs. Wells also phoned their newsroom with her apprehensions.

Just in case the station might somehow overlook one nano-shred of a sensationalistic possibility, Homer Hardwick, nighttime anchor-to-be (in his dreams), was dispatched to garner all the gory details. He also left after getting nothing.

The afternoon wore on toward closing time punctuated by a call from Mrs. Wells every half hour or so asking for anything new and Wells' secretary asking what she should be doing. Stanley had no trouble keeping busy. The firm's biggest case of the year would begin in a few days. Since partner Wells wasn't there to help, he had to carry the entire load.

Driving home, Stanley punched on the radio. Through the mish-mash of blather, suddenly he heard, "There is little to report on missing attorney Lowell Wells of the law offices formerly known as Smitter, Bryson, and Wells, now Smitter and Wells. It appears that this firm may have suffered a second tragedy in less than a year. Last summer, the body of Benjamin Bryson was found by U.S. Coast Guard divers off the shore of Lake Michigan.

"Despite recent repeated calls to local police to obtain additional information about Bryson's mysterious disappearance, none have been returned. If viewers have any information about this case, please call the number on your screen." Stanley smiled.

****

Edith Ann met her husband at the door. "Stan, what in the world is going on! Two TV channels have been calling all afternoon about Lowell Wells being missing. And Mary Wells has called about fifteen times asking if I've heard anything. I've tried your office about ten times, but the line is always busy. What's going on, Stan? Where's Lowell?"

"Slow down Edee, slow down. You know as much as I do. There's nothing we can do. Hate to say it, but I'm not too surprised that he ran off. I haven't said anything about it, but I'm going over the books tomorrow. It seems to me that some of the figures aren't panning out."

"You mean...."

"I don't know a thing for sure. Just don't say anything to Mary. If something's out of order, we'll get it straightened out."

"My word! I never imagined..."

"Relax, it may be nothing."

While Stanley poured a double scotch, Edith continued, "That's not all that happened this afternoon. Some awful man called about cutting down our tree. He said it might take a little longer since he had to make preparations about protecting the grass and shrubs. Stan, you know how I feel about that tree. Have you made arrangements to get it cut without even asking me! If you have, you can just call him back and cancel them!"

Stanley downed another generous gulp. "Edee, I called him when I noticed some strange stuff growing on it. Didn't look like the same stuff we've seen before. I didn't want to upset you, so I called an expert to look at it. He scraped it off and took it to a lab. Turns out it's fairly common to old maples in the process of dying. Only problem is, it's a form of scale that's easily transmitted to other trees. Edee, if we don't have it removed, all the rest of the trees may go, too. I was going to talk to you tonight."

"Are you *sure*? What about the squirrels?"

"Knowing how you feel about them, I asked the man. He said something I never thought about. He said with trees that've been struck by lightning so often, it's only a matter of time till it happens again. Said we'd be doing the squirrels a favor to take out that tree. When lightning strikes again, they'll all be killed. He also said he's never seen it to fail that when he cuts down a tree with nesting squirrels, they find a new home the same day."

"Stan, that tree has been a part of our lives for a long time."

"I told the man that, and here's what he suggested. He'll save a good part and we can have something made from it to put in the house. That way, we'll have a reminder of what it's meant. He said most people have a decorator clock made. That would be good for us, too."

"You sure the squirrels would be all right?"

"Edith Ann, I wouldn't go ahead with it otherwise."

"Well...." The phone interrupted. "That's sure to be Mary Wells. What do I tell her? You want to talk to her?"

"It's best if you do. Tell her you've talked with me and everything's going to be all right."

****

With the phone calls from Mary Wells, the police coming in every other day, and the continuing news coverage, Stanley became increasingly nervous. In particular, Channel 14 tightened the pressure with suggestive implications. He tensed at any sight of a police car. Most indicative of his edginess, the weekly scotch supply dwindled ever more rapidly.

His change in behavior did not go unnoticed by his wife. "Stan, what's troubling you? You miss not having a partner to help out? Don't worry, you'll have another one pretty soon."

There was more. His answer to all of it was to pour another double and go outside. He began walking the beautifully groomed gardens just as a helicopter passed overhead. Startled, he almost dropped his drink. Could they be spying on him? He shook his head vigorously. *(Snap out of it, Smitter! What in blazes is the matter? Everything went off without a hitch. He'll never be found. Can't understand it. I had a few jitters after the first one, but they didn't last long. Now, get it together before you do something really downright stupid.)*

Stanley drained his drink and started back inside, glancing at the soon-to-be-gone old maple. *(You'll soon be one less aggravation pestering me. Just like all the others.)* One more step, and he could swear he heard a reply. He whirled, then caught himself. *(Ye Gods! Now, I'm hearing the wind and thinking a tree's talking!)*

He turned again toward the house. This time he was sure. It wasn't the wind! It *was* that confounded maple. "I may be gone soon enough, but so will you. They know what you did."

Panic-stricken, Stanley raced inside, jerked the doors closed, and leaned against them. The shuddering finally stopped, and he regained a measure of control. *(Relax Smitter, relax. All the kerfuffle stirred up by that TV outfit's getting to you. It was just the wind. What I need is a drink to calm down.)* He got to the liquor

251

cabinet before realizing he must've dropped his glass outside. No problem, he poured the triple into another one.

****

An incessant ringing awakened Stanley. Obviously, Edith Ann had already gone. It was his secretary, Marie. "Mister Smitter, the lawyers in the Fallon v Chester case will be here in an hour. Just wanted to remind you."

Stanley shook away some of the fog. "I'll be there. We're all set aren't we?"

"Yes, sir. All set."

"OK. See you." (*Marie, too? Might as well be after me. Everyone else is.*)

A quick face-rinse and shave and he was ready to leave, but he had one thing to do. That tree business last night was the last straw. He didn't need a snootful of scotch and a breeze playing tricks on him. He phoned Kelly's Tree Service.

Kelly answered from his cell. "Kelly, this is Mister Smitter. You're planning to take down a tree for us in a few days?"

"Yes sir, Mister Smitter."

"Well, there's been an emergency. Last night, my wife was out there and a big limb fell off and nearly hit her. Probably the wind. Anyway, I want that confounded tree out'a there. Can you get at it anytime today?"

"Golly, Mister Smitter, we're covered up. I don't see any way it'd be possible."

"Listen here Kelly, everything's possible. Let's don't play games. This is an emergency. What's it gonna cost to get it done today? Surely you've run into this before."

"Well, I guess I could see if my next job will OK changing his time with yours. Won't cost extra if he does."

"Good man! By the way Kelly, my wife bought that squirrel story you told me. That and a tale I told her about using part of the wood out of that old pest to make a clock. A reminder of what the tree meant to her. You know anybody that can do that?"

"This is funny. I don't know any clock makers, but I had the exact kind of thing happen before. The guy's wife wanted something made out of an old oak. A'course she couldn't tell one oak from another. We saved a slab for him to show 'er. Then he took it away, and after a few days, he went to a clock place and bought an oak one. She never knew the difference. Maybe that'd work for you."

"Great idea! Save a piece of the maple. When will you know if your next job'll go for changing his time?"

"You wanna wait a minute, I'll call him from here."

Stanley waited impatiently, but Kelly was back sooner than expected. "Mister Smitter, there's good news. We can get on the job later this morning."

"That *is* good news! Just get the tree down and out of there. Don't worry about filling the hole and laying down sod today. Say Kelley, my wife's away, but if she comes back, lather on the lard about the squirrel story. Don't say a word about a limb almost hitting her. She's still very upset."

"Gotcha, Mister Smitter. Big on the squirrel story, mum on the limb fallin'. We'll get the tree out'a there pronto and take the downed limb, too. It must'a been pretty far gone. I didn't know of much wind last night."

"Pretty far gone, all right. You don't have to take it away. I did that last night. OK Kelly, send me your bill."

"Will do, and thanks a lot, Mister Smitter."

Stanley rang off and went to his car, *(Clown'll probably charge an arm and a leg for changing the job to today. Worth it though to get that mouthy beast out of the yard.)*

253

****

After weeks of barely controllable tension, Stanley sat relaxing in the den with his only scotch of the evening, Now that the old maple was gone, the hole filled and sod laid, things were much better. It also helped that Edith Ann thought the phony clock was such a wonderful reminder of the lying brute. Then, too, Detective McCord was no longer bugging him with the same old questions about the missing partner. Chanel 14 also found other victims to persecute. Even Wells' wife stopped calling so often.

Two minutes into the news, Stanley's good feelings crashed and burned. A bit was being featured about a resort under development up north in the deep forest. It was to be a get-away-from-it-all, up-scale, complex for recharging the batteries of executive-suite types. A body had been discovered, but was as yet unidentified. "More on this as the story unfolds."

Apprehension exploded. Stanley frantically dashed to a laptop to do a map search of the area they described. He couldn't be positive, but it looked *awfully close* to a certain place he once knew where nothing would ever be found. (*What in the name of heaven could anyone in their right mind be thinking! Build a resort there? Nobody will ever go. The fools!*)

He rushed for a scotch and downed three fingers, then poured another. What to do? What to *do!* Heading back to switch to another news channel, he tripped and barely avoided crashing into a desk. From the other room, Edith Ann called out, "Everything all right, Stan?"

He corralled his thoughts enough to reply, "Yes, everthing's OK. Just tripped on the rug a little."

There was no other news about the resort. Tension, already on the launching pad, rocketed into a nearly uncontrollable orbit. The second scotch didn't help much, so he went for another. (*Careful now, you drunken idiot. One more stumble and she'll be in here whining about the scotch.)*

Violin-string taut and not knowing what else to do but wanting to stay clear of his wife, Stanley stepped out into the moonlit garden and was greeted by a freshening breeze. Even in his condition, he admired the scene. *(Like something out of a movie. With that old beast gone, it's perfect.)* He took a deep drag from his glass and walked to where the tree once stood. *(So peaceful now. Gotcha, you old bastard. Talk to me wouldja? See what it gotcha. Why don'tcha say somethin' now?)*

Glass drained, he cocked his head and listened for a reply. Hearing none, he stumbled in triumph toward the house. Four steps later, he heard it. "Soon, Stanley Smitter, soon."

Paranoia fueling panic, Stanley took two steps and went sprawling. Scrambling up and staggering on, he made it all the way to a side door and through the kitchen area into the garage, locking the door behind him.

Finally, he convinced himself it was just the wind and mastered enough composure to go back to his den. Another scotch in a still shaking hand, he slumped in his chair and thanked his lucky stars Edith had gone to bed.

****

Although boozed up, sleep wouldn't come until hours after midnight. Then it was only sporadic, interspersed with vivid visions of "missing" partners Ben Bryson and Lowell Wells. Only one-fourth awake at 9:20, he nursed coffee he somehow managed to brew. Coffee did nothing to erase his night terrors. However, switching on the three different 24/7 news channels and hearing nothing more of the discovery up north, he felt a bit better. No news was good news, but his anxiety eased only a little.

Recalling the main reason both sneaky partners had to go helped some. *(Almost from the very start, I could tell they were out to get me. There's enough people in the world going for your jugular without someone on the inside doing the same.)*

Finally dressing for work, memories of last night's garden episode added to his apprehension about the body-discovery up north. He sat on the bed and studied his shaky hands. Maybe a short scotch would steady them. It didn't, but a second short one seemed to help some. He started down the hall to the garage, passing the reminder-of-the-maple clock.

At the garage door he heard it. "Soon, Stanley Smitter, soon."

He whirled, rushed back and clawed the clock from the wall. *(I'll fix you, that's what I'll do!)* At the garage door, he hurled the offending clock out onto the floor, followed it, and kept slamming it down until it until he was exhausted. Then, he attacked the remains with a hatchet until it was in almost unidentifiable pieces. Sweeping them into a shovel, he carried them to the outdoor incinerator, tossed them in, turned on the gas, and pushed the button to ignite it. Satisfied the clock was totally destroyed, Stanley left for work with a final shot at the clock. *(Told you I'd fix you, didn't I?)*

As he drove toward the exit gate, Stan glanced at his watch. *(Ten forty. Mail's already come. Might as well pick it up.)* Window down, he reached and pulled open the mailbox. He was wrong, the mail hadn't come, but before he could close it, a voice called out, *"Very soon now, Stanley Smitter, very soon now."*

Instantly, Attorney Stanley Smitter threw the SUV into reverse, slammed it back into drive, shot forward smashing the mailbox into scrap. Then, he repeated the process before roaring off down the street.

****

Channel 14 interrupted regular programming for breaking news. "We have just received word that prominent local attorney Stanley Smitter of Smitter and Wells has died in a spectacular car crash. Witnesses report he was being pursued by police while he was speeding and dragging what may have been a mailbox. They also report that he ignored the stop signal at the intersection of Mason and Morgan streets and was struck broadside by a semi-trailer truck. A reporter is on the way and we'll have more later.

"In other news, a body discovered at a construction site in the northernmost county of the State has been identified. It is that of Harold Beecham, a hiker who may have lost his way and died from exposure. More later."

THIS HERE'S IT– LAST'A THE BREAKIN'

THIS BE CLARABELLE. CAIN'T TELL Y'ALL HOW GOOD IT'S BEEN BEIN' WITH Y'ALL FOR SOME WHILE. IT WAS SO GOOD I'M GONNA COME OVER AND THROW ROCKS IN Y'ALL'S GARDEN.

I RECKON I HAD OUGHTA 'SPLAIN THAT'S A SAYIN' AMONGST MY KINFOLK. Y'SEE, MOST'A OUR GARDENS GOT LOTS'A ROCKS IN 'EM. COMIN' OVER'N THOWIN' ROCKS *IN* Y'ALL'S GARDEN DON'T MEAN WE'LL PITCH ROCKS *INTO* IT. MEANS I'LL HEP THROW THE ROCKS *OUT'A* Y'ALLS GARDEN. SEE? IT'S A WAY'A THANKIN' FOR A FAVOR'N PROMISIN' TO DO ONE BACK.

ANYWAY, ME'N THE JUDGE WANNA GIVE YA'LL A GREAT BIG THANK YA FER SO KINDLY GOIN' ON READIN'N GUESSIN'.

ADDRESSING YOU IS THE HONORABLE JUDGE HAROLD HAND WHOM YOU MET AT THE BEGINNING OF THESE ANECDOTES. I WISH TO THANK YOU FOR SO DILIGENTLY PERUSING THESE FINE LITERARY OFFERINGS.

NOW I SHALL CALL TO YOUR ATTENTION ANOTHER MATTER. I AM RELIABLY INFORMED THAT A MEMBER OF THE LOCAL LEGAL COMMUNITY AND MY NEWEST LEGAL AIDE, MADAM CLARABELLE CADWALLADER, WILL SPEAK TO YOU AT THE CONCLUSION OF THIS SESSION REGARDING A POINT SHE WISHES TO STRESS.

"LOOK DOWN, ISAAC, LOOK DOWN!"

Now 12 years old, Isaac Mather was growing up in a fundamentalist-religion family in which a saying or rule was part of daily life. They were repeated so often that he knew most by heart and probably when they'd be quoted. Many were reserved for special situations, some for about any occasion.

"Always look before you leap," "Your sins will find you out," "Pride goeth before a fall," "Think about what other people will think," and "Brag dog's no good, hold fast is better" were only a few of a vast repertoire. A favorite often used by Isaac's father was, "Always try your very hardest to do your very best."

There were times it seemed to Isaac that the incentives for adhering to each and every rule of the day were not hearing more of them. Except for rare instances, tangible rewards were few. However, an unlikely one was attending a three-ring circus. Whether it was Hagenback and Wallace, Ringling Brothers or Cole, his mother, Ella, just *had* to attend. This year, Isaac would get to go along as a reward for "minding his p's and q's."

Circuses were Ella's only "vice." Just how this genteel farm lady developed such a passion for them was a mystery. Perhaps it was due to not having opportunities to see one as a child.

Whatever the reason, when the first advertisement appeared in the local newspaper a full six weeks before the scheduled performance, she began planning. Right away, a bit of money from selling eggs, her "special fund," would be put aside weekly for tickets. Having no automobile, she needed enough for her good friend's ticket, the widow Naomi Niedlinger, who would provide the Model "A" Ford transportation.

Two weeks before the bars of the traditional opening march, *Entrance of the Gladiators* (the "screamer" in circus terms) trumpeted forth, planning was complete. Every single item on Ella's "to do" list was checked and re-checked. Once again, she reviewed it with Naomi to be *absolutely* sure nothing was missed, including what would be in the box lunches taken along.

Merely arriving for the opening acts was out of the question. To get the full measure of pleasure, they'd arrive at the circus grounds in time to see the tent being set up and other preparations.

Everything went according to plan. No sooner had they entered the grounds, elephants were led into place to help erect the massive middle poles upon which the tent canvas was centered. Kids were allowed to stand fairly close, and being in such proximity to those immense beasts, which Isaac only saw in pictures, was indeed a tremendous thrill.

To Isaac, one of the most amazing scenes occurred when large steel stakes for anchoring the tents were driven into the ground. Assuming side-by-side positions a few feet apart, men with sledgehammers encircled a stake. At a signal, man number one raised his hammer and brought it down forcefully, generating a resounding steel-on-steel, almost musical, ringing tone.

The rest of the men followed suit, so perfectly synchronized that a hammer struck the stake every second or so. 'Round and 'round, up and down, the visually mesmerizing circle of flashing hammers created a wonderfully choreographed symphony. In no time, the stakes were driven.

The entire preparatory procedures were unbelievably efficient. Isaac later learned that Kaiser Wilhelm of Germany dispatched several military officers to observe just how circus workers did so much in such a short time. He wanted to adapt their methods for troop movements.

Once the tents were up, the three early birds walked about and saw some of the acts rehearsing their routines. Of special interest was watching the trainer put the big cats through their paces. He even came over and talked to Isaac, then invited him to join in. He declined, all the while keeping a firm hold on his mother's arm just in case the trainer persisted.

Just before one o'clock, they presented their tickets and took seats on bleachers inside the enormous tent. More than an hour before the opening act there was only a handful of other spectators, but eating the box lunches helped fill the time.

Finally, the big show began. The stands filled to capacity, the fanfare rang out and the ringmaster, bedecked in his flashy uniform, came striding in. In full theatrical baritone, he announced the opening acts for all three rings. In bounced the clowns and everything was underway.

To Isaac, it was *magic!* Each act seemed to outdo the previous one. The trapeze artists performing so high in the air without a safety net down below was particularly breathtaking. And, those riders standing upright on their circling horses–how'd they keep their balance?

Isaac's mother warned that when lady performers who wore nothing covering their "lower limbs" appeared, he was to look down when she said, "Look down, Isaac, look down." Apparently, she had no inkling that bare limbs of girls were no mystery to any grade-schooler. The chant "I seen London, I seen France, I seen somebody's little pink pants," was often heard when girls stood up on their swing seats, pumping hard to soar higher.

Isaac tried looking down, but it was awfully hard not to see the bareback riders' "lower limbs." Then, during the trapeze acts, he also tried not to, but soon learned how hard it was to keep from rolling one's eyes skyward while bowing the head. And, being seated high up in the bleachers didn't help in avoiding "lower limbs," either.

All too soon, it was over. What a day it had been! Isaac's expectations were sky-high, but today they were exceeded. His father was already home from the fields when they arrived. First his mother, then Isaac, took turns describing everything. His mother also told how she made sure Isaac looked down at the proper times.

As Isaac walked with his father to the barn to help with chores, he kept babbling about the day's events. During one infrequent pause, his father inquired sternly, "You do as your mama said? You looked down at all the right times, Isaac?"

Uh-oh. What was he gonna do! (*I gotta tell the truth—can't lie. Maybe I can pretend not to have heard.*)

No luck. His father repeated his question, louder this time.

There was no way out. Now, he was gonna catch it! What to do? *What to do!* Finally, he managed, "Father, I tried my hardest to do my very best. You always say to do that."

His father asked, "*Every time,* son?"

"Yes sir, I tried my very hardest to do my very best every single time."

They walked on. With a small smile, his father responded, "Glad to hear you tried your very hardest to do your very best."

WHAT'S IN A NAME, INITIALLY?

Occasionally, vehicles from over on the Interstate wound up in rural Taylor at **HELPFUL HARRY'S** "convenience" store (coffee, donuts, gasoline, and rest rooms). Now and then, a seedy character approached, and after an overenthusiastic greeting, attempted to hit them up driver and/or strangers for a buck or two.

Today, the name Harry Johnson used when chasing away the panhandler, "Threesy" interested the rotund passenger from the chauffeured limo. Around a donut he asked, "That his real name?"

"Nope, it's Charles–Charles Munsen. Went from *Charles* to *Maggothead,* then to *Threesy.*"

Chubby picked up another donut. "Know how it happened?"

"Takes a while to tell."

"I have the time if you do, tell away."

****

Mrs. Clara Bydel couldn't understand it. The hens all appeared to stop laying eggs simultaneously. Eggs were very important at the Bydels. Not only did the family rely on eggs as a food staple, the sale of any extra provided the wherewithal for Clara's "egg-money" jar which was set aside for discretionary spending only.

Try as hard as they might, Clara and husband Jake just couldn't figure what caused the hens to go on an egg strike. Were they upset over something? The old saying was, "A happy hen is a laying hen." They checked, but it didn't seem as though the free-roaming hens were upset about anything. They were singing up a symphony. Could it be the chicken feed? Didn't seem so. They were the usual eager eaters.

Day after day, the diminished egg count evidenced during the egg-gathering routine continued to increase both mystery and anxieties. Instead of the usual three dozen eggs, now there was a maximum of half a dozen. This was barely enough to supply the needs of the family–not even close to enough to sell. The hens weren't paying their way, and the chicken-feed bin was running very low.

Another week passed. The Bydels tried everything. Nothing worked. Would the time come when the flock would have to go? Would they be reduced to buying Leghorn eggs? With few exceptions, area farmers were now raising those skinny white chickens because of their greater egg-producing reputation. Clara's reaction was unvarying. "Not on your life!"

She wasn't done. "Pale white things! If I can't eat a wholesome brown egg, I'll do without! No wonder they lay those tasteless things–cooped up day and night!"

Just when it appeared she might be forced to eat her words, things took a turn for the better. The missing egg mystery was about to be solved.

****

The phone rang and Clara was surprised to hear that it was Mr. G.R (Got Rocks) Lewis phoning from his grocery. "I've shilly shallied 'bout callin' you, but a couple'a things've been goin' on for the past little while that're startin' to bother me considerable."

"What might they be, Mr. Lewis?"

Well, you've been bringin' me eggs for a long time, but then you stopped all of a sudden. I thought maybe I'd done somethin' to cause offense. Then, that Munsen fellow, the one I believe they call

268

'Maggothead,' started bringin' in eggs every afternoon. Like everbody else, I don't like 'im, but good eggs are good eggs.

"Still, I thought it was funny, him bringin' in eggs, since I heard he don't live at his folks anymore. I phoned 'em to see was he bringin' their eggs, anyhow, but they said not. Durin' my call, they mentioned they'd started in to raisin' Leghorn chickens, and a'course, this got me to thinkin'. He's been bringin' in *brown* eggs. Leghorns only lay *white* eggs."

Lewis passed, then continued, "Now I don't wanna cause no ruckus, but you and the McHenrys are the only ones I could think of still raisin' brown-egg-layin' chickens. And, Missus McHenry don't often sell eggs. That just leaves you. Now, like I said, I don't wanna cause no ruckus, but it does seem pretty unusual you not comin' in with eggs and Munsen startin' to bring in brown eggs.

"Question is, am I just nosin' in where I oughtn't? Just tell me, and I'll butt right out."

BINGO! Lightning-bolt clarity struck. There was the answer to the egg mystery! After reassuring Lewis that he was certainly *not* nosing in, she thanked him twice more for phoning and hung up.

Then, she began verbally eviscerating that "...*thieving Munsen scoundrel!* My husband knows he's no good, but he just *had* to hire someone to help catch up on farm work now that he had to take a job until harvest time. That *egg thief* has been working mornings the past few weeks, and this is the thanks we get! He's been sneaking into the hen-house and stealing eggs after he's finished for the day at noon, then selling them!"

If Munsen's ears were burning because someone was torching him in absentia, by now they'd be cinders. Finally, she wound down, but not before repeating some of her previous invectives—even more scalding this time around.

****

Folks had nothing good to say about Charles Munsen. From the very first day elementary school, he did everything within his power to make teachers rue the day they chose their profession and the other kids despise him.

One of a multitude of odious actions teachers took exception to was particularly revolting. On more than one occasion, he put what the horse left behind in a teacher's desk. (Friday, after school, to remain and ripen over the weekend.)

The old *Double-D*, Dirty and Dirtier, his classmates could tolerate. But, such things as cheating at marbles, stealing from lunch pails, and sneaking up behind girls to shove them into a mud puddle were over the line.

Kids hung all sorts of monikers on him before one finally stuck. First it was "Ferret-face" and later "Skunk-nose," but neither seemed to do him justice. Nobody could remember why or when he got tagged with it, but "Maggothead" seemed to have about the right ring, and "Maggothead" it remained.

When Munsen took a permanent recess from public school, Truant Officer Marvin Mahon didn't even *think* about going after him. Word went around that teachers were even talking of naming Mahon "Educator of the Year."

Munsen's post-school activities soon attracted the attention of local law. His reputation throughout the county was that if anything Munsen wanted to steal was nailed down, he'd also steal what it was nailed to. Whenever any crime short of an in-jail-for-life variety was reported, Deputy Sheriff Dorhagen's automatic first suspect was Maggothead.

Many believed an in-for-life felony was a distinct future possibility. He was arrested so often that the checker players at Fats Phillips' store made a sign for Dorhagen to hang on a cell reading, *RESERVED FOR MAGGOTHEAD MUNSEN.*

270

****

Home after work, Jake Bydel barely set down his lunch pail before Clara apprised him of Got Rocks Lewis' call. Still steaming, she repeated it, just in case he hadn't gotten the details the first go-'round. This time it ended with what was more a demand than a question. "...and just what do you intend to do about it!"

Ever the peacemaker amid touchy situations, Jake had to agree that Maggothead was indeed the source of the egg problem. Everything pointed to him, including why their dog hadn't raised a racket. He knew Munsen because he was working around the farm.

Again, Clara asked. "Just what do you intend to do about it?"

"Clara, let me sit a minute and think about it."

The silence grew heavy. Finally, he began, "Well, Munsen's pretty stupid. We not only gotta stop his thievery, we gotta be sure he don't try somethin' later on. I have an idea how to do both."

Of course, Clara was on him like a duck on a June bug to reveal what it was. He did, explaining the roles Clara and their son Tommy would play. Sounded a little scary to the boy, but exciting.

****

From the vantage point in his tree house across the driveway, Tommy could easily see the route Munsen would have to take to avoid detection when coming from his job in the west pasture to sneak alongside the long back wall of the chicken house. He'd be well concealed all the way, only exposed very briefly as he rounded the corner of it to enter.

As chief scout, Tommy was to shinny down quickly and alert his mother that Maggothead was enroute. Then, he'd shoot back up to his post and signal with a dishtowel when Maggothead actually entered the chicken house to commit his egg snatching mischief.

271

Clara's assignment was hurrying down to the chicken house to shut and bolt the door from the outside. That was it until Jake returned from his job that afternoon.

Clara asked "Is there any way for him to escape–maybe retaliate in some way?"

"No way for 'im to get out with the windows havin' those heavy mesh screens. Can't get out through those little openings allowin' the hens to go in and out, either."

"Jake, you're sure he'll be all right?"

"Certain-sure. If he needs water, he can get it from the chicken's trough, and it won't hurt 'im to go without food till I get home. Remember now Clara, no one's to go near that chicken house no matter how much racket he raises."

Everything went hunky-dory. Tommy *did* take a header in his haste to tip off his mother that Munsen was sneaking up to the chicken house. But, it didn't screw up the plan.

****

Waiting for Jake to come home from work made the next few hours seem a day long. Shouts from the locked chicken house, demanding at first, grew more plaintive by the hour. Banging on the walls also lessened in intensity as the afternoon wore on. Refraining from responding was difficult for Clara, but she managed. After all, the prisoner *was* a criminal, an egg-thief.

Jake arrived as usual shortly after 4:00 p.m. Clara was almost as eager as Tommy to see what was going to happen. But, it would have to wait. To his extreme disappointment, his dad's daily routine was going to be followed. "Soon as the cows are milked and we get supper, I'll tend to our egg thief."

Supper over, Jake instructed, "Clara, fry me up about half a dozen'a those eggs you have left and make a sandwich."

"Half a dozen? That's about all we have."

272

"There'll be plenty tomorrow. Go ahead."

Off he went with the sandwich in one hand and Tommy's baseball bat in the other, Tommy trailing just far enough behind to avoid a "Go back to the house" order. At the sound of someone at the door, the noise inside ceased. Jake ordered, "Get away from the door and stay away." Muffled agreement.

Jake went inside, and Tommy slipped up to a window. Maggothead looked considerably the worse for wear. He started to brazen it out, but had a speedy change of intent when Jake held up the bat. "You thievin' scum. One more step and you'll be buzzard bait. Now shut your big mouth and listen. I know you're hungry, so eat this sandwich. If you need water you can scoop some from the chicken's trough."

"What's in the sandwich?"

"Why, it's your favorite...eggs."

"Eggs!"

"You seem to like 'em so awful much, I thought you'd like a six-egg sandwich."

"Six!"

"Start eatin', egg thief. You're gonna need your strength for a little chore when you finish. And, if you got any ideas'a runnin' off on account'a me bein' a site older, might as well forget 'em. With that gimpy leg you got from Jim Robinson wingin' you when you were stealin' from his watermelon patch, I can still run ya down easy enough."

Jake held up the bat and shook it. "Wouldn't mind a'tall addin' a second gimpy leg."

Around a crammed-to-the-max mouthful, Munsen managed, "What chore ya talkin' about?"

"Keep eatin'."

"There's too many eggs. Can't get 'em down."

273

"Teach you to steal eggs. Take a drink'a chicken water and keep swallowin'. Speed it up, there's work to be done."

Choking down the last of the sandwich, Munsen whined, "Gonna lemme go now?"

"When you finish your chore. Pick up that shovel. Pick it up and get to work! I been meanin' to clean out this chicken house, anyway. *Start shovelin'!* And don't fret the roostin' hens.*"

"*Criminitly!* There's a ton'a that peat-moss stuff you cover the floor with'n straw mixed with chicken crap!"

"Won't take longer'n a couple hours if you hustle. Keep right at it so those hens millin' around out there—too scared to come in can go to roosting. Shovel it out through that window I just took the screen off."

It was nearly dark before Maggothead finished, mumbling curses and bellyaching all the while. Off he went for town, Jake's demand and offering ringing in his ears. "Munsen, don't ever come near here again. By the way, wanna take a few eggs along to eat later? I'll get a sack." Munsen kept walking.

Of course, Clara bombarded Jake with questions when he came back into the house, beginning with, "Any trouble? Exactly what happened? How did he take it?" Etc, etc.

Jake waved for a chance to respond, then related the entire episode ending with the saying he sometimes used to emphasize a person's ultimate reaction. "Should'a seen 'im when I opened that chicken-house door. Looked like death eatin' a cracker."

"Jake, you're *baaad!*"

****

Next afternoon, Deputy Dorhagen drove in and greeted, "Howdy Jake. I heard from Got Rocks you been havin' some egg stealin' goin' on."

"Some, I reckon. All taken care of."

"That a fact. You sure?"

"I reckon."

"Can ya give me a little hint?"

"I reckon not."

"Aw c'mon, Jake."

"Looks like I'm gonna hafta if you're gonna keep whinin'."

"Consider it a favor." Jake told him the tale, Dorhagen smiling and chuckling.

****

Happy Harry Johnson's corpulent customer washed down the last of his fourth donut with a second coffee and responded, "Quite a funny tale all right, but how does it explain how that fellow you called 'Threesy' got that name?"

"Well, a'course the tale was too good for Deputy Dorhagen to keep to himself. When the tale first got around, folks started callin' Charles 'Maggothead' Munsen 'Chicken Crap Charlie.' But before long, all three words got too much to use in conversation, so they got to callin' 'im just 'Three-C.' After a while, even *Three-C* got easier as only *Threesy*.

The obese stranger thought a bit before responding, "Odd custom—forming a nickname using the first letter of another name or nickname. Never heard of it. Common around here, is it?"

"I reckon lots'a places. Never heard it in school? Just where'd you go to school?"

"I didn't attend a public or private school. Mother hired a tutor for my sister and me."

"That could accounts for you not hearin' about it before."

"Don't get it, but what's that got to do with anything?"

"Nothin' maybe. By the way, tell me your name again."

"It's Stark—Frederick Allison Theodore Stark."

275

MARKERS MARK

Kenny Marshal hated the kid. Always had. Even before he was born, Kenny hated him. When Alice Ann told him she was pregnant, he began hating him. He tried to get her to "do something" about it, but she refused, saying maybe having a baby would be good for both of them. She was wrong. It only made things worse.

From the start, Kenny felt that the kid was to blame for *everything*. Money was tight, and he needed *everything*. Stupid kid was dumber than a box of rocks. Even after several wallopings for the same screw-up, he never learned a thing. Locking him in the closet all day didn't teach him a blamed thing, either.

Kenny said the kid's stupid behavior wasn't limited to home. In the first grade, he was nothing but a jerk. The same since. The school called so often that neither he nor Alice Ann paid attention to them anymore. The truant officer had their number on speed dial. Recently, the Juvy cops were on his and Alice's butt about the kid's shoplifting and other mischief. Little clown was only ten and already a thief. "Oh yeah, the kid's a born loser."

****

When beer-buzzed Kenny arrived after last-call at the Hooty-Owl tavern, Alice Ann was waiting to tick off the day's news. The cops had a report from school that the kid showed signs of physical abuse and were asking lots of questions. Court actions were a possibility. If the report proved correct, the kid would be placed in a juvenile facility. Charges could also be filed against them. Children's Protective Services would be coming soon.

The problem was temporarily solved by moving to another state the following weekend. But, only a few days passed before local law came pounding on their door about the kid. Alice Ann was beside herself and put her foot down. She wasn't gonna let that brat spoil her life anymore. For once, Kenny agreed with her. Clearly, it was time to take care of things.

****

In mid-afternoon when Johnny Marshal came out of the restroom at the roadside rest park, he froze. Where was dad or mom! Where was the car his dad borrowed for the trip! Very street-savvy for a 12-year-old, Johnny displayed no panic and walked the length of the parking area. Maybe dad moved the car. But, there was no sign of it or his parents. OK, they'd figure out pretty quick that he wasn't along and come back. But, they didn't.

****

After an hour, Johnny's belief that his parents' would return was slowly being replaced by growing anxiety attempting to take over. However, he employed a protective strategy developed during past experiences with his father and others. He immediately retreated into a great sense of calm any time he faced a threatening event or situation. Accompanying this today were the sprouting seeds of what would become a life-long, ever-present, rage.

Johnny carefully considered his predicament. He could go to an attendant, but the chances were they'd only call the cops. Past encounters with the cops, however minor, made him wary.

Distrustful of all strangers, Johnny avoided contact with them, so explaining his situation to one was out of the question. They'd call an attendant who'd call the law.

Sometimes contact with a stranger couldn't be avoided. On his second tour of the roadside park, a uniformed attendant spotted the same kid sitting by himself and paused to ask some questions. He was especially interested in how he got all those bruises on his arms and that cut over his eye.

He went on his way when the kid told him he'd been in a car accident and his parents were in the johns. The next trip around, the kid was gone, and the attendant gave it no more thought. Nor did he mention the incident to the second-shift attendant when he came on duty.

In spite of Johnny's protective calm, desperation reared its ugly head higher as the day wore on. Another demon he couldn't ignore also began competing with calmness. Gnawing hunger.

To avoid further inquiries, Johnny walked along with other families, looking as if he belonged. On one of his many trips, he passed a family preparing food and commented, "Boy, that really looks good."

They gave him a sandwich and started to ask him a question, but he thanked them and hurried off, explaining that he had to get back to his parents.

On his way to a distant table, he passed a tour guide feeding coins into a soft drink machine and placing the sodas on an adjoining table for the dozen clients milling about. They came up one short. It went well with Johnny's sandwich.

Hunger partially satisfied, Johnny Marshal's survival instincts took over once again. It was time to get really serious about all his problems. What about food? What about sleeping out here in the open? What about tomorrow? Where was he, anyway? Hitchhiking was out. Who'd pick up a kid? Even if they did, bad things could happen or they'd turn him in. As twilight approached, he briefly considered hiding in the trunk of a car, but it'd probably be locked. Besides, they'd do the same as the others.

On and on he went, each thought shoving him closer to panic.

Even a smart kid of 12 couldn't see his way out. Just as panic was about to take over completely, a big yellow solution drove into the rest park.

****

Veteran Camp Silver Springs bus driver, Max Turner knew when the kids got quiet, probably only a couple things were responsible. One, they were getting sleepy. No chance. Way too early–only around eight. They were about halfway home from their field trip to the city's museums. No doubt it was the second reason, potty-break time. He pulled into the next rest park followed by the second Silver Springs busload of field trippers.

From a spot well back in the trees, a non-camper observed the action, and a light flashed on. Quickly, Johnny moved to the rear of the restroom building, then casually rounded it and mingled with the hundred or so scattered pre-teeners. None appeared to notice just another Camp Silver Springs summer-camper.

Fervently, Johnny hoped there would be an extra seat on the second bus. It mattered not that he hadn't the slightest idea where it was going. At least it would be away from this now nearly vacant place. Looking neither right nor left, he joined the others when driver Turner sounded the "all-aboard" horn.

To his great relief, there were three empty seats near the rear. He chose the one nearest the window. Another couple hours and the chatter lessened. Johnny's pretended sleep became reality. After what seemed only minutes, he was awakened by renewed chatter and the bus being bounced about on a bumpy road.

Suddenly alert, Johnny saw the others taking down overhead belongings. Obviously, they were near wherever this Silver Springs place was. Must be back in the woods over a rough road. Who cared? At least it was away from that place where his dad left him to die. Growing rage flared.

****

Twenty-four-year-old Johnny Marshal lay waiting amid the shrubbery for the stranger he met at the Phoenix bar last night. This one was a bit different. Most of the time, he didn't meet them, just encountered them accidentally. It mattered not. The guy was just one more to be dealt with.

As usual, the lurking rage burned white-hot as Johnny relived the year, month, day, hour, and minute it became his destiny to see that no one looking like his father would ever do the same awful things to another boy. They were all alike.

His target was just leaving the bar. Johnny was about to squeeze off a shot from his spot across the parking lot but abruptly lowered the weapon. And, not one instant too soon. A patrol car rounded the corner. Now, he'd never have another chance at this one. He had to move on early next morning.

Oh well, there were plenty more who looked the same as his dad and would do the same things to their kid. He'd just have to wait till the next one came along. Waiting only added to the satisfaction later, anyway. Lately, though, between times the satisfaction was shorter and the burning rage came back sooner.

Yeah, he'd just have to deal with waiting till the next one. Sometimes it took a fair amount of time to find others. Others like those up there in Montana and Washington. Frisco, too. They couldn't all be like Portland's and that other one he couldn't remember just where. After he headed his rig east on Interstate 10, he'd take a look around as soon as he dropped off his load at the mid-west terminal.

****

Passing the front gate upon finishing the full eight-year stretch with no time off for good behavior, departing con number 7768212 looked up at the guard tower and gave the old one-finger salute, a gesture so common that the guard barely noticed. Besides, he'd get his chance later. Most of them were soon back inside.

Eight years gives plenty of time to plan. Those other fools could talk all they wanted about going straight, he knew exactly what and how he was going to get a permanent address on easy street. He and a recently paroled short-timer were going into the major-chain business. Who had more money on hand at any given time? Oh sure, there'd be lots of security around, but good planning and a quick in-and-out would take care of that.

First things first. What he needed right away was a drink of good booze to wipe out the taste of that rotgut they managed to brew inside. He'd been thinking about it all day, but it was late afternoon before all the paperwork was finished. Later still, he neared town and went looking for the closest bar. He had the lousy twenty bucks they doled out to each guy when sending him on his way. That, plus what he hadn't blown on meth of the peanuts he earned working in the laundry would get him by.

****

The last leg of the trip to the mid-west terminal was pretty boring, but even though it was past 8:00 p.m., Johnny Marshall arrived in good spirits, feeling rested. Unlike some, he didn't use uppers and downers to keep rolling. Increasingly, the only stimulation needed was thoughts of completing another mission.

After checking his load in, he registered at the Trucker's Rest, then showered and shaved. Another half-hour and he was on his way toward town in a rented car. Just in case he was lucky enough to happen upon another one, he took along a sniper rifle just like the others he always wiped clean and left behind. Doing that and wearing latex gloves always worked even if they found the rifle.

Having been in the area so many times, he was soon at his favorite bar, the BIDE-A-WHILE, set well back in the trees just outside of town. At this hour, the only seat available was at the end of the bar. He sat and ordered his customary beer. As he waited for it, he looked up and down the bar. Halfway along, he stopped as if struck a sharp blow. Could he be that lucky! Were his eyes fooling him in the dim light? He rubbed them and looked again. They *weren't* fooling him! There sat a guy who was the absolute spitting image of his father!

Blinding rage exploded. It was all Johnny could do to hold himself in check. Carefully, very carefully, he finished his beer and ordered another. Only part way into his fourth, he observed his target counting out what appeared to be the last of his change. Was he getting ready to leave? Rage still barely under control, Johnny set down his beer, left twenty bucks on the bar and hurried out. No way was this one going to get away with abandoning his son by the side of the road after beating him all his life!

****

Chief Inspector Imhoff was incredulous. "You telling me one had no ID and the other one's ID was phony?"

"Yep, Chief. The one offed right outside that dump next to the city limits didn't have any ID on 'im. The one we found just at the far side'a that big woods surroundin' the bar had the phony. No idea what he was doin' in there. Maybe drunked up and takin' a leak. Was headin' back across the road to his car when the Buick took 'im out."

Any scoop on a motive for the shooter?"

"Nothin' yet, Inspector. Early yet, though."

"Detective, first thing tomorrow, see that DNA samples get sent off to the lab. We got a new arrangement with 'em to do rush jobs. Be sure that's called to their attention. Meantime, we'll just hafta keep both of 'em on ice." He smiled at his analogy and added, "OK, keep on detecting, detective. And lemme know if you get lucky and stumble onto something."

****

The phone rang on Inspector Imhoff's desk. "Imhoff here."

"Inspector, this is George Merkins at the DNA lab. Any reason for the funny stuff? Trying to test us out or something?"

"What'n blazes you talking about? Drunk on the job already this morning, George?"

"*Funeeee,* Inspector! Those samples of the two wipe-outs you sent us? Well the first one's in the data base as Kenneth Marshal. But, get this! He got out of the pen the same day he caught one."

"Well, how about that! Didn't last long. Could be someone was just waiting."

"There's more, Inspector."

"Pretty interesting so far. You have something better?"

"Hold onto your hat. The other one's his son."

"Holy Ned! His son! You sure'a that?"

"Sure as sure can be. DNA markers don't lie."

"Is that ever hard to believe! They didn't look one little bit alike. Their features are totally different and the older one has black hair. The one you're calling his 'son' is a blond."

RIO WHAM BAM

In the board room of New York based **AMALGAMATED INDUSTRIES**, the weekly meeting of top officers was in progress. From CEO Jacob Meriweather's demeanor, it was obvious he wasn't a happy camper. "As you have seen by the last three analyses, there are numerous problems with production at the plant in Rio De Janeiro. It's never met projections for the first year of operation, and now it's dropped even more.

"Something's gotta be done to fix it, *and right now!* I'm sending two of you down there this week to see up and close what's needed to get things going."

He made a quick eye-to-eye sweep around the long table. In the silence, there was considerable shifting about as they waited for the next shoe to drop. All of them played roles in the Rio expansion and knew all about the disappointing production reports. Who might be under the gun? Who was he going to send?

"In the absence of enthusiastic volunteers for the job, I'm sending Jeff Winston, Vice-President for Development, and Emery Nelson, V.P. for Personnel." The others relaxed and breathed a mental sigh of relief.

Smiling, Merriweather added, "They already knew they were going, of course, but I couldn't resist a little fun watching the rest of you wiggle around hoping it wouldn't be you that'd be jerked out of the lap of luxury for a month." Forced chuckles all around.

Additional business concluded, Winston and Nelson went with Merriweather to his office for a final briefing. Instructions finished, the boss concluded with, "Bring me some good recommendations and a little of that Rio Wham Bam I've heard so much about. Always wanted to try it. I'm not too old to have a go."

****

During the first hours of the flight to Rio, the two company fast guns went over the production problems plaguing the newest factory in the world-wide Web of AMALGAMATED INDUSTRIES.

Finally Jeff Winston snapped shut his laptop and declared, "Emery, every which way I look at it I see the same thing. The root of the lack of production is not as much a personnel problem as it is one of a completely dysfunctional raw materials procurement snafu. Whataya think?"

"That's exactly my diagnosis, Doctor Winston. Long treatment period you think?"

"Not long at all. Here's what I suggest."

Nelson outlined a program to which Winston responded, "Once again proving great minds run on the same track, I agree completely with your thinking."

Winston continued, "Okey doke. Now, with the trifling job taken care of, let's get on with the important mission."

"That is?"

"Do you not recall the boss giving a direct order to bring back some Rio Wham Bam?"

"Jeff, you think he was serious? You believe the stories about that stuff being the world's most powerful aphrodisiac? I know lots'a guys have heard about it since they were kids, but I thought it must be just talk. You know exactly what is it and how it works?"

"Don't know if the stories are true or much about it. A couple guys at the club were bragging that they got hold of some and the

KID SLICK

This morning, young Cliff Peterson was about to begin his very first job, a clerk at the Apex Coal Mine company store. His brief orientation was a lecture by the manager on company policy combined with a list of rules. The usual stuff. The customer is always right. Clerks are expected to work hard and not carouse around. Clerks must get along with the other clerks. Clerks are expected to be at work fifteen minutes before the store opens at 6:00 a.m. and fifteen minutes after it closed at 6:00 p.m.

Finally, the company treats you right if you treat it right. Benefits were pay, a room over the store, plus breakfast and supper down the way at the Dew Drop Inn.

That was it except that the newest clerk had a "special responsibility" and there was a company bonus plan. Cliff was tossed an apron and told to go to work. He already knew about many of the rules, No so, the "special responsibility" and the weekly bonus items.

The extra chore he inherited as the newest clerk was interesting but didn't seem too tough. The arrival of the morning and afternoon trains was of major importance in town, usually called the "coal camp." Mail delivery, supplies transferred to north and south trains, and passenger business was routine, but there was more to the trains' stopover. They were the high social events of the day, and everyone who could possibly arrange it was there.

Cliff's "special responsibility" was to remain on duty at the store on the small chance a customer might come in during the train's arrival. Everyone else trekked on down to the depot located about a football field away.

The explanation of the weekly bonus plan was simple. The clerk who took in the most money during the week got the bonus. After closing time on Saturday, the manager assembled the clerks, reiterated a few rules, then paid out a cash bonus to the winner.

Cliff was warned that he probably wouldn't be in the running for quite a while, he being so new. He replied that he understood, but thought (*Newest clerk or not, I'll get that bonus soon enough!*)

****

Cliff's first day began routinely. Then, about 8:30, he looked out and saw two men carrying a door down the street. That wasn't so unusual, but what they carried and how they carried it was. They held the door horizontally as they might've done with a stretcher.

Matter of fact, that's exactly what they were using it for. A man was stretched out on it. Stretched out and not looking so good, either. Looking very much the worse for wear, he was. Maybe the brownish looking stuff all over his shirtfront had something to do with that.

Cliff rushed back to the small glassed-in-island office in the rear. "Hey! Two fellas are out there are carrying a man on a door! *Looks like he's been hurt real bad!*"

The manager glanced up, then continued with his paperwork as he talked, "Yeah, he's a federal revenue agent. Ever since the guvment got the plumb dumb idea they're gonna put on a big drive to shut down moonshinin', several'a them agents they sent down here come to no good end.

"Folks didn't pay much mind when the damfool guvment started movin' in on the other counties 'round here to dry 'em up. But, since they're talkin' 'bout comin' into *this* here county, most everbody's taken notice and let it be known they're payin' attention to things now. Real *close* attention, y'all might say."

"You're not gonna do somethin' 'bout the man on the door?"

"Nothin' I kin do. Somebody's already doin' 'bout all a'body kin. The guvment kin stop sendin' agents down here to keep meddlin' in other folks' business, that's what'll help. Y'all are deep in 'shine country, son. Don't tell me y'all don't know 'bout 'shine. I know they got it 'round your home place, too. It's a natural act. It's a natural act everwhere."

The manager paused to transfer some figures, then added, "Ain't good to mess with nature. Makin' 'shine's as natural as things git. God wouldn't let mash ferment iffin wasn't natural. Nope, can't tell what'll happen when ya go to mess with nature."

Cliff did indeed know about moonshine. Everyone back home did. Probably no one in the whole state who didn't know about it and had probably tried it. He even did so once along with his pals.

Needles shot up and down his neck, and for a second, he thought his teeth would clamp shut on the jug. Talking with his buddies about it being "good stuff" was fun he supposed, but all things considered, they didn't sound too convincing, either.

****

The morning train came and went without incident. Cliff supposed the poor ventilated federal man was shipped off to the hospital or undertaker. He never learned the outcome of the agent's "messin'" with nature.

He continued "minding the store" during each train's stopover, all the while thinking of plans for winning the weekly bonus. With no one coming into the store, it didn't take long to see it might be a wee bit more difficult than he first figured. He hadn't taken in a dime for the company when the trains were at the depot.

Even when the trains weren't there, no matter how much effort Cliff put forth to be of service, customers almost always wanted to be helped by another clerk, including the kid who only wanted to buy a penny peppermint stick. Even local kids leaned to watch an "outsider" a bit before accepting him as trustworthy.

Six weeks passed, and Cliff remained shut out of the bonus. Customers only went to him if the others were busy. He thought he heard a snicker or two from the veteran clerks each week.

****

This afternoon, it was the same old routine. At a quarter to three, the other clerks began taking off their aprons, preparing for the train stopover. Once again, Cliff would tend the store by himself, but what good would it do? There wouldn't be any customers, anyhow.

The others left, and it grew quiet. Cliff puttered around, killing time until the train departed. Amidst rearranging this and that, sweeping the already clean floor, and more rearranging, the hanging doorbell above the door jangled as two customers walked in. *Glory Hallelujah! Miracle of miracles!* Now he'd take in some money for the company and be on his way to the bonus. Bustling over, he gave them his best, "Afternoon gentlemen. Can I be'a help to y'all?"

Neither answered. Instead, the tall one with the jet-black beard stayed near the front door, looking up and down the street. Then the short chunky one walked toward the back room, and Cliff became a little nervous. He eyed the two. *(Rough lookin' pair, 'specially Blackbeard. But then, everybody else 'round here is pretty rough lookin', too.)*

His "little nervous" became "very nervous" when the one at the front asked, "Anybody upstairs or in the basement? Anybody 'round 'cept y'all?"

Cliff felt his neck hair elevate, and his throat throttled back on its ability to swallow, but not only because of what the fellow said.

When he turned back toward him, Cliff spotted the handle of big hog-leg revolver sticking out of his pocket.

It looked a lot like a stickup, all right. Good time for it too, with everyone at the train station. A trickle of sweat inched down Cliff's back. Just as he was about to say something, a voice from behind him inquired, "Y'all got very much sugar in stock today?"

The company's newest clerk nearly levitated! He hadn't heard Blackbeard soft-shoe up behind him. Shock, a suddenly dry mouth, and a constricted throat prevented an answer. Cliff's first rational thought was, *(They're gonna rob the company, and this jughead wants to know how much sugar we got on hand?).*

The sugar question was repeated. Cliff finally managed a bit of saliva. "Ssh-ssh-ssshugar?"

"Yeah."

(Sugar! Not money?) Things were so completely daffy that Cliff didn't respond.

The bearded one grumbled, "Y'all deef? We'uns wants'ta buy three hundert pounds'a sugar."

"Three hundert pounds," his short partner echoed.

(Buy! Did he say 'buy!') Cliff may've been scared nearly speechless, but quickly realizing how far so much sugar would take him toward the bonus smeared his fears into faint smudges.

****

Before Cliff could spring into action, the front door exploded open. Blackbeard whirled, and Shorty sprang forward. In a flash, two very large and loud-talking agents of Messrs Smith and Wesson, calibers .44, were looking eyeball to eyeball with the intruder. Cliff gulped, probably for two reasons. There was going to be a shooting, and that was bad enough. Worse still, there went the big sugar sale.

Blackbeard lowered his revolver. "Oh, it's you, Charlie. Whataya want?"

Cliff's breath whistled out in relief. Obviously, they knew the new "customer." There might not be a shooting after all.

The newcomer was nearly breathless. *"Good Lordamighty! Somethin' awful's just happened! Noah Miles Hinshaw jist got offin the train. He's headed right this'a way!"*

Cliff couldn't believe what transpired next. The two hardcases looked as though they might become melting blobs of jelly and ooze down all over the floor. Eyes bulging and lips quivering, their arms fell to their sides, guns dangling. Blackbeard managed, *"By Jehosiphat!* How'd he know we was gonna be here right now?"

"Reckon it's plain enough. Somebody's done tipped 'im off y'all got them stills up yonder, and you'd be in here today when the train come in. He's gonna grill ya to find 'em. Whataya gonna do? Kin ya make a run fer it out the back way through the woods?"

"Ain't no way we kin make it a'foot to the team in broad daylight. It's hitched way up yonder in a maple thicket. What'll we do! *What'll we do!"*

****

Cliff knew why the mere mention of Noah Miles Hinshaw could inspire such fear in the hearts of the two gunslingers–especially if they were helping God along with fermenting a little mash. Hinshaw was the most notorious and feared revenue agent in the history of the sport. Oh yeah, about everyone both north and south of the Mason-Dixon line knew of Noah Miles Hinshaw.

Suddenly, a great number of things became clearer to Cliff. Then, it didn't take long to guess why the two gentlemen wanted to buy so much sugar. It takes sugar to make moonshine. From the amount they wanted, these two must be some of the biggest "white lightning" entrepreneurs in the State.

Other things fell quickly into place. For instance, the new law mandating stiff sentences for certain citizens caught with handguns.

Many said it was passed just to help get at the moonshiners. That must be why these two were so terrified. The world's greatest 'shine hunter come to blot out one of the last of the really big 'shine centers in the State, and there stood two of the kingpins with "Roscoes" stashed in their "overhalls."

With his knowledge of 'shine scoundrels, Hinshaw would no doubt recognize these two on sight. So, even if he hadn't caught them at a still, he'd search them anyway and nail them for carrying guns, then grill them to learn the whereabouts of their stills. It certainly looked as though he would be getting more headlines.

****

For a second, Cliff thought that maybe the distillers would try to shoot their way out, but then he saw what the soon-to-be-prisoners saw. About five armed deputies were trailing along in Hinshaw's wake.

Shorty began to make funny sounds, and Blackbeard snapped, "Shut yer yappin' face, Melvin. We'uns is caught, so let's don't give that big-eared divil the pleasure'a seein' any snivelin'." Cliff thought, *(Melvin! A famous moonshiner named Melvin?)*

Under a full head of steam, Noah Miles Hinshaw closed to within 100 feet of the store. On he strode, the juices of the righteous flowing in the craggy old bloodhound.

Melvin sniveled a final snivel. "Mebbe we kin hide these here pistols somewhere in this here store. Or, mebbe if'n we jist stick 'em under our shirts, he won't see 'em."

"Won't be no help to us, Melvin. He'll search us'n everwhere else in here."

****

Funny thing about decisions affecting life. Often, they're made on the spur of the moment. Later, it's nearly impossible to explain why someone acted as they did. Now was one of those times for

Cliff. He was about to do something that would dramatically change things.

In another twenty seconds, Revenue Agent Hinshaw would be up the steps and through the door. Out of the blue, Cliff extended both hands to the dazed and doomed duo. "Gimme y'all's pistols, boys!" Meekly, they quickly complied.

The old still smasher was on the porch as Cliff whirled and rammed each well-polished weapon deep into a big barrel of pinto beans. Just as he jerked out his hand and smoothed the beans, the doorbell clanged and Noah Miles Hinshaw charged in.

****

Noah Miles felt *gooood!* There stood Melvin and Percy Smith. *(Percy! A moonshiner named Percy?)* Hinshaw recognized them instantly. He already knew they had stills, in the hills somewhere around, and from their reputation, they just *had* to be packing pistols. He just *knew* it!

"Well howdy, gentlemen. I come all this way down here representin' the legal law of the United States of America jist to meet up with y'all. Looks like we both done picked a fine day for it, ain't we?" He was enjoying this, but they weren't. "Reckon y'all know why I'm here, don'tcha? It's to rid up this here county'a the likes of sneaky, *slimy-snake* lawbreakers such as yourselves." Noah was never much for beating around the bush. Melvin and Percy stood limply, stricken mute.

Hinshaw was so thrilled with his stage that he began hamming it up. Pulling out a huge pearl-handled, nickel-plated revolver and circling them slowly, he advised, "Now, you knotheads surely ain't gonna be so all-fired jackass-stupid as to try to slow me down in my work, are ya? Jist save us both lots'a time 'n take me out to your stills so's ya can get on with your punishment.

"Y'all know I'm gonna find 'em, anyway. It'll jist go worse if I don't get no cooperation." He brandished his revolver, then holstered it under his duster once he saw it had the desired effect. The two miserable creatures before him were so terrorized that Hinshaw was forced to ask them about the stills again.

Since it appeared Hinshaw was going to talk and not shoot them on the spot, Blackbeard recovered somewhat, "What stills would that be, Mister Hinshaw?"

Noah *despised* insolence from lawbreakers. He roared into Percy's face, ***"Don't gimme no sass!"***

Both culprits recoiled, but managed to somehow hold their ground after falling back a step. "Ain't got no stills, Mister Hinshaw," Melvin offered.

"Well now, ain't that interestin'. They's stills all right. Big ones, I'd venture, and I'm gonna find 'em. I *never* miss. *Everbody* knows that. Anyways, I got you conivin', suck-egg-dogs, red-handed. I know y'all gotta be packin' pistols. We'll just take care'a that little matter first. You'll get five to ten for that alone!" He pulled out his revolver. "Now hand 'em over!"

In chorus: ***"Ain't got no pistols!"***

"Horse dabble! Grab hold'a them skunks, boys. We'll find their shootin' irons soon enough. They got 'em. You can betcher life on it. None'a these low-life's can live without 'em."

****

Noah Miles and his merry men frisked the pair and found no weapons aside from fearsome pocketknives, which didn't count. Then, they went over about every square inch of the store looking for the weapons he *knew* were hidden somewhere.

By then, the clerks returned and stood about in awe of the renowned revenuer. When the manager determined what was going on, he called Cliff aside and asked whether he knew about any guns. Cliff shrugged and played dumb. This wasn't too difficult, considering his panicky second thoughts about what he did upon witnessing Hinshaw in action.

After another round of searching with no results, Hinshaw stormed and raged at fate in general and the Smith brothers in particular. He bellowed every threat of dire consequences known to man and added a few creations of his own. Percy and Melvin had the good sense to keep their mouths shut, and pretty soon there was nothing Hinshaw could do but deliver one last volley and his personal promise about their sure-fire fate.

"You two scalawags may think y'all put one over, but I'll *D-double-damn personal promise* y'all that you two **slimy, miserable, low-down, yella bellied weasel-dabbles** are both gonna be in jail **ferever** and this D-double-damn county'll be dryer 'n spit in the fiery pit after I find your stills. 'Fore I leave here, too. This here *illegal, sinful, Godless* 'shinin's gonna stop ferever'n you're gonna rot in jail! ***Hear me? ROT… FEREVER!*** I tell both'a you *and **all*** them thinkin' they kin hep sorry shiftless skunks, too." Cliff's eyes glazed over.

Hinshaw bellowed some more and finished, "I wanna tell y'all agin, I d-double-damn garantee it personal…***personal!*** So, no matter how long it takes, I'll get all'a ya and your kind!"

Still-smasher Hinshaw roared out in the state of pious indignation of a good man temporarily thwarted in his intentions of right-doing. (Thwarted big-time in the old ego, too.)

The Smiths left soon after, no doubt to partake of healthy portions of their own product. Cliff stood rearranging the same horse harness until the manager asked his newest clerk, "Since y'all've rearranged the same harness till two sets'a reins are about wore out, wouldja like to start on the bridles?"

Not much more happened except the news that one or two of the Smith "cousins" who ratted them out to Hinshaw left the area.

Talk was it would be an extended journey. Cliff was standing around, not selling enough to pay his keep, and he thought the manager was getting nervous about it. Either that or Hinshaw's repeated visits to inquire about the pedigree of employees.

****

A few days later, things took a sudden upward turn for Cliff. Hinshaw let up on the manager about the gun episode being an inside job. With a "D-double-damn" personal promise to return and catch all the moonshiners for sure, he left on the morning train to look for whisky farmers elsewhere.

The same afternoon a customer, rough-looking even for these parts, walked in and asked for Cliff. He hadn't seen the man before, and here he was asking for *him!* The other clerks nearly had a stroke, and the store came down with a case of instant quiet.

Cliff rushed over. "Yessir, how can I be'a service, sir?" In his eagerness, the rookie clerk caused the man to take a step back.

He passed the time of day with a wildly curious Cliff until the normal noise level returned and then inquired, "Figger y'all might sell me 'bout ten scoops'a pinto beans? And kin y'all put 'em in this here bean bag'a mine?"

Well, it didn't take a brick outhouse to fall on Cliff to enlighten him as to what was going on. The damning evidence was still in the bean barrel. He was so scared that he left both guns there, hoping to sneak them out during a train stopover and hide them in the woods.

But, each time he lost his nerve, and every passing day added to his anxiety. The barrel was nearly half empty. It seemed everyone wanted pinto beans lately, and he had to shove the weapons deeper into them almost daily.

"Yessir, I can put the beans in y'all's bag. Just gimme it." Cliff somehow got between the beans and the other clerks and managed to scoop out the now grimy and dusty guns without spilling any. "Here ya are, sir. I'd be pleased to help if there's anything else I can do for y'all."

"Reckon ya'all could sell me fifty pounds'a flour if'n you're a mind to fetch it out to my wagon yonder. Cain't do no carryin', gotta bad back."

Cliff hesitated. The guy looked hale enough. Was he up to something? Maybe something about the condition of the guns? The heavily-bearded flour buyer eyed him intently. Cliff swallowed hard. "Be more 'n happy to." After paying, the customer followed Cliff shouldering the flour to the wagon, apprehension mounting with every step.

****

The manager may've noticed a thing or two, but kept them to himself. Things like how, as a light sleeper, every once in a while from his living quarters in the rear of the store, he heard a whippoorwill calling during the wee hours after midnight.

And, how just after that, it sounded like one of the clerks headed very quietly down the stairway outside their rooms over the store as if on the way to the privy.

And then what sounded like a team and wagon moving every so quietly out back by the storage shed.

And, how much extra sugar he needed to order lately.

And how (smiling), (*Some folks say sugar's used in makin''shine.*)

And, how Cliff's cash drawer was extra full the day following the "whippoorwill."

And how the other clerks had taken to calling Cliff "Kid Slick" when he began winning the weekly bonus so often.

(*Well, reckon I might could investigate. But later. Lots later.*)

"You're not gonna do somethin' 'bout the man on the door?"

"Nothin' I can do. Somebody's already doin' 'bout all a'body can. The guvment can stop sendin' agents down here to keep meddlin' in other folks' business, that's what'll help. Y'all are in deep 'shine country, son. Don't tell me y'all don't know 'bout 'shine. I know they got it 'round your home place, too. It's a natural act. It's a natural act everwhere."

The manager paused to transfer some figures, then added, "Ain't good to mess with nature. Makin' 'shine's as natural as things get. God wouldn't let mash ferment if it wasn't natural. Nope, can't tell what might happen when ya mess with nature."

Cliff did indeed know about moonshine. Everyone back home did. Probably no one in the whole state who didn't know about it and had probably tried it. He even did so once along with his pals.

Needles shot up and down his neck, and for a second, he thought his teeth would clamp shut on the jug. Talking with his buddies about it being "good stuff" was fun he supposed, but all things considered, they didn't sound too convincing, either.

****

The morning train came and went without incident. Cliff supposed the poor ventilated federal man was shipped off to the hospital or undertaker. He never learned the outcome of the agent's "messin'" with nature.

Cliff continued "minding the store" during each train's stopover, all the while thinking of plans for winning the weekly bonus. With no one coming in, it didn't take long to see it might be a wee bit more difficult than he first figured. He hadn't taken in a dime for the company when the trains were at the depot.

Even when the trains weren't there, no matter how much effort Cliff put forth to be of service, customers almost always wanted to be helped by another clerk, including the kid who only wanted to

299

buy a penny peppermint stick. Even local kids leaned to watch an "outsider" a bit before accepting him as trustworthy.

Six weeks passed, and Cliff remained shut out of the bonus. Customers only went to him if the others were busy. He thought he heard a snicker or two from the other clerks each week.

****

This afternoon, it was the same old routine. At a quarter to three, the other clerks began taking off their aprons, preparing for the train stopover. Once again, Cliff would tend the store by himself, but what good would it do? There wouldn't be any customers, anyway.

The others left, and it grew quiet. Cliff puttered around, just killing time until the train departed. Amidst rearranging this and that, sweeping the already clean floor, and more rearranging, the hanging doorbell above the door jangled as two customers walked in. *Glory Hallelujah! Miracle of miracles!* Now he'd take in some money for the company and be on his way to the bonus. Bustling over, he gave them his best, "Afternoon gentlemen. Can I be'a help to y'all?"

Neither answered. Instead, the tall one with the jet-black beard stayed near the front door, looking up and down the street. Then the short chunky one walked toward the back room, and Cliff became a little nervous. He eyed the two. *(Rough lookin' pair, 'specially Blackbeard. But then, everybody else 'round here is pretty rough lookin', too.)*

His "little nervous" became "very nervous" when the one at the front asked, "Anybody upstairs or in the basement? Anybody 'round 'cept y'all?"

Cliff felt his neck hair elevate, and his throat throttled back on its ability to swallow, but not only because of what the fellow said.

300

When he turned back toward him, Cliff spotted the big hog-leg revolver stuffed partly into his pocket.

It looked a lot like a stickup, all right. Good time for it too, with everyone at the train station. A trickle of sweat inched down Cliff's back. Just as he was about to say something, a voice from behind him inquired, "Y'all got very much sugar in stock today?"

The company's newest clerk nearly levitated! He hadn't heard Blackbeard soft-shoe up behind him. Shock, a suddenly dry mouth, and a constricted throat prevented an answer. Cliff's first rational thought was, *(They're gonna rob the company, and this jughead wants to know how much sugar we got in on hand?).*

The sugar question was repeated. Cliff finally managed a bit of saliva. "Ssh-ssh-ssshugar?"

"Yeah."

(Sugar! Not money?) Things were so completely daffy that Cliff didn't respond.

The bearded one grumbled, "Y'all deef? We'uns wants'ta buy three hundert pounds'a sugar."

"Three hundert pounds," his short partner echoed.

(Buy! Did he say 'buy!') Cliff may've been scared nearly speechless, but quickly realizing how far so much sugar would take him toward the bonus smeared his fears into faint smudges.

****

Before Cliff could spring into action, the front door exploded open. Blackbeard whirled, and Shorty sprang forward. In a flash, two very large and loud-talking agents of Messrs Smith and Wesson, calibers .44, were looking eyeball to eyeball with the intruder. Cliff gulped, probably for two reasons. There was going to be a shooting, and that was bad enough. Worse still, there went the big sugar sale.

Blackbeard lowered his revolver. "Oh, it's you, Charlie. Whataya want?"

Cliff's breath whistled out in relief. Obviously, they knew the new "customer." There might not be a shooting after all.

The newcomer was nearly breathless. *"Good Lordamighty! Somethin' awful's just happened! Noah Miles Hinshaw just got off the train. He's headed right this'a way!"*

Cliff couldn't believe what transpired next. The two hardcases looked as though they might become melting blobs of jelly and ooze down all over the floor. Eyes bulging and lips quivering, their arms fell to their sides, guns dangling. Blackbeard managed to rasp, *"By Jehosiphat!* What's *he* doin' here?"

"Reckon it's plain enough. He's after y'all, that's what. Somebody's done tipped 'im off y'all got them stills up yonder, and he's gonna grill ya to find 'em. Whataya gonna do? Kin ya make a run fer it out the back way through the woods?"

"Ain't no way we kin make it a'foot to the team in broad daylight. It's hitched way up yonder in a maple thicket. What'll we do! *What'll we do!"*

****

Cliff knew why the mere mention of Noah Miles Hinshaw could inspire such fear in the hearts of the two gunslingers, especially if they were helping God along with fermenting a little mash. Hinshaw was the most notorious and feared revenue agent in the history of the sport. Oh yeah, about everyone south of the Mason-Dixon line knew of Noah Miles Hinshaw.

Suddenly, a great number of things became clearer to Cliff. Then, it didn't take long to guess why the two gentlemen wanted to buy so much sugar. It takes sugar to make moonshine. From the amount they wanted, these two must be some of the biggest "white lightning" entrepreneurs in the State.

Other things fell quickly into place. For instance, the new law mandating stiff sentences for citizens caught carrying handguns.

Many said it was passed just to help get at the moonshiners. That must be why these two were so terrified. The world's greatest 'shine hunter come to blot out one of the last of the really big 'shine centers in the state, and there stood two of the kingpins with "Roscoes" stashed in their "overhalls."

With his knowledge of such scoundrels, Hinshaw would no doubt recognize these two on sight. So, even if he hadn't caught them at a still, he'd search them anyway and nail them for carrying guns, then grill them to learn the whereabouts of their stills. It certainly looked as though would soon be getting more headlines.

****

For a second, Cliff thought that maybe the distillers would try to shoot their way out, but then he saw what the soon-to-be-prisoners saw. About five armed deputies were trailing along in Hinshaw's wake.

Shorty began to make funny sounds, and Blackbeard snapped, "Shut yer yappin' face, Melvin. We'uns is caught, so let's don't give that big-eared divil the pleasure'a seein' any snivelin'." *(Melvin! A moonshiner named Melvin?)*

Under a full head of steam, Noah Miles Hinshaw closed to within 100 feet of the store. On he strode, the juices of the righteous flowing in the craggy old bloodhound.

Melvin sniveled a final snivel. "Mebbe we kin hide these here pistols somewhere in the store. Or, mebbe if'n we jist stick 'em under our shirts, he won't see 'em."

"Won't be no help to us, Melvin. He'll search us 'n everwhere else in here."

****

Funny thing about decisions affecting life. Often, they're made on the spur of the moment. Later, it's nearly impossible to explain why someone acted as they did. Now was one of those times for

303

Cliff. He was about to do something that would dramatically change things.

In another twenty seconds, Revenue Agent Hinshaw would be up the steps and through the door. Out of the blue, Cliff extended both hands to the dazed and doomed duo. "Gimme y'all's pistols, boys!" Meekly, they quickly complied.

The old still smasher was on the porch as Cliff whirled and rammed each well-polished weapon deep into a big barrel of pinto beans. Just as he jerked out his hand and smoothed the beans, the doorbell clanged and Noah Miles Hinshaw charged in.

****

Noah Miles felt *gooood!* There stood Melvin and Percy Smith. *(Percy! A moonshiner named Percy?)* Hinshaw recognized them instantly. He knew they had a still, probably more, in the hills somewhere around, and from their reputation, they just *had* to be packing pistols. He just *knew* it!

"Well howdy, gentlemen. I come all this way down here representin' the legal law of the United States of America jist to meet up with y'all. Looks like we both done picked a fine day for it, ain't we?" He was enjoying this, but they weren't. "Reckon y'all know why I'm here, don'tcha? It's to rid up this here county'a the likes of sneaky, *slimy-snake* lawbreakers such as yourselves." Noah was never much for beating around the bush. Melvin and Percy stood limply, stricken mute.

Hinshaw was so thrilled with his stage that he began hamming it up. Pulling out a huge pearl-handled, nickel-plated revolver and circling them slowly, he advised, "Now, you knotheads surely ain't gonna be so all-fired jackass-stupid as to try to slow me down in my work, are ya? Jist save us both lots'a time 'n take me out to your stills so's ya can get on with your punishment.

"You know I'm gonna find 'em, anyway. It'll jist go worse if I don't get no cooperation." He brandished his revolver, then holstered it under his duster once he saw it had the desired effect. The two miserable creatures before him were so terrorized that Hinshaw was forced to ask them about the stills again.

Since it appeared Hinshaw was going to talk and not shoot them on the spot, Blackbeard recovered somewhat, "What stills would that be, Mister Hinshaw?"

Noah *despised* insolence from lawbreakers. He roared into Percy's face, ***"Don't gimme no sass!"***

Both culprits recoiled, but managed to somehow hold their ground after falling back a step. "Ain't got no stills, Mister Hinshaw," Melvin offered.

"Well now, ain't that interestin'. They's stills all right. Big ones, I'd venture, and I'm gonna find 'em. I *never* miss. *Everbody* knows that. Anyways, I got you conivin', suck-egg-dogs, red-handed. I know y'all gotta be packin' pistols. We'll just take care'a that little matter first. You'll get five to ten for that alone!" He pulled out his revolver. "Now hand 'em over!"

In chorus: "Ain't got no pistols!"

"Horse dabble! Grab hold'a them skunks, boys. We'll find their shootin' irons soon enough. They got 'em. You can betcher life on it. None'a these low-life's can live without 'em."

****

Noah Miles and his merry men frisked the pair and found no weapons aside from fearsome pocketknives, which didn't count. Then, they went over about every square inch of the store looking for the weapons he *knew* were hidden somewhere.

By then, the clerks returned and stood about in awe of the renowned revenuer. When the manager determined what was going on, he called Cliff aside and asked whether he knew about any guns. Cliff shrugged and played dumb. This wasn't too difficult, considering his panicky second thoughts about what he did upon witnessing Hinshaw in action.

After another round of searching with no results, Hinshaw stormed and raged at fate in general and the Smith brothers in particular. He bellowed every threat of dire consequences known to man and added a few creations of his own. Percy and Melvin had the good sense to keep their mouths shut, and pretty soon there was nothing Hinshaw could do but deliver one last volley and his personal promise about their sure-fire fate.

"You two scalawags may think y'all put one over, but I'll *D-double-damn personal promise* y'all that you two **slimy, miserable, low-down, yella bellied weasel-dabbles** are both gonna be in jail *ferever* and this D-double-damn county'll be dryer 'n spit in the fiery pit after I find your stills. 'Fore I leave here, too. This here *illegal, sinful, Godless* 'shinin's gonna stop ferever'n you're gonna rot in jail! *Hear me? ROT... FEREVER!* I tell both'a you *and all* them thinkin' they kin hep sorry shiftless skunks, too." Cliff's eyes glazed over.

Hinshaw bellowed some more and finished, "I wanna tell y'all agin, I d-double-damn garantee it personal...*personal!* So, no matter how long it takes, I'll get all'a ya and your kind!"

Still-smasher Hinshaw roared out in the state of pious indignation of a good man temporarily thwarted in his intentions of right-doing. (Thwarted big-time in the old ego, too.)

The Smiths left soon after, no doubt to partake of healthy portions of their own product. Cliff stood rearranging the same horse harness until the manager asked his newest clerk, "Since y'all've rearranged the same harness till two sets'a reins are about wore out, wouldja like to start on the bridles?"

Not much more happened except the news that one or two of the Smith "cousins" who ratted them out to Hinshaw left the area.

Talk was it would be an extended journey. Cliff was standing around, not selling enough to pay his keep, and he thought the manager was getting nervous about it. Either that or Hinshaw's repeated visits to inquire about the pedigree of employees.

****

A few days later, things took a sudden upward turn for Cliff. Hinshaw let up on the manager about the gun episode being an inside job. With a "D-double-damn" personal promise to return and catch all the moonshiners for sure, he left on the morning train to look for whisky farmers elsewhere.

The same afternoon a customer, rough-looking even for these parts, walked in and asked for Cliff. He hadn't seen the man before, and here he was asking for *him!* The other clerks nearly had a stroke, and the store came down with a case of instant quiet.

Cliff rushed over. "Yessir, how can I be'a service, sir?" In his eagerness, the rookie clerk caused the man to take a step back.

He passed the time of day with a wildly curious Cliff until the normal noise level returned and then inquired, "Figger y'all might sell me 'bout ten scoops'a pinto beans? And kin y'all put 'em in this here bean bag'a mine?"

Well, it didn't take a brick outhouse to fall on Cliff to enlighten him as to what was going on. The damning evidence was still in the bean barrel. He was so scared that he left both guns there, hoping to sneak them out during a train stopover and hide them in the woods.

But, each time he lost his nerve, and every passing day added to his anxiety. The barrel was nearly half empty. It seemed everyone wanted pinto beans lately, and he had to shove the weapons deeper into them daily.

"Yessir, I can put the beans in y'all's bag. Just gimme it." Cliff somehow got between the beans and the other clerks and managed to scoop out the now grimy and dusty guns without spilling any. "Here ya are, sir. I'd be pleased to help if there's anything else I can do for y'all."

"Reckon ya could sell me fifty pounds'a flour if'n you're a mind to fetch it out to my wagon yonder. Cain't do no carryin', gotta bad back."

Cliff hesitated as the heavily-bearded flour-buyer eyed him. He looked hale enough. Was he up to something? Maybe something about the condition of the guns? Cliff swallowed hard. "Be more 'n happy to." After paying, the customer followed Cliff shouldering the flour to the wagon apprehension mounting with every step.

****

The manager may've noticed a thing or two, but kept them to himself. Things like how, as a light sleeper, every once in a while from his living quarters in the rear of the store, he heard a whippoorwill calling during the wee hours after midnight.

And, how just after that, it sounded as if one of the clerks headed very quietly down the outside stairs leading from their rooms over the store to the privy.

And then what sounded like a team and wagon moving every so quietly out back by the storage house.

And, how much extra sugar he needed to order lately.

And how (smiling), (*Some folks say sugar's used in makin' 'shine.*)

And, how Cliff's cash drawer was extra full the day following the "whippoorwill."

And how the other clerks had taken to calling Cliff "Kid Slick" when he began winning the weekly bonus so often.

(*Well, reckon I might could investigate. But later. Lots later.*)

THE FELLOWSHIP SEWING CIRCLE

Homer Jelke discovered a new way of housing chickens to hold down costs so his egg prices were lower than everyone else's. Customarily, hens were housed in long, narrow, one-story buildings and permitted to range outside freely. Jelke kept them penned in large two-story chicken houses twenty-four hours a day. Well, not exactly two-story chicken houses. What Homer did was adapt his two-story *barn* to accommodate chickens on both levels.

His idea worked so well that he was soon shipping State-wide, and inquiries about purchasing them were coming from wholesalers several states away. It looked as if he produced more eggs, his burgeoning business could become a truly great success story during a depressed economy.

To expand, Jelke needed more facilities and more help. He solved the facilities problem by buying surrounding farms that had suffered foreclosure during the economic depression at the time.

Banks holding these properties were only too happy to finance Homer when they got a look at his books. The extra space requirement was solved. Solved some problems for the banks, too. Besides the profit possibilities, they got rid of maintenance expenses for each farm.

Next, Homer activated his plan for obtaining workers and paying them. They'd only receive meager money, but there was a perfectly good vacant house on each farm. He'd house them rent free as part of their wages. Then too, there'd be all the free eggs a family could eat. Obviously, he could hire no locals. They all had housing and the wages he offered were next to nothing.

For workers, Jelke went south. In areas even more severely depressed than those farther north, there were families eager for any kind of relief. Jelke had no trouble choosing three families with the most sons. They could work, too.

Having thought of everything else, Jelke purchased an old school bus for transporting his recently contracted hired hands to their new homes. The same bus would pick up everyone to attend Sunday service at his church, The Temple of The Truest Believers. That was part of the deal.

****

No sooner had the bus deposited the newcomers than they were given their dawn to dusk (often later) work assignments. Naturally, such a schedule allowed few opportunities to socialize or otherwise become assimilated into the community.

The sudden appearance of so many destitute-appearing "outsiders" caused hesitancy on the part of long-established residents to become acquainted. Consequently, the nearly thirty "outsiders" lived in a world of Homer Jelke's making. Other folks knew of them, but that was it. There was seldom any contact.

****

At the monthly meeting of the Fellowship Sewing Circle, the conversation turned to attending the wake for little Clementine Haney, one of the new farmer family's young daughters.

When Freda Fenway spoke, no one had any trouble hearing. She wasn't known far and wide as "Foghorn Freda" for nothing.

"Well, I'll tell ya, ladies, in the case'a that egg farmer's little girl dyin', I know it's the custom to visit durin' the wake. And, I know that bunch'a hillbilly down-and-outers losin' a little daughter is tough. But, I don't reckon they'd expect anybody from around here to come callin'. They don't know us and we don't know them. They'll always be egg-farmer types and never mix in. It may be they don't even know what a wake is, anyhow. "

Mrs. Amanda Farley responded, "Now Freda, what difference does it make whether they know us or not? They're folks with a heavy burden right now and need all the comforting they can get, egg farmers or not. Maybe if we go out of our way a little they'd *'mix in'* as you call it."

"Mandy, don't be naïve. They're just not our kind. You and everyone else knows there are those that just don't fit in and never will. I've lived around here long enough to know what I'm talkin' about. It'd be better for everybody if the county council passed an ordinance keepin' certain kinds out. Think about it. In the long run, the egg-farmer types would be happier, too."

Wow! Did the fur fly after that! The other ladies jumped all over Freda. Back and forth they went. Then Freda challenged them one by one, asking whether they intended to attend the "egg-farmer's" wake. Each had "other plans" for the evening or offered various reasons not attending the wake for little Clementine.

This went on for a while before Freda admonished, "See there, every last one of you feel the same way in spite'a how you've been criticizin' me. At least I'm honest enough to say things like they really are and not be hypocritical. Now, how about the rest of you? What about you Matilda, you plannin'…."

A resounding voice interrupted. It was Sarah Pratt, recognized elder "stateswoman" of the group. "*Enough! Shame* on you Freda Fenway! I can hardly believe my ears! There you sit, spewing out the most *un*-neighborly and *un*-Christian malarkey I've ever had the terrible misfortune to hear. Those you call *'egg-farmers types'* are human beings, too."

311

Sarah's sewing sisters didn't escape her wrath. "And shame on the rest of you! Just listen to what you're doing! You're a bunch of so-called *Christian* women sitting around hearing Freda's mouthy claptrap and pretending to disagree. But, you're really agreeing by making all kind of idiotic two-faced excuses not to go see those poor folks. Again I say, *shame on you!*" She had plenty more for the Fellowship Sewing Circle.

In the stunned silence, Sarah addressed Freda again. "Freda, as for your high and mighty prattle about the county doing something to keep out '*egg-farmer types,*' it's true your people have lived around here a long time. And, I've heard all about your grandfather's moonshining and thieving activities. And, if my ancestors, who came here years before yours, did what you want this county to do about keeping out "*egg-farmer types,*' you wouldn't be here today!"

Mrs. Pratt drew a deep breath and finished. "Every one of you can use whatever invented hypocritical excuse you please to avoid visiting that poor grieving family. I'll not be a part of your prejudice and intolerance. Amanda and I are going to visit those troubled folks and offer what comfort we can."

She stood, gathered up her sewing and added, "Now as I think of it, maybe I don't care to be part of a group who thinks so cruelly about other humans. Come on Mandy. Let's get clear of this diseased room before we catch something."

****

On their way home, additional planning took place. Arriving at a wake without food offerings was unheard of. Earlier, Sarah and Amanda considered the number of kids in the Haney household and the possibility of other egg farmers visiting without much of the customary food. They decided Sarah would make a large kettle of soup and plenty of freshly baked bread. Several dozen sugar cookies, too. Amanda would prepare two traditional casseroles, one macaroni, the other escalloped potatoes with ham.

****

Buford Haney answered Sarah's knock. Clearly, he was taken aback by the scene before him. Written all over his face was, "Who are these four people and whatta they want?"

Sarah stuck out her hand and introduced themselves as the Pratts and Farleys who came to express their condolences for the loss of his daughter, adding, "Mister Haney, we've brought along a few offerings to help out in your time of sorrow."

Buford Haney hadn't recovered. From behind came, "Buford, what is it? Somebody out there?"

Still staring at the two couples facing him, Haney managed over his shoulder, "It's people sayin' they come to tell us how sorry they was about Clemmy Mae and to bring vittles."

Norma Virginia Buford moved around her husband. She too, looked very surprised, but instructed, "Well Buford, don't just stand there in the way, have those kind folks come in." As they entered, she informed, "We don't get much company, and the other farmers ain't comin' over till after their chores get done. We do thank y'all for comin' by. It helps a heap at a time like this. Won't y'all take a seat?"

Mrs. Pratt suggested that she and Mrs. Granger could help set out the food they brought. Soon, kids from everywhere appeared. Mrs. Haney introduced all nine of her freshly scrubbed offspring and told them to go into the other room. She'd tell them when they could have some of the 'fixin's."

One child declared as they left, "Sure looks good. Don't look like there's lots'a eggs in it, neither."

The ladies finished and Mrs. Haney told the kids they could have some food, but, "Be careful not to spill nothin' and don't take one bite more'n y'all can eat."

****

After Mr. Haney led the visitors into the room where the casket sat for the "viewing," they returned to the adjoining room. Mrs. Haney began crying as she spoke softly about how "precious" Clemmy Mae was. Said she was only eight years old, but she was curious about almost everything and into everything. Said she was only sick for just a couple weeks, "Then she left us."

Mr. Pratt asked what the sickness was, and Mr. Haney said at first it seemed like only a little bellyache, then it got worse. When she got real bad, Dr. Johnson came and said it was probably appendicitis and she needed an operation right away. But, before they could figure out where in the world to get the money, she died. The undertaker arranged time payments. Sarah Pratt was aghast. Later she'd have plenty to say at church and everywhere else about the little girl and no money for an operation.

Mrs. Haney continued to weep as she talked of the dead child. One of the other Haney daughters, Martha Jean, came and sat beside her on the couch. Then, the tiny girl put an arm around her mother and pulled her close. To further comfort her, she said, "Don't cry Mama, there's lots more of us."

That was too much for Sarah and Amanda. They rose as one and rushed over to lean down and embrace both. The four remained so until Mrs. Haney's sobbing ceased. Wiping her eyes, she stood. "Y'all'll kin never ever know how much y'all comin' here's helped. I'll never fergit it. And whatcha y'all jist did I'll never fergit, neither."

She reached down and picked up Martha Jean. "And you, little one, I know there's lots more'a y'all, and I'll keep right on lovin' ever last one'a ya more'n ever."

The other egg farmers began arriving, their day's work finally over. After introductions all around, Sarah Pratt said she expected it was time to be going. Mr. and Mrs. Haney accompanied them onto the porch, both thanking them over and over for being so thoughtful and such good neighbors.

****

As the two started toward Amanda Farley's Ford, other cars began pulling into the driveway. Several. Amanda questioned, "Now, who in creation can all those folks be?"

Then she answered her own question. "Why Sarah, those looks like Fellowship Sewing Circle cars! And guess who just got out of the first one! *None other than Freda Fenway, that's who!"*

They kept walking and Amanda added, "Look Sarah, not only are they here, several are bringing food."

At first, there was no response of any kind. But, as they passed on by, Amanda was pretty sure she saw a trace of a smile as Sarah Pratt, head held high and looking straight ahead, commented, "Hope Freda Fenway had sense enough not bring those deviled eggs she's always so proud of."

PARTNER, PARTNER, WHO'S MY PARTNER?

The weekly meeting of the River Bend Bridge Club was in session in the Order of the Beaver hall. Often recognized area-wide as a club not only organized 55 years previously, it was also noteworthy that the original members were still playing, several with near-perfect attendance.

Nothing stopped or slowed the weekly game. Neither wars, economic downturns, fires, floods…nothing. As one of the waiters at Bill's remarked to a rookie after he served them late-morning coffee on his first day, "Nothin' stops 'em. They're just like all bridge-club players–all a little out'a round. Gotta be or they couldn't be one. Cut their teeth on a deck'a cards and never let go. I play once in a while, but I'd never join a club, believe me.

"Don't mess with 'em. When they say 'jump,' just ask how many times and how high. Couple years ago, some dimwitted managing editor down at the newspaper decided the football team needed more coverage, so he left out the how-to bridge column one week. He's writin' obits somewhere in Canada."

The River Bend bunch had such a ferocious reputation that other bridge players in town instantly manufactured any excuse imaginable to avoid substituting for a club member in the unusual happenstance of their rare absence. Once when asked to sit in, Pete Zenger remarked that a *few* bridge players might cut your throat to take a trick, but River Bend Club players were different. *Every one* of them would.

Its members played together so long that there were no more secrets, playing, or personality-wise. On rare occasions when a member varied from the expected and committed what was called by members "an unpardonable," they didn't hesitate to offer comments–snippy more often than not. This past year or so, snide remarks occurred frequently when 94-year-old Ezra Peters lost track of the bidding.

Peacemaker, The Reverend Samuel Wallace, sometimes came to his defense. Lately, however, he was twice the victim of what was becoming known as the "Peters Peril" and said nothing when his partner made more than a few surly asides about the elderly gentleman's play.

Today, many members were becoming annoyed with all the talk of Matilda Mattingly's sudden passing. Sure it was tragic. Sure she was a founding member. Sure it had to be hard on Al Hariday, now that he no longer had a partner. Just look at him sitting there and not knowing what to do next. It's not every week you lose a partner of fifty-odd years. Gotta be tough, all right, but stuff happens. We came to play bridge. Let's play. We've delayed too long already.

When others began to talk about hands that Matilda played over the years, Jeff Mandel cleared his throat preparatory to reminding them that they were there to play bridge, but he refrained when Al Hariday spoke up. "I just can't believe she's gone. Been bridge partners ever since I can remember. Until today, I can't recall the last time she missed. Bet nobody else in here can either. She was the best partner I ever had. 'Course she's the *only* one I ever had."

He looked over at Velma Sturgess and continued, "Vel, I know you and Matty had a few falling-outs over your bidding, but now that she's gone, I know you'll have to say that she was a great bridge player."

Not quite ready yet to go that far, Velma paused a long moment before replying, "Well Al, I can't quite say she was *great*, but I will say she was a *middling-good* player, all right."

"Thank you for that Vel. I know she'd be grateful."

Clohe Chamberlin joined Jeff Mandel in expressing his impatience by tapping her cards on the table. "Now listen, we all miss her a lot and we'll get to say lots more at the eulogies. But, knowing Matty, I'm sure she'd want us to go on."

Rhonda Robertson responded, "Exactly right Clo. If the shoe was on one of our feet, I know whoever couldn't be here would want us to do as we always have. Don't you think we should get on with the game, Al?"

"Yes, I'm sure that'd be the case. We just better go on without her now. She'll never be back. There's a little problem, though."

Ezra Peters slapped the table smartly. *"Problem!* What *problem!* My bid was perfectly proper."

His long-suffering partner calmed, "No, No, Ezra. You did just fine. What's the problem Al?"

"Well, don't you see? What'll I do for a partner?"

After a chorus of "By golly, he's right," Cynthia Byron offered, "No reason not to go right on. We could get that older waiter to sit in. I heard him say once that he played a little. He could get us by till Al can find someone else, and Matilda's hand is right there on the table. After all, she collapsed right on top of it. Don't look like a single card's disturbed."

319

PRG AND LRX VISIT No. 623

P rg and Lx, 1,437[th] cousins on their mother's side floated, levitating in the highest court of all before the highest ruler of all, *MASTER OF THE UNIVRSE,* ZOG-ZZZ. Worst. Convicted of violating intergalactic law a millennia earlier they expected the.

Now, they were suspected of conspiring to learn more than the two hundred different languages allowed each young citizen of Cali-shicka-pata-rosch-ay, the meteor lying just beyond the outskirts of the galaxy Microalegria on the planet Telamania.

Their fate was of intense interest every Cali-shicka-pata-rosch-ayan. For the last eonaterra, an inner-beaming module was tuned to station **ZZZ-PLC** the official antenna beamer of the *MASTER GALAG.*

The ruling was far more terrible than Prg and Lx could imagine. They were banned to the speck on the map of the total universe so far out that it was only a number. Number 623, not yet explored. Every antenna snapped fully out at its mere mention. Not even a language-translation mega-computer could retrieve enough nano-bits of its odd language floating about in space to name it.

There was more. Since they seemed so interested in learning more languages than allowed, they were to remain until they exhausted every conceivable effort to find any trace of the heretofore indecipherable language that may've been used there.

Should they find any, they must translate it completely before being beamed back to Cali-shicka-pata-rosch-ay.

Prg and Lrx were immediately transferred to, and placed in, the most advanced beaming-outward-configured centrifugal-ultra high-intensity-inter-galactic module. The signal given, away they were beamed for light years of travel.

For communication, they were fitted with the latest thought-transmitting equipment by which their stored thoughts would be collected in Cali-shicka-pata-rosch-ay's intergalactic library system. But, they would not be allowed to have any thoughts whatsoever of their home galaxy, for there would be no two-way thought allowed that might interfere with their searches.

****

Prg and Lrx didn't think No. 623 was much different than Cali-shicka-pata-rosch-ay, including a totally smooth and powdery surface. It seemed nearly inconceivable that they'd find any trace of a language used on No. 623.

However, on one of their many trips completely around 623, a full two centuries later, Lx sank deeply into the dust and felt a very unusual object. Excitedly, he extracted it. At last they found something that might hold clues to a language!

Equally excited, Prg examined the strange object. It was flat like some of the stones he saw on Planet Jupiter on an inter-planetary trip from school. But, it was not solid like a rock. It had many thin things attached at the back and loose at the front. On each of the thin things were strange marks of all kinds laid out in rows. On the outside were other strange marks in rows, but not as many and much larger. The marks looked like some of the bits floating about in Cali-shicka-pata-rosch-ay's galaxy. Bits like "pg," "ltr,," and "wd." Could these be part of a language?

****

For centuries, Prg and Lx tried every strategy they possessed to determine what this thing was and what the strange marks one after another meant. Even the ban on thoughts of Cali-shicka-pata-rosch-ay was lifted, so great was the two-way-thought curiosity.

Just as it appeared identification of the strange object might never happen, Prg made one last try in his most advanced cranial archive filing system, and there it was! Earlier, the system hadn't retrieved what just might be the key to the mystery.

Prg and Lx took turns working on the problem. Occasionally, one or the other would find marks that might've been part of a pre-galactical language. On and on they studied the problem. After another century or so, they had to be extremely careful when handling the object. Many of the thin things fastened at the back had come loose and almost too worn to see the strange bits.

Suddenly, Prg shrieked*!*. *"Smklls.* Lx, *smklls!* Ysll j" jrl;l'kkx. Nlfls llsg, xt, qlwg! *Jll- l'ff! *Q!vvpkkl, Lx, Q!vvpkkll!!* **ZMNMCKQR**, Lx, **ZMNMCKAR!"**

****

When news of Prg and Lx's finds was beamed throughout Cali-shicka-pata-rosch-ay, exuberation erupted. For light years, many attempted to solve the mystery of the missing parts needed to join the bits of language floating about. Now they knew there *were* none. How lucky Prg and Lx were to find this object they named "bk," and find in it that the true name of No 623 was "Wrld."

In the report for **MASTER OF THE UNIVRSE,** Z!*k Gz, Prg titled it with the last two wrds in the bk, those showing it was surely the last one written on Wrld. For it and the full report, Prg used the language Lx and he translated. Both thought it a dandy idea for illustrating a complete, not just a partial, report.

Master Gz loudly declared it stupid and not even the title could be spoken, so Prg shouted it in the language Lx named "Txtng.

ND!

ND!

THIS HERE'S CLARABELLE COMIN' ATCHA ONE MORE LAST TIME. I BE TALKIN' FER *ALL* THE FOLKS IN THESE HERE TALES'N 'SPECIAL FER MY NEW BEST FRIEND HAROLD. WE BE GITTIN' ALONG FINE. SPEAKIN'A GUESSIN', WHO IN THE WHOLE WIDE WORLD WOULD'A GUESSED THIS COULD'A HAPPENED?

ANYHOW, EVER LAST ONE'A US-UNS BE THANKIN' Y'ALL A HEAP'A ROUNDED-OVER BUSHELS FER READIN'N GOIN' ON PLAYIN' THE GUESSIN' GAMES. D'RECTLY, WE'UNS'LL ALL BE COMIN' 'ROUND TO THROW ROCKS IN Y'ALL'S GARDEN.

BLESS Y'ALL'S HEART.

IN CLARABELLE'S WORDS, "THANK Y'ALL A HEAP'A PILED UP REAL HIGH BUSHELS FER READIN' THESE HERE TALES. ONE DAY, I'LL COME'N THROW ROCKS IN Y'ALL'S GARDEN."

D. D. Huddle

ii
19
3 1
3 3
3 4 —
4 4 — ?

Proof

Made in the USA
Charleston, SC
09 January 2015